smarty girl

smarty girl

DUBLIN SAVAGE

Honor Molloy

BOSTON

First published by GemmaMedia in 2012.

GemmaMedia
230 Commercial Street
Boston, MA 02109 USA

www.gemmamedia.com

Printed in the United States of America

16 15 14 13 12 1 2 3 4 5

978-1-936846-10-8

Library of Congress Cataloging-in-Publication Data

Molloy, Honor.
Smarty girl : Dublin savage / Honor Molloy.
p. cm.
ISBN 978-1-936846-10-8
1. Girls—Ireland—Fiction. 2. Dublin (Ireland)—Fiction. 3. Domestic fiction. I. Title.
PS3613.0465S63 2012
813'.6—dc23
2011052992

Cover by Night & Day Design

Author photo by Silvia Saponaro

Cover photo courtesy of the author

For Shivaun

For John

For Yvonne

"From magic we come
To magic we go."

—Frank O'Connor

Contents

The Fine Days

1965

laughing apples

We're going to see the dancers. I'm skipping up the lane, dragging my daddy's hand and yanking him along Tolka Row toward the taxi-rank.

I'm terrible-excited 'cause we're going to the ballet. Come-on, come-on. We'll be late. *We're going to see the dancers.* That's my dancing song. I made it up myself. *The dancers, the dancers—*

My big sister Fiona and big brother Des stomp the footpath in disgust. Des pulls the red velvet hat off my head. My electricky hair cracks the air.

Going to see—

Showoff, Fiona hisses.

Dancers, I sing, louder than loud, in her face. I'm wearing my new gray coat from my American Gran. High white socks and shiny black shoes. Clack-clack-clack. I'm marching on the footpath towards Merrion Row.

When we do catch a taxi, it's Paddy the Cabby—Daddy's friend from years ago. He's a burly fellah. Asking, *where to?*

The dancers, I sing to him. *We're going to see the dancers.*

Honestly, Noleen. That only annoys, Mam says, all American-like, 'cause my mam is from America. *Will you please stop singing and look out the window?* Mam holds her head like she's getting a pain in the brain from my song.

She'd give headache to an aspirin, Daddy tells Paddy. *Couldja take us to the Gate.*

Please, I shout. *Take us to the Gate, please.* 'Cause I am politer than Daddy. I stand on the brown leather seat, better to watch Dublin go by. Stephen's Green where I play every day. Then Trinity College where Mam went to school. We zip and roll over O'Connell Bridge, under the dazzling advert signs jumping with life. Orange and green, Club Orange, Esso, and Players, Please! Then the Pillar with Lord Nelson on top. Past This Is The Happy Ringhouse shop with the flashing boy and girl, getting married. The wife has a flip-do under her wedding veil, and the daddy's got a top hat and swallow tails. There's two horseshoes side-down-up for luck and love. Above them is a diamond ring winking on and off. And on. Lucky flashy ringhouse, happy flashy ringhouse. Lucky flashy dancers. *We're going to see the dancers, the dancers, the dance—*

Noleen O'Feeney. What did I say? Mam warns.

We're here, Daddy calls as we reach the spiked iron railings standing tall as soldiers front of the Gate Theatre. Sometimes my daddy does his plays here, but not today.

Today is the dancers, the dancers. We're going to see the dancers.

I jiggle the door handle to Paddy's cab; it's locked. He takes a huge-long time coming round to open it. I race up the walk, turn back, and Mam's climbing out slow as a crab.

Daddy's chatting with Paddy. I run to him, hug him at the knees. *Come onnn.*

Give Daddy a chance to pay the fare, Mam says.

I squinch my lips side to side and side to side like a bunny squinching his whiskers. 'Til at last, until finally.

Bye, Paddy. We'd better embark—woof! Daddy catches my hand, swings me up the steps and into the theatre.

I'm angry 'cause Daddy talks with the doorman, the ticket-seller, the coffee lady, and the usher. He knows everyone in Ireland 'cause he's an actor on the stage. He's even on the telly. Every night, after the news, my daddy comes on wearing a long coat that falls to his shoes and a newsboy's cap. He's not my daddy anymore, he's Mister Mac, peering over a pair of wire spectacles, talking real high and squeaky like an ould fellah. People believe he's an ould fellah telling jokes and stories. He's like out of the olden times, so all of Ireland loves him.

Mam steers us to our seats, middle of the row. I'm lost in legs, spangly stockings, heavy coats, and pointy knees. The seats flang up, slap 'em down. Spring up, slap 'em down. Spring up—

Stop it. Fiona swipes at my frock.

Missed me. I laugh, give her a kickapoo.

It's velvet, the seat. So soft. I run my fingers on the seat so soft. My fingers tickle forward like Paddy's cab driving us cross O'Connell Bridge all the way to the Gate Theatre where we'll see the ballet. Smooth my fairy dress. Kickle wiggle kickle. Smack my shoe soles together with a solid *plap.* Twist the lace at the top of my socks so they're straight'n'perfect, so they're gorgeous, so they're good.

Where's the ballet? I want to know. The theatre is packed-chaos. There's a stampede of posh people in furs and tweeds. Everyone's ready for the show. Where is it?

Then Fiona asks, *Can I buy sweets?*

I'll go, Daddy says. *You'll get lost in the crowd.*

Daddy vanishes out the door. We wait. And wait. He's taking too long.

Mammy, can I go find Daddy? Fee says. *Maybe he's lost.*

There's Daddy, Des says.

I see him signing autographs, ignoring me. *Daddy,* I yell.

He wags a box of Milktray chockies, points us out to his fans, keeps talking. I slip off my seat, crawl under'n'over, ducking diving dodging 'til I reach my da.

Here's my Noleen. He's boasting about me.

Isn't she an angel? purrs a lady with a slinky hair-do.

She's a bother and a nuisance, a terror and a scourge, Daddy says. *Listen to her voice. Say hello to Miss Dazzo.*

Good evening, Miss Dazzo. Showing him I'm not a nuisance and a bother, a terror and a scourge. Not at all.

Oh my, Miss Dazzo chuckles. *What a croak, like a little bullfrog.*

I have the lowest voice in the world for a girl. That's from being born early with mucky lungs—bronchitis. And from playing in the Green, where I rage and I roar louder than anyone. Louder than Fiona and Des. Louder than the kids in our gang.

Listen to her. Listen to this. Daddy taps Miss Dazzo's wrist. Twice.

I watch her looking at my daddy, at his sleek black hair, his bony face.

Miss Dazzo has on fishnet stockings. She catches fishes in her legs.

Born with a voice like Tallulah Bankhead. He says.

She's dripping fur with tails and fox-faces, glassy black eyes. If I could, I'd sink them fox teefs into her cheek.

G'wan, talk in your Tallulah-voice, Daddy orders. *Don't be shy.*

I go into our Tallulah act. *Why hello, dahh-ling.* I talk down in my boots and draw out the words.

Miss Cleverality. She leans close to Daddy, dips her chin. A sly, foxing smile.

Have an exxx-quisite day. This is the act Daddy makes me do for all his pals. He taught me how to say the words, where to move, when to stop.

Isn't she a scream?

I pinch my forehead, flutter my eyes. *If the bloody ballet doesn't start, I shall go insane-insane-insane-insane-insane.*

Brilliant. Absolutely brill-O. Miss Dazzo says. *You're very funny. Will you be a comedian like your da?*

And I say yeh.

That's enough, Noleeny, Daddy says.

So I stop. 'Cause I want to be the best, the special, *his* best.

You've her trained like a poodle-dog. She's devoted to you, Miss Dazzo says. *How old?*

Almost five.

Five going on fifty-five. She's clutching to the arm of Daddy's jacket.

"She's from before." My mother says. Daddy drops his hand over her hand. Drums his fingers.

"That child was here before." Is what Granny says. About me.

We've to get back. Daddy gives Miss Dazzo a wiggle-waggle of the eyebrows. *See you at interval?*

When we get to our seats, Mam and Daddy sit me 'tween them so's I won't escape again.

Then the lights go out and a spotlight pops, a circle on the curtain. I ruggle on the seat in excitements. *The dancers.*

Sit down. Daddy mashes me into the seat.

I can't seeeeeeeeeee.

On my lap. So I sit in his lap where he hugs me.

A lady steps into the spot. *Good afternoon ladies, gentlemen, patrons of the National Ballet. Today's matinee promises to be a great treat. We'll start with a smattering from the company's repertoire.* She glimpses at a scrap of paper, clasps her bosoms with the fervor. *The second portion of this afternoon's program will feature the world premiere of "Nuala's Twelve Weaklings"—a legend from our folk culture. Ah, the noble Nuala—*

Bit loo-lah that name Nuala. Must be Irish.

I'm proud to say that this ballet was commissioned specially for our talented dancers—

Yes, the dancers, I shout. *Where are they?*

There's a gasp, a big-huge pause. The whole audience is gawping at me.

The dancers. I howl. *We want the dancers.*

The lady tries to speak but no one can hear. I'm that loud.

Daddy claps his hand over my mouth but I keep at it. *Mmm-mm the mmm-mmmz.*

I know we're impatient to see the ballet. However, I must ask—

I wriggle and minch. *The Dancers, the dancers, we want the—*

The little girl is right, a man says.

We want the dancers, Miss Dazzo calls.

Bring out the dancers. The audience yells. *The dancers, we want the dancers.* The theatre throbs with the beat.

Daddy shrugs and lets me go. *The dancers, the dancers.* I step onto his hand with my shiny black shoes. He pushes me high into the air like a circus girl. I'm far over the peoples squashed in their velly-vet seats. *We want the dancers.* I wave my hands like I'm leading a showband.

We want the dancers, the dancers. We scream and kick and belt. Lift the roof off the place with my song. *We want the dancers, bring on the dancers.*

You win. The lady holds up her arm, sweeping it towards the curtain: *The dancers.*

And everyone is delighted, especially meeeeeeee.

The theatre goes bang-black, the curtain lifts, sudden color screams, the dance is on. I open my eyes wide as wide to gather everything in: the music, the magic, the dancing all round. An orchestra sits in a teeny side stage with a curtain all its own, violins lashing out the melodies. Girls spin by on tippy-toe in tutus made of fairy floss. One does eight double turns in a row. She doesn't get dizzy and she doesn't fall. O, them girls and their specktakular feets. It's wonderful-wow.

When the house lights go on for intermish, do I eat my HB ice cream cup? N O, no. Stead, I wait and I wait for the ballet to begin again.

And there it is. Twelve poor boys tear about the stage,

wearing tayto sacks. They grab their bellies with the hunger, clearly starving. A tall lady swans on, real regal, even though her dress is tattered and ratty. The poor boys cling to her dress, snatching at the flitters of her worn-out apron. She's their mammy. They hold out their hands, begging her for food. Their mam bites her fists in flusteration 'cause she's nothing to feed 'em.

The lights turn green and eerie, the boys fade behind her, and she's tearing through the deep woods of a forest, searching in the roots of trees for mushrooms, berries, something to feed her kiddos. She comes upon a red-red apple, she picks it up and kisses it—gives it a big ould schmoocher. She finds another apple, and another. She grows glad and gladder with each one she slings into her apron. Soon her cooking apron is bouncing with twelve giddy red apples. Out of the dark woods she gallops, happy-go-lucky, home to her sons. The stage lights broaden and wink, go golden. And the mam, triumphant, arrives—her apron bursting with apples. The lads rush for the apples. They jig with glee, pegging apples at each other, juggling them over their mam's head, 'til, one by one, they toss the apples back into the bowl of her apron. Then they leap and they soar out of sight.

The mam stands alone. She stands and stands a longing time, waiting for her boys to come and eat their apples. She crashes to her knees then, clawing at her apron, the apples, all bulge-y, look like cobbles, look like stones.

Then she opens her mouth and she's screaming. But no sound comes out. Instead, a viola plays a sorrowful tune, mournful. The mam lets loose her apron hem. The apples roll and gambol down the stage. They come to a stop in a clever lip, a dip, a gutter. But for the one apple that bunks and pops high over the audience to land—*thwuck*—in my lap.

Ping-black. Lights come up. The dancer boys bow and ballerinas curtsey. There's flowers, more bows, and cheers. Kick-kick hooray. Kick-kick hooray.

Then it's blinking bright and ever-over. The audience pulls on their coats and furs and files out the doors.

I stand on my seat looking at the closed-up curtains and the story gone.

What do you think of the dancers, Noleen? Daddy asks.

Put out the lights. I want to stay in the dancing and never go back to the really worlds.

I want to be a dancer when I grow up.

Wouldja like to go backstage with me? Daddy asks. *Give them back their apple?*

No. I cup the apple in my hand. It's light-so-light. It's sparky red. And it is mine.

It's not a toy, yeh know, Daddy explains.

I know. It's a pretendy apple. I could borrow Mam's apron and dance a dance all me own in the garden. I could dance about apples. I could dance about mams. I could wear a Tayto Crisp sack and be a dancing boy.

Give it to me, Nolee. Daddy reaches for the apple. *They need it for their show tonight.*

But I don't give it back. I won't give it back. 'Cause I need it more.

Noleen's father, the actor Oliver O'Feeney, is whistling, jetting along the granite pavement by the General Post Office. He's after recording four adverts for *Radió Éireann*: Fanta, Silk Cut. "Small world, big airline. Pan Am makes the going great." And verse better than Shakespeare anys-the-day: "People who know the difference choose Black & White, the whiskey with the smoother flavor."

Smooth tobacco, smoother whiskey, smooth-smooth-smooth. That's what life is for him. I mean, what a run of luck today. At twenty-five pounds per ad, that's one hundred quid hot in his pocket. What'll he do, what'll he do with this money? He still owes the stoney for putting the chimbellies into their house. There's the Rotunda fees for the new babby coming. Or? He could put it back into his shows—Olly O'Feeney Productions. *Gaels of Laughter*, his new revue, opens next week. Dress rehearsal tonight. He's on a ninety-minute break. Just enough time to run home for tea. Soup and prawns, Gina's brown bread. What a peasant, cooking the bread in a pot oven over the fire like they do down the country. Gina's done up their home like an Irish Cottage, using an actual milking stool for a coffee table. Mad.

Gina, his Pennsylvanian wife, producing, directing, working the stage lights, polishing his shoes. Gina and her American ideas. Inviting the critics for some afters, after the afters. Asking them in to their mews down the lane at the back of one of them Georgians on Tolka Row. And Olly's shows at the Gate are packing 'em in.

If only his father had lived to see this. Him, top the pops. Him, in his hand-tailored, sleek gray suit—with the secret padding under his right shoulder, meant to bulk out the back ribs, make him whole. *Chuh*, that's laugh. But with the new suit, who'd know that he'd spent eight years in and out of hospital? With the TB.

From the age of sixteen to twenty-four, he was in the sans, the sanitoriums, the chest hospitals of Ireland. Prisons of the medical kind. Each of 'em a horror show in real life. But that's all one. For today, white cuffs at the knuckles, his thin black tie. His slick-dark, divils-the-hair. His schnonky nose with the donkey kick to it, like someone pushed it to the side on her way out the door. Olly grins. Ah, lookit his teefs, that was back when he had 'em. "People who know the difference." That's him, that is Olly, indeed.

Bounding trouserly down Merrion Row, Olly's deep in his own jolly world, when the door to O'Donoghue's pub swings wide.

Olly. Paddy the Cabby grabs Olly by the suit jacket. *You're wanted on the phone.*

Me?

It's the RTÉ.

For me?

They rung just as you were passing, Paddy says. *Might be a new part, heh?* Producers often call O'Donoghue's 'cause the O'Feeneys don't have a phone. *What're you drinking?*

I'll have a Black & White, the whiskey with the fluther savor—Bollocks. Let me at that again. Olly jokes. *I'll have a Black & White, the whiskey with the smoother flavor.* The ad flows from his mouth butter-easy.

And Olly's into the pub.

Say "fuck."

Fuck, I say.

Say "shite-boak-shite-fuck."

Shite-boak-shite-fuck, I say.

Don't you have a curse of your own? Young Eamon's digging through the props in the scene shed when he finds Daddy's prop sword.

Toilet. There's two ways to say toilet. Number one: *Toilet* with a sharp T at the end like I do when I'm at school. I'm in Babies Class with the under fives. And Number two: *Tile-eh* like the kidgang in the Green.

S'nothing. Young Eamon scowls.

Po. Potty. Pope's bum. Shite. I say, getting nowhere. And so add: *Smellrump-boaking-wanker-mickey-like bitch.*

Stewwww-pid.

Young Eamon has the poor teeth rotted out of his mouth. He's rotty down to the teef-roots. He's got twine looped through his waistbelt. Young Eamon's got a yellow bubble of snot blowing fat with each breath. He presses his snotting nose right in my face. *Fuck is the boldest word ever. So, say fuck. G'wan, say it.*

Fuck, I say.

Hello, yeh fucked duck, how are yeh? He's using the tin sword to scrape grass from between the cobbles on the floor of the shed.

Just grand, rotty fuckteeth.

Young Eamon points the sword at my eye. *That a jeer about me teeth?*

Not jeering, I'm not jeering.

I'm the king of the castle and you're the dirty rascal. He has the sword over his head like a heathen. *Repeat after me, "Bleeding Jesus, sin no more—"*

Bleeding Jesus—

"Look down on us shitefuckers, you blasted bastard."

Sin no more—I try to catch up, I really do.

"Bleeding belly." He's stabbing zigzags in the air with Daddy's sword. *"Tear me side with a sword same as Jesus. Our Father's Son. Him that bled into fuck."*

Young Eamon charges out of the shed. He darts through the Georgian door up our lane.

Dung-arsed mucker. I roar and rush to the lane but he's vanished entirely. Young Eamon's gone straight into fuck.

Out on the lane, high on a mossy wall, someone nailed a birdhouse to the stone. There's a weeshy bird-head popping in and out. Then a slitter of feathers and a fly away, fly.

Over the wall I can see up into the offices of No. 11 Tolka Row. We live in an old stable that used to be part of that big house. It has businesses on all five floors. When them office peoples is working we must play quiet and stay outta the side garden. We must play on the cobbles of our courtyard or out in the lane.

Hi-yeh, says Young Eamon's wee sister Aoife. She's real pale. Skinny and all. Sucking the two middle fingers on her right hand. Them fingers is the only clean thing on her whole body. Even her teefs is dirty. Aoife has brown stubs of teeth lining the top of her smile. She has so many-many freckles on her face it looks like diseases.

Have you done your Haitch Com? Aoife asks.

What? Not sure I want to talk with her.

Your Holy Communion when you marry Christ the King

and become a Bride of God. I done me Haitch Com, didja know. I've a white handbag, white gloves, white prayer bewk. But I don't have me dress anymore, 'cause Daddy put it in the pawn.

Aoife takes a big breath, talks faster. *After you do yers Communion, you go up to Mass and eat His Body. After you done Communion, youse are up there every week, drinking the very blood of Jesus Haitch Christ. Have you done your Haitch Com?*

No.

Why haven't you?

Dunno.

How many are you?

Nearly five.

You've to be seven. When you're seven, you'll marry Jesus Haitch Christ.

Aoife's already seven, but you can't tell 'cause she's a runt. She's so small she fits in the frock Granny Volk sent me from America. It was a new dress of my very own and never was Fiona's first. 'Cause we do, after all, wear hand-me-downs. We are not rich, though we look posh in our American clobber. Mam made me hand-me-down my Kate Greenaway dress to Aoife before I'd grown out of it. That's 'cause Aoife's frock was raggedy and 'cause her da'll be singing tonight in *Gaels of Laughing*, my daddy's show.

Tonight is a special show to get money for the tinkers to buy better houses. We're not s'posed to say tinkers, though that's what they *are*, tinkers—Big Eamon, Young Eamon and Aoife. Mammy says it makes tinkers feel bad when you call them tinkers. So tinker is a really worse word than po-po or damn. I bet tinkers is as bad as fuck.

In the house Big Eamon's practicing music for Daddy. Light, jangly tunes fly out over the birdhouse high on the wall, into our lane. Big Eamon's known for his singing, all in Irish, over the wall. We're going to the show tonight, two families together. 'Cept Aoife and Young Eamon don't have a mam. They live with just their da in a caravan, him singing all the whiles. Wish I had a caravan for going Ireland's allover. I'd live in a campsite down the country and cook my dinner over a fire, banana sangitches and smokey tea. Wish I'd a caravan. I'd go with Daddy and we'd make a show.

Caw caw. Young Eamon calls from the carpark in the rear of the lane. He's hiding near the stables where the office people park their cars. Back behind them stables is a wet muck of lane with gicky puddles of black water. Mammy says we mustn't play back there or we'll get polio. I peep round the corner and find Young Eamon rooting in the muck with Daddy's prop sword.

Aoife and I hug the damp stable walls, picking round a wide pool of black water. Just then she pulls her fingers from her mouth and presses into her wee-wee.

What's the matter? I ask.

I've to piddle.

Shut it. Young Eamon smacks her hard. Aoife whimpers. He grips her mouth with dirty hands.

We can't go in the house when they're rehearsing. I'll be killed. I'm terrible-worried Aoife will go up to the house.

Daddy'd roar at me then, 'cause he told me to take the kids outside so he can get some work done.

Aoife's clutching the front of the hand-me-down frock I had to give her, pushing it up into her pee-hole, jiggling foot to foot when I get the idea. *Let's have a wee race. See whose wee reaches the puddle first.*

You're on. Young Eamon unzips his trousers.

I squat, yank my frillies to wizzz out fast. That Aoife and her freckles—even on her beam-end. Here we are—Aoife and me—underpants to knees, pissing at the rear of the stables. All these are real-true stables. Horses lived here once. That's why we've a half-door. In the olden days, horses reached their noses over the door and ate oats out of a feedbag sack. We can break our front door in half. There's a latch middle of the door. Throw the catch, the latch, the middle and they go together into one door. Or you can take them apart. When the top is closed and the bottom's open, it's a small door for kids. Big peoples must bend to run in under or they'll bang their heads and die.

I won, you pissers. Young Eamon hits the puddle first.

Pissss. Hate to lose. Pull up my drawers, smooth the wrinkles from my frock. *Will I get a wedding dress?* I ask, remembering the excitement of Communion.

When? Eamon squints at me suspiciously.

When I do Communion.

You will never do a Communion. Eamon is suddenly furious and I don't know why.

Course she will. Aoife says. *She'll have a beautiful dress of white with flowers at the waist and a veil spattered in diamonds.*

She will never do Communion. Young Eamon repeats, louder now. *'Cause her mother is a Yankee-Prod.*

That right?

Eh—I say. *'Spose so.*

Do you believe Mary was the mother of God? Aoife asks with a serious frown. They both surround me, their eyes all mean.

I dunno.

Proddy-woddy go to hell. Young Eamon taunts, pressing me 'gainst the wooden stable.

My daddy is a Catholick, I say. *A full-on one, so I'm half.* Though really, Daddy's atheist. He believes he created himself. He used to be a good Catholick, Granny says. Wish I was a whole Catholick, I'd get a school uniform and a gabardine coat.

Proddy-woddy go to hell. Young Eamon whacks my bare legs with Daddy's sword.

Proddy-woddy go to hell. Aoife screams.

This is just the end. *Take off my frock, you tinker-runt.*

I punch her in the eye and they clobber me.

Eamon O'Bearla, the best *Sean Nós* singer on this little island, is standing in front of the granite fireplace, eyes shut for the feeling.

Sho-ho-een. Ein-een-ee, ein-een-ee. Eamon's last note, a haunting thing, murmurs in the air for a full minute after he's done singing it.

There's the painting of John Millington Synge, Gina's personal saint, above the mantle behind him. Johnny Synge looks on in approval. This is good. This is very good. It was Olly's own idea to bring Eamon in from the encampment in Carlow and have him sing plaintive Irish songs. That'll put the perfect button on the end of act one.

It'll be exclamatory, Olly says. *We'll raise a mint for itinerant housing.*

Do yeh think? Eamon is asking, when the bottom half of the stable door blasts open and there in the squat doorway is Noleen, howling in her raspy growl—the little gurrier. Splashed heels to crown with wet black muck. Muck splattered over her dress. Muck down her socks.

Ah-flip. He told her to take the childer outside, keep them outta his hair.

Yeh dirty, filthy child. What did your mammy say? Olly says sharply. *You'll catch your death from playing in that polio water. Git up.* Hitting the rafters with a knuckle as he points toward the stairs. *Get into a hot bath. Now.*

In the square light of the bottom half-door, Aoife's face tips into view. Real nosey. What did that one do to his Nolee? The freckelly feck.

Don't forget to turn on the hot water heater. He calls to Noleen as she skitters up the stairs. Ah, the pet.

Lookit their house, gleaming. Everything ready for the press reception tonight. In the one big downstairs room, what looks like a bar is really a kitchen. Tucked under the counter is their gorgeous fridge. Olly dreamed that up, he designed it. When they first came to Tolka Row, there was no running water, no electrics, no stairs. They went up to bed in the loft by ladder. He laid the drains, the floor, the lino himself.

There's a commotion outside as the kids return from the markets, putting an end to him and Eamon's brief rehearsal. Des pushes through the Georgian door into their courtyard. *We bought everything in the shops,* Des announces, pulling the fambilly's red wagon behind him, parking it in the yard.

Gina and the gang are back from their shopping expedition, loaded with packages from Byrne's Butchers and Magill's. They even stopped into the specialty shop next to the American Embassy for a few packets of Birds Eye frozen corn on the cob—costs a fortune. Fiona, at ten, is wheeling Ely in the pram. Amazing thing, this having of children. Fee's got the fair skin, the red hair of Olly's brother Dominick. But lookit Ely's big brown peepers, like his very own eyes staring back. For Ely is the spit of Olly and that's why Olly detests him. Joke! Only a joke.

Ely, fat as butter, is in his fire-engine-red playsuit, picking at the brown paper parcels of meat crammed in around him. He's squeezing 'em, sinking his chubby hands into the soft mincemeat. Lifting a brown paper parcel and tossing it out. Ely stands in his pram and looks over the side, bewildered. The wheels spring up, and Fee quickly pushes him down before the pram spits Ely onto the stones. That's funny. Keaton or Chaplin couldn'ta done it better. The acrobatic precision of his son: the standing, the looking, the bounce of the wheels almost toppling him. Then Fee kicking to action before castrassophy struck.

He could put that in a sketch. Build a gigantic pram, dress himself as a brat. Execute an elaborate series of flips and turns—give the audience the fright of their lives while they split their guts laughing. This could work, yes it could. Olly is always on the lookout. Gathering people, gathering material, gathering acts. Although they open tonight, Olly's already working on his next big show. And there's the audition this coming Wednesday. *In the Clover,* a new telly series on *Radió Teilifís Éireann.* But don't think of it. He could pox the job.

Leave the food in the bag, Fiona shouts.

What now? Ely's munching on a bright green cooking apple. Fiona grabs the half-eaten thing, digging into his mouth for the remains when Ely bites her wrist with his baby teefs. She swipes his chin with the back of her nails.

Leave my children alone, Gina yells. *When you grow up and have kids of your own you can hit them all you like. But leave mine alone.*

Uff, the kids. All over the place, Eamon's as well. Interfering. Never shoulda had 'em. Why did he? Was Gina, she wants children in her life—that great desire for creation. And another coming in three months, four.

Gina's carrying the dry cleaning high off the ground. She's got Olly's new suit, the old one he's lending Eamon, and two clean white shirts.

Bring this into the house, Gina says, easily managing Young Eamon. She dumps the dry cleaning into his arms and unhooks the clothesline. *It's a British latrine in here. Fee and Aoife, put the food away.* She walks across the frontyard, looping the clothesline like a lasso, giving orders all the while. Olly loves how strong she is, how smart. A successful American.

Des, polish Daddy's good shoes. Young Eamon will polish

the brown pair for his daddy. Shove newspaper in the toes so they fit. Gina hangs the clothesline on the whitewashed wall above her rose garden. *And he needs decent clothes for tonight. Give him something of yours.*

Couldn't do it without her, Olly thinks. Grinning at his glamorous wife, the perm fresh on her head. Once she has everything sorted, she'll pop into her black cocktail dress, slip lipstick over her smile. He craves her. Yah-bastardins, he'd like to take her. Right there on the cobbledy stones.

There's a shrill whistle and a *heya Olly.*

It's Boots, the day barman from O'Donoghue's, a jaunty slacker. Boots works days so's he can do music nights. He plays the tin whistle like a fiend. Pipes, recorder, reeds. Anything tootley. Boots. He's young. He's loud. He's Boots. An easy-going rip. He's rolling a barrel of Guinness over the cobbles, delivering their O'Donoghue's order out the back of a van. There's Paddy's, wine, weeshy bottles of tomato juice. Gina's thought of the lot, even a crate of glassware rented for the night.

The postman bashes the brass knocker on the Georgian door. *Telegram for Mister O'Feeney.*

Olly gallops to the lane and signs with a flourish.

"Break a leg, Olly." Gina's brother Donald in Hackettstown, New Jersey. What an imagination on him. Break a leg, I ask you.

And there—bedammy. What's his prop sword doing out in the lane? Nolee and them savagers, playing with his things.

O-Jesus. Who is this? Clattering down the lane in her heels and her mini. Must be the new babby minder come to look after Ely. Her-legs, her-legs, her legs go miles up under that little bit of skirt. Olly sucks a breath, purses his lips. Stop-stop-stop. Not a hair over sixteen, wouldja stop.

Nothing to do about it, but—He could skip to the loo for a wank. Yeh-yeh-yeh.

Inside the house, pandemaniahhhhh. Olly mounts the stair four steps at a time.

I'm making faces at myself in the curved metal of the bath-taps. Watching my nose grow fat and my eyes disappear. When I move back and forward with my mouth open, I look like a cartoon fish.

I lie on my tummy, kick my legs and I'm swimming. I'll swim in the sea. I'll swim to America, all the way to Penn-sly-vaniah where my mam grew to tall.

Stop playing in there. Daddy thumps on the door.

Not done. I'm all soapy.

He marches into the room, lets out the water, pulls me from my bath. And the black polio soil skirls down the bung hole. He kneels on the floor and rubs me with the towel.

Your eyes are awful from crying. Daddy says, wiping my face and ruffing my white blonde, electricky hairs. *What'll you wear to me show tonight? The frock with strawbelly embroidery?*

I want a Communion frock.

No. You wouldn't be wanting that.

What?

Being a Catholick. School with the nuns. They'd beat you blue.

And over his shoulder like a sack of spuds. One step: into the hall. Two steps: into the MamDad room.

Alley-oop, Daddy shouts, tossing me high in the air over their bed. I pike and spin into a forward tumblesalt, springing off the mattress into a back flip, and a back flip, one more, one more. 'Til I plop on the bed with the dizzies. Daddy tickles me and tickles me. He likes me most of all the kids in our family, I know it. Then he rolls me up in the big white towel, so I look like a cigarette. With feets.

sixpence the stars

On Christmas Eve afternoon, Aunty Mara carries our radio cross the room. *Your mammy's going to tell Ireland a story.* She sets the radio down on Mam's writing desk next to our Christmas tree wrapped in red and green paper chains we made this afternoon. We worked for hours gumming and gluing, little circle of red, slipping a green through to glue, then a red through to glue, then a green into red into green. Now there's a big cross of chains over our downstairs home. Kitchen to fire corner, Mam's desk to the foot of the stairs. It looks so holly, so jolly-lay-loo-lia.

We even wrote our Santy letters. Here is mine:

DEER SANTY,

WILL YOU BRING ME A PURR OF RED BALLY SHOES SO I CAN DANCE TO THE MUSIC ON TELLY AND TAKE LESSONS. I WOULD LIKE A DOLLY AND A COOKERY SET TO MAKE HER CHRISTMAS TEA AND SUPPER. MY LITTLE BROTHER WANTS A TEDDY AND A LITTLE COAT FOR THE TEDDY BEAR TO KEEP IT WARM. HE CAN'T WRITE HIMSELF SO I HAVE TO FOR HIM.

You must be quiet when your mammy's on. Aunty Mara says. Aunty Mara is Daddy's big sister. She's minding us today on account of Mam is in the studio telling her story in the radio part of *RTÉ*. Skinny Aunty Mara wheels the dial, making it loud so we can hear when Mam comes on.

And Mam will tell us soon. She will tell a Christmas story, 'cause Santy Claus is tonight and tomorrow's Christmas.

Wait—that's our mam coming out the radio. Sounds like she's inside there. Is Mam in the radio? Sitting on the lino, I lean back to see. Course not. Mam's far too big to fit back there.

When I touch the spongy brown cloth where the sound comes out, I feel her words on my fingertips.

Don't touch the wireless, Noleen. Aunty Mara shovels food into Ely's mouth.

No touch, Yeeny. Ely arches his back and almost pulls the highchair down on top of himself like he did last week.

Sit down and listen. Fee slaps my hand.

Her slap stings, so I cry. But stop when I hear my mam. Even Ely is quiet so we can listen to soft America in her voice. America, warm, here in her words. America, warm, here in the room.

Christmas on an Island

—Radió Éireann Broadcast - Dec. 1965

The first Christmas I spent away from my home in Pennsylvania, I had come to University in Dublin for a Ph.D. on John Synge. I wanted to get a glimpse

of Synge's magnificent Western World. So I set out for the West at Christmas time. An actor-friend invited himself along. You may know of him: Oliver O'Feeney. We hitchhiked to Galway to catch a curragh bound for Inishmaan. Olly and I collected at the pier with young Islanders returning from navvying and nursing in England. They gave us a look, watching us as the curragh drew up. O'Feeney and I pretended we were able for it, feigning confidence-supreme that such a flimsy vessel made of bark, canvas and tar could weather the wilds of that sea. We were tossed up and down on a mad see-saw. Terrifying waves crashed six feet in the air. It took five miserable hours to travel thirty miles to Inishmaan.

When we reached shelter, a spinsterish landlady held out a delicate cup and saucer. "Get this into you. Black tea, so strong a mouse could walk across it. Better than medicine after that voyage."

Her tea calmed me so, I managed to thank her. She recognized my accent.

"Sure, how could you be American and you so horribly healthy? Now. How long will you be needing accommodations? And are you married-like?"

"Do you mean Olly and I would sleep in the same bed?" I was flummoxed because company-keeping with O'Feeney had never crossed my mind.

She put me in a room off the pub to keep her eye on me. And stashed O'Feeney in the attic, so there'd be no occasion for sin.

Now, that's a funny thing, I'm thinking. Mam and Daddy 'fore they got married. Not sleeping in the same bed? 'Cause that's all they do, climb in the bed together. Like they can't wait for that time with each other. After us kids is asleep, with Daddy home from his plays, they twist in. Arms up and round each other in their dreamings. Daddy snoring, Mam humming quick words—have no meaning—into his ear.

I know this, I know. 'Cause in the early morning-time, I open their door and watch them, dopey in sleeps.

Them. Daddy turning in to Mammy's holding.

Them. Tucked into each other. Two rabbit babbies. Breathing and pawing in their dreams.

The next morning—

From out of the radio box, Mam takes me back to *Inishmaan*. She's bringing people sitting round the wireless, dunking bikkies in their tea, carrying all of Ireland further inside her Christmas story.

Olly and I set out for a thatched cottage at the far end of the island. In the west country, the day moves every twenty minutes through the four seasons. Along our way we picked strawberries, wildflowers, exquisite shells. We waded in waves of a Christmas Eve.

"I've never known such peace as with you," O'Feeney said to me.

"Isn't it the island?" I tried to joke him.

"No, it's you," he said most seriously.

And then it came—our first mad kiss. His gift, one wild red rose.

"O, love," he said. "O, life. These are the fine days and us in them."

Des sticks out his lip and pouts. That's 'cause he always turns away when Daddy hugs my mam. 'Cause Des wants Mam all to himself.

Hsst, says Aunty Mara, plucking at Des's shirt. She *loves* love stuff 'cause she's never had a boyfriend. Unless you count Mickser Murphy—Daddy's best friend from the san. The Murphs tried to court Aunty Mara years ago but she spurned him on account of he went into the Pigeon House Hospital at the age of eight.

"Sure, yeh wouldn't want her." Daddy said to Mickser Murphy. "She's up to her ears in rosary beads."

"Hasn't the health to be a nun." Mickser sneered. "Racking and hucking with the catarrh."

"If she saw a bare langer, she'd die." Daddy told him and they sniggered together like schoolboys. "She'd be safe on a troopship." I was under the dinner table, earwigging. "Noddy Big Ears" Granny calls me. Gran is wrong, it's Noddy *and* Big Ears. They write super books. Mickser and Daddy were having their tea. I only adore Mickser Murphy, 'cause he's not much taller than me. He has black Irish eyes like my da, and he does magics, yes he does. One time he zapped a silver sixpence under my teacup. It just appeared there, most magically.

The cottage where we stayed was freshly whitewashed for the season and had a fine open hearth. Bridgie—wrapped in a traditional red petticoat, striped with a black ribbon at the calf—crouched in the light of the fire, smoking a clay pipe.

As O'Feeney rolled a fresh cigarette, Bridgie knocked ash to a saucer. "Would you give me a knuckle of tobacco for my pipe? Tobacco's better than dried tea leaves, God love you."

We were treated like family that night. A great bottle of whiskey was put down for us, cork tossed into the fire. The children came in. Shy at first, they soon loosened up over lemonade and sweets.

"Where'd you come from?" A young girl asked.

"America."

"Would you show me on the globe I got for Christmas?"

And I traced my route: Pennsylvania to New York to Cóbh, then Dublin. Dublin, Maynooth. Maynooth to Galway, Connemara. Over the sea and over the sea, to Inishmaan—this tiny island.

"I was on the mailboat to Galway once."

"And what did you think of it?"

"Tis not a bad thing to see a bit of the world."

Settling down that Christmas Eve, I was content to see her bit of the world.

Long before dawn the town headed out for Mass. Their church was a gray stone fort lit only by candles. Women gathered down front, and men sat together

at the rear. The service was in Irish and there was no music. Not one note.

After Christmas dinner, all the island came to meet us. The school teacher, the priest, his mother. "Tis a wonderful thing having a son a priest. And nice, too."

It was then Bridgie turned to me. "Did you ever by strange chance meet my son? The favorite. He's out there in America. A man by the name of Padraig. He drove a tram in Boston, Massachusetts for twenty years. He drove that tram for all them fine Americans. But he have no English on him. Having no English, just the same, maybe you wouldn't know him."

Bridgie sat back in her chair, drew genuine tobacco from her pipe. Shook her head, glanced to the stone hearth, polished smooth by years of fire-tending. "No-no. You wouldn't know him, surely."

I wish I could have said, "Yes, I know your Padraig, your most-loved, the favorite."

Bridgie's children—all twelve—left the island for the states decades before. I asked her how she lived with such loss.

"You see, it's a very lovely thing to get the letters. The children grow and leave you, they do. They leave you. They must go away from the island. But they send back the letters. I don't know what we'd do on Aran if it wasn't for the letters."

Mam stops talking, her story's done.

Then a song plays. A girl sings for Bridgie cross the waters on Aran. Bridgie of the old days, the backyears, the ago.

O happy the mother who ne'er reared a son
For little did she ere think what hardships would come
Not a quilt nor a blanket for to cover her skin
But an old broken sentry-box where the tide's drifting in

The instruments after:

Flute alone, a guitar answers.

Then they gather, flute-guitar together, rippling on the sands of Connemara.

As for himself? Olly's at the rail in Paddy O'Donoghue's Pub in Merrion Row, listening to his wife on the wireless. Olly recalls that "first mad kiss." The wooden hug, her hard schmooch. Like she could catch it off him. But after a time, she melted. 'Til they were living in each other's mouths.

"You cure me," He remembers her saying. No-wait, he's after telling a lie. That was himself saying, "you cure me."

Before he met Gina: a world of begrudge and torment. Sneaking off the ward, slipping outta the Pigeon House on the sly. Snatching the bus from Ringsend into the Nelson Pillar. Performing at Madame Cogley's pocket theatre, playing to eight, maybe ten people in that damp basement. Standing round the walls, drinking wine from jam jars, eating cake out of the hand. Then he met Regina. The style of her, tall in her American coat, silk scarf, her knock-me-over red high heels.

"Never known such happiness," He said to her. And it was true. Is true, is true.

It wasn't just her love of words, of books, of music, of

plays. It was how she opened to him. Opened up her smashing self. He could tell she'd not done that before. Open so fully like that and allow him to walk in. When he—*Hah.* Olly opens and opens to anyone wandering by. He has ardent and eccentric attachments to working men, barkeeps, unemployed hacktresses. Anyone with a story and a wanting. 'Cause Olly finds himself in their wanting. As for Gina? She needs nothing but him. O, her pure belief in him.

"Why me?" He asked her.

" 'Cause you are a great rarity, Olly O'Feeney. You are so far above all the others."

And right there with them words, she pulled him from out of his dark self and into a big-big world.

"You cure me," He said then. Tossed his streptomycin to the waves, walked away from the TB wards for life. 'Cause Regina loves him full. She loves his all.

Quite the wife, Olly, remarks Boots the day barman, a full glass in his brown-stained fingers. Curious. Olly notes the acid-bitten sleeves of Boots's jumper. What's this he's setting on the counter? Harp Larger with a foamy head.

That she is, Olly says, pushing the glass aside. *I've to run home for some spondoolies.* Each year at the Christmas, Gina gets her soybean check. One of her uncles? A spinster aunt? In-anyway, *someone* died and left her shares of stock in a soybean farm in What Cheer, Iowa. What Cheer is right. Thank the naked Jesus for that check 'cause he lost out on that job in the new *RTÉ* series—*In the Clover.* Went to that fellah with the big fuzzy eyebrow, Milo O'Shea, yeh. Bloody amateur. *Roll Me Over,* they should call it, *and Fuck Me.* Gotta get home, nab some a that dough afore it vanishes.

Out in the scene shed. I'm out in the shed and she's in the house with the rest of them. Fee. My enemy. Big pig sister. So smacky. She bashed me hard in the face. Hate her, hate her forever.

Would you stop your screeching? Aunty Mara said to me. *Your behaviors is not very Christmassy.*

That's 'cause Noleen is Chriss-messy, Fee taunted.

So I came out here, with my Chriss-messy self.

I'm alone in the scene shed where the turf is bricked high for winter and the scenery flats are stacked 'gainst the walls. There's a wooden board cut in the shape of a princess couch. The back of the board is knotty wood, but the front is painted like a scarlet sofa. There's a head cushion with a smiling pink button. I put a bench hind the painted sofa and lie down. I am Princess Chrissymess, lounging on my princess couch. Barefoot servants pare my nails, brush my hair three thousand times. When all of a sudden, Daddy comes home. I see him through the grubby window. He ducks under the wet clothes limp on the line and he's into the house.

Back in a quickwink, he dodges through the courtyard door. I'm out and I'm after him. At the street end, he turns left, heading for O'Donoghue's.

On Merrion Row there's a weensy hole in the street. No one knows about it but me. I squeeze a pebble through the gap. Wait forty seconds and *pah-lunk.* There's a river down there, far beneath, far benunder, rushing under the cars on the road. I press my lips to the hole and call: *hellooooo.*

Noleen. The river answers.

Hello.

Noleeeeeen.

Better get out of the street 'fore I'm hit by a lorry.

After ages and ages, Daddy ambles out of O'Donoghue's with a man wearing a long-to-the-ground coat and a high-crowned bowler hat. He looks like the real-life version of Mister Mack. Did Daddy get his idea for Mister Mack from this ould fellah? 'Cause Daddy's all the time stealing from peoples for his shows. He took my lollypop shop for Mister Mack. "Lookit he's back, it's Mister Mack. With his trif-fick makey-uppers. Gather your children round, it's Mister Mack." And Mister Mack taught the people watching how to make a lollypop shop out of a fridge box. What you do is get a fridge box, sellotape lollypops all over it, and sell 'em to your pals. That was *my* lollypop shop. Daddy stole it.

He catches me under my arms and tosses me up into laughing. Daddy tips me high overhead, pushing me up-up-up into the day going down and the night coming up which is Christmas.

Daddy-Daddy-Daddy, where you going?

Wisher's taking me to pick up Mammy at Radió Éireann *and you're coming, too.* He says, turning to the man in the long coat, *This is Noleen, my pucksy girl.*

He's my favorite daddy.

Hope I'm your only daddy.

Tis a pleasure and a treasure to meet you. Wisher talks

high in his nose. He salutes from his bowler, bends to shake my hand.

In the lane at the side of O'Donoghue's, Wisher has a horse and cab smartly painted green and gold.

There y'are, me auld segotia, me lovely picture postcard. Wisher the Cabby lifts me so I walk my feet up the small steps into the carriage. He wraps me in a green velvet blanket with gold tassels. Wisher is, I do believe, Mister Mack-the-really.

Daddy climbs in, sits on the leather seat beside me.

Is this a horsey cab from the olden days?

The horse isn't, but the cab is. Daddy's watching the world go by.

Were you in the olden days, too, Daddy?

I'll olden-days you, I'm a very young actor.

Whoa there, Flossy. Aisy does it. Wisher flicks a switch at Flossy's bum and cartwheels whirl the spingles. The night spins into *on*. And we're off to pick up Mam at the studio.

It's bell ringing time above, bell ringing time. The tower bells is thringing their songs for Christmas Eve. Everyone's out and they are shopping. There's a family sticking prezzies in the boot of a car.

Are you having the happy-happies? Daddy asks me.

Yes, I am happy, deep through my all-of-mes. *This is a fairy night.*

Then put on your wishing cap, for tonight all wishes come true at the gift of the Fairy, Wisher says as we wind our way to Capel Street Bridge.

Janey, one-way streets. It's a world of one-way streets.

Iron lampposts hang over them in big black question marks. *Where're we going, where?* I ask the lanterns.

Why, here, the lanterns answer, opening a way through the violet blue.

Water's coursing under the Ha'Penny Bridge.

Water slaps the river walls.

When I crinkle my eyes at shops and lorry lamps, the neon signs go starry.

Colors streak cross the shivering Liffey.

And the gulls swoop and scream, swoop and scream.

As we turn onto Henry Street, Wisher curses, pointing to Lord Nelson up his pillar. *Jayzus-indade, lookit that hellion.*

Lord Nelly? Daddy asks.

The British dog. With his down-the-nose sneer at the little country, like it's him rules Dublin. Military hero, I don't think. We should give him the boot.

What an idea. Daddy laughs hard as a donkey. *For the fiftieth birthday of the Easter Rising. What about that?*

Wisher jerks the reigns and Flossy claps to a stop by the General Post Office. There's Mam, paisley scarf tied over her hairdo. Mam got her hairs rollered and set yesterday at the Swan Room, a House of Hair and Beauty Culture. She's got the lipstick on for her radio talk and for Christmas.

Noleen, what are you doing here? Mam says.

I found her playing in the scene shed, says Daddy. He is lying. I was outside of O'Donoghue's.

What a beautiful cab. Mam's smile is fierce. Daddy kisses her right on the street in front of Dublin.

Thanks for the lift, Daddy says.

I'll love you and leave you. Wisher takes Daddy's pound note, touches the brim of his bowler, clicks his teeth. Flossy plods towards the bustle of O'Connell Street and Nelson up his pillar, looking down.

Daddy and Mam each take my hand, haul me up between. Daddy steps in rhythm with Mam. Left leg, right leg, then we run. Them on the ground, me in the air. I'm kicking my legs into the air. Running past shop windows in the air. They run me over the spangling path. Over the streets and over the roads, they run me all the way to Moore Street.

Moore Street—the Dublin markets where the shawlies sell fruit and things off their stalls. Shawlies is called shawlies on accounta they all wear shawls.

Can hear 'em far before we arrive. A roar of voices comes.

Buy your lovely little fir tree here.

Canary tomatoes.

Shilling a bunch the celery.

There y'are, me ould flower. There's a dirty girl talking to me. Her voice is skranky. It scrapes up outta the gutter from which she comes. Though she's small like a girl, she's a mam 'cause she's got a sticky milky babby sucking milk from her diddies. The Dirty Mam crouches in a doorwell. Her feets're bare and covered in half-healed cuts. She's rough and her nails is broke. One hand's under her baba's head, the other hand's holding a cardboard begging box. Inside is holy medals and cards of the saints.

The Dirty Mam tugs Daddy's trousers. *Spare a few shillings for the babby?*

Daddy drops a tenbob note in her cardboard box.

Thanks in the thousands, Mister Honey. I'll pray for your special intention as Dublin lights the blessed cangle this Holy Christmas night.

We move through the stalls.

Three halfpence the goldy apples.

Jumping monkeys, get the last of the jumping monkeys.

Downlow, peoples bump me with parcels. Hands swing in my face. Down near the coat hems and trouserlings is filth. A man brushes the street with a treebranch broom, a real-true witch's broomstick. He's sweeping torn lettuce greens, a plum tucked-still in purple papers. The sweep taps it into a neat pile, but it soon gets trampled, so he gathers it up all-the-overs again.

Hello me darling girl, Nolee. Isn't it Jacintha, the fir tree shawlie. She knows Mam and Daddy from when they used to live in Blather Alley, the market dealers' neighborhood. She nudges Mammy's elbow, asking, *When are yeh?*

Excuse me? Mam says.

Looka, Gina, it's clear you are in the club. When's it coming?

O. Mam blushes. *April.*

Mind yourself, Mister Mack. Or you'll have babbies hanging offa yer eyebrows. She wags her finger at Daddy, calling him Mister Mack like he's on the telly right now, like she forgets his really-name. *Here's half a crown for your Christmas box, alana.* And she hands me half a crown. Terriff. *Christmas trees, get your Christmas trees.*

We already bought our tree, I tell her. *From you, don't you 'member?*

Christmas trees, are you buying? She bellows.

Heya Olly, here's a bit of the bartley for your Christmas box. A man throps down two bulging burlap sacks. *There y'are. Turnips, parsnips, and spuds.*

Starlights and balloons.

Little oranges two shillings the box.

Mechanicalized toys.

Stars, sixpence a star.

Stallkeepers box-up their cartshops for the night. The Christmas market's vanishing. The cartsellers're collecting their crud in bockety prams. The market cries grow desperate, grow louder than loud.

Christmas crackers ten shillings a box.

Stars for the top of the tree.

Mechanicalized—

Angels and—

Stars—

Silver bells for your sweet fir tree.

The shawlies and their roadcalls ring from Moore Street, far to the old city walls.

Two shilling the box the little oranges. Buy the little oranges for the kiddellies.

And there on a cart—trays and trays of tangerines, that's what Mammy calls 'em. I pick one up, hold it fat in my hands, pull it to my nose and smell.

Daddy, I whisper. *Can we get tangerines for the Christmas?*

A box of tangerines, please, Mam asks the Tangerine Shawlie.

Come here 'til I tell you, when are you?

How does everyone know she's having a babby?

It'll be April.

Gorgeous. Please God yiz'll have a son now for Ireland. And she turns to me. *Like the little oranges, wouldja?*

I'd like them little oranges, the whole box.

Sacrum Jaysoo-kin, youse must have the little oranges at Christmas. 'Cause on that first Christmas Eve... Have youse not heard the story?

The Tangerine Shawlie pulls her shawl tight to her bonnets so her chests look big as Sugarloaf Mountain. She breathes a deep gulp of night.

And...

Way back in bible-days there was Mary and her husband Joe, a carpenter. Mary was a spouse most chaste. And yet, in the mystical body of Mary, a great swell was astirring. For Mary is going to have a babby, and not just any ould babby. This will be God and Mary's son, Christ the King, the Lord of everything. Loollay-loollee. Ah, Mary. Sorrow-sick and sorrow-worn—

Must I hear it again? Daddy shifts his feet, dropping our burlap sacks. Rutabagas and spuds thunk the cobblestones.

Tush, you ould stager. Where was I? Yeh, Mary and Joe. Over they go, over the living roads, slouching off to Bethlehem to have the babby borned. They knock at every stable hall and inn and bang-nothing. No rooms left. O Gates, them landladies—a brood of vipers—don't care if Mary and Joe go to the gutter.

Anyways—la-la. Doesn't night come in a frock of blue moonlight and blacklace. There's the moon going "hoo-hoo" and flocks of stars o'erhead, gala-exx-stacies of *stars.*

At the veriest edge of sky, Precious Mary spies the one winky star. And that one winky star says to her, "Folly me, Mary."

Mary says to Joe, says Mary, "Holy Joe! Folly that star."

So they folly that one winky star cross desert sands and rock 'til they reach a cowshed.

"Are you mad, woman?" Joe asks her. "This cowstall's no place for a bleeding babby."

"Shut it, Mister Joeboy. That one winky star has found me a nest for to birth Christ the King, the Lord of everything. Loollee-loollay."

"Super-doopers," Joseph mutters. "Amn't I nearly killed-knackered from all these goings-on? Leading that manky donkey. And such." He spreads fresh yelly straw in the cow trough. Now the cow trough is surrounded by aminals: the white sheep with the coal eyes, oxen, piggies—a pair of them—all peering about, most curious about these lunatics clearing up their cowpen.

Once Joeboy's got the field-straw tucked in, Mary stands. Gone are her slothy clothes. She's wearing a petticoat of damask red under a holy blue holy wimple.

When—Sacra Fa-milly-ers—doesn't God part the heavens, hurl down the star. Doesn't that star come screaming through the ceiling, and plop, land in the cow trough.

There's a whirling wheel of light and by jingo, star of mercy, star of grace—there in the field straw is the naked Baba Jaysoo. If yeh saw him, yeh'd eat him like salt. His dimples and yelly locks, pink mickey flopped 'gainst his leg.

Howandever, at the selfsame time, there was a gang of fellas from the valley of kings follying the very same pointy star. And didn't that pointy star point them king-fellas in the direction of Mary's cowstable.

They joyed to find they'd arrived at the spit-second Jayzoo fell to earth. Ah-yeh, there's the Sacred Enchanter getting his chubby chins tickled by his Mammy-in-Gloriam.

Begab-begob, that cowshed was mental, absolutely mental. 'Cause there's tribes of aminals what came with the kings—a menagereeee. Lions, ostriches, griffins and peahens. A harpie fluting the pipes, the priest swinging his chazoo-bells, and far back at the rear was a young shepherd lad and his doggy, Patch.

On that first Christmas Eve, all the guests brung their gifts to the Great God Babby Divine. There was gold, and frying pans, and more.

After everyone had given their prezzies, the little shepherd boy inched up to the Babby in the straw. He was sneaking his prezzy on the pile, see, 'cause he was shamed. Shamed it was far too insignificant next to the gold frying pans, for it was only a weensy basket of little oranges. Soon as he set out the basket, didn't the Babby Divine grab up and gobble down all the little oranges, flinging peels at the peahens, spitting pips and wiping his sticky hands on his swaddly clothes.

Telling yeh, Christmas wouldn't be Christmas without the little oranges. The Tangerine Shawlie settles a tray of little oranges in my arms—each one wrapped in silver foil like a present.

Mam and Daddy and me carry our Christmas food and our gifts and our gifts and our gifts over the glittering Liffey to home.

Moore Street cries at our backs.

Jumping monkeys, get the last—

Fading dazey far behind.

Stars for the top of the tree. Stars, get your stars.

I'm browned off selling, take the lot.
All the stars for sixpence, sixpence for all the stars.

Her Uncle Dominick O'Feeney, a fair and punchy bachelor, is on the ferry over. Standing at the deckrails in the bow, he's the first one facing shore. His beige raincoat is belted high over his stomach like a prig. His square red beard emphasizes the cut of his jaw. The ciggy, set crooked in his teeth. *To Dublin to Dublin to Dublin.* Can't get there fast enough. *To Dublin to Dublin to Dublin.* He whispers into the splintering flash of sun on the sea.

And Dublin comes in, Dublin comes at him.

He wants off the boat, wants home.

He just can't get over the beauty of Ireland, the Wicklow hills, every one known to him, for he'd crawled all over them as a boy. Howth on his right, the breakwater. The Three Rock Mountains of *Dún Laoghaire* and the harbor, granite-clean. In England, he misses the granite, the silverglint off the paving stones, magical colors on a wet day, Georgian houses and their multi-shades of brick, such a change from London's gray. Seaweed twists and slithers in the shallows. There's that fug, that Dublin fug: turf smoke and grass.

He is home.

Making his way down the gangway, scanning the crowds on the granite pier, Nick O'Feeney is eager for the Christmas faces of Olly and his tribe. Gina, tall, dark, with a tan like a fil-um star. Fiona, his favorite, since she minds him of himself, ginger-haired and gawky, standing to the side.

Then the boys who is just boys, nothing more. And wee Noleen, the little savage.

He's so excited 'cause he's loaded with prezzies. A Matchbox Motorway Set of replica cars for Des, a teddy for Ely made of genuine fur. For Fiona, a Parisian beret, and he'd searched and searched since Olly asked him: a bright pair of red ballet slippers for that savage Noleen.

Killing-bladder-hell, shoulda pissed before. But he couldn't miss the first glimpse of the fambilly—Olly's brood. So good to be staying with the gang on Tolka Row, even if it means sleeping on the couch. In a day or two, he'll go out to Dean's Grange for a visit with the Ma. Grim bitch. With Mara home from the san at the moment, there's no bed for him in the bungalow. "The invalid daughter," his mother calls her. Dossing down on a daybed in the parlor. No place for Nick but a rusty cot in the garden shed. Olly slept there on and off for years. Each time he'd a spell from the Pigeon House, he was exiled to the tool shed with the pissing cats.

"When he's on the bones of his bum, it's home to the Ma-zer." The blondie twat. Olly was sick, never mooching.

Fuh. Nick sips his breath back through his teeth. It's skonchy in his leg, the left one. Near his bollocks, not quite a pain, but—*Skonchy* is what. Where are they? Olly, yeh prick. Always late.

Noleen's mam, Regina Volk O'Feeney, is sitting on the toilet, flat to the seat. Alone for the minute, having a rest. Taking a break from the mayhem down the stairs. The cabbage, the ham, Birds Eye corn on the cob. Christmas dinner at the ready in the kitchen. But here she is hiding, taking breath. With the support hose tight at her knees, she hugs herself at the calves and breathes. *Ugh.* There's urine stains under the bowl. Lily their housekeeper missed a spot. But how can Lily keep up? How can she keep up? Could have been Des, Olly for that matter, or Uncle Nick who has had too much to drink already. He arrived off the ferry from Holyhead, reeling and singing. Ten o'clock in the morning and Olly's matching him one-on-one. Perhaps, after dinner, they'll head out for a saunter and she can pull the house back to order. It's demolished entirely.

Mammy. Ely toddles through the door, like a fat baron in his new teddy bear coat, yellow paper crown from the Christmas crackers. *If-ta go weeee.*

Stay out, she says to him, tugging the hose over her swelling belly. Can't wait 'til it's over and the baby's come. These legs, these legs—murderous. Her varicose veins, the pinching heat, such tightness, such pain. It's hard for her to admit she has pain, even to herself. Never mind anybody else.

As she lifts Ely to his potty, out the window in the garden, there's a flash of red on the winter grass. She sees it through the branches on the elderbelly tree. Funny, how the children's words have replaced the originals in her mind. The kids are turning her into a moron. She's forgotten everything she learned in school. Elder-berries. Elderberry tree.

And there's her Noleen, hair wild, dancing in the garden with the ballet shoes Nick gave her for Christmas.

She's flinging and leaping, tumbling and rolling in the grass. Noleen's got Lily's stainy apron on. Gina stands still for a moment watching her bold girl. She's plucking stones from the rockery—discards of Wicklow granite John the Stoney had left over from building their fireplaces. Noleen's plopping them into the bowl of the apron. Noleen clutches the apron of stones to her breast, a pregnant mammy.

In the bowl of me apron is twelve goldy apples.
Though twelve goldy apples have I, where are my boys?
Where are my sons? Off to England every one.
Ochón agus ocón ó.

Gina chucks her tongue and gets it. Noleen's imitating the ballet they saw weeks ago. The famine story, Nuala and her sons.

Ochón agus ocón ó.
Where are my boys? Where are my sons?
Off to England every one.
So I run up the trunk of the sycamore tree.
I dive and fly and fly away free.

on tolka row

In Februaries, it is cold. Wet nights smather on the windowpanes outside. Me and Des rush freezing from our bath into the MamDad room.

Des leaps onto the bed, grabs a pillow and whacks me. We bounce naked on the bed, scuffing the bedcovers in a jolly pillow fight 'til I get the shivers and drop belly-down on Mam's side of the bed near the clothes press. Sometimes I play inside there. Open up the double doors, empty the shoes, push the hangers to the side and make a play all my own in the little theatre that happens when you open up them doors.

Mam hauls Ely into the room, and Fee pounds through the door in her sockedy feet.

Settle down kids, or you'll get no story. Mam plunks Ely on the bed. Fatso Ely, not yet two. Squirmy kicker, never stays in place. Mam's holding onto his kicky legs, pink from his bath. Mam reaches for the powder, but I get there first. *Powder me too, Mam?*

Powder is for babies, Des says. *It's called baby powder, dopey-head.*

Fee tosses Des his 'jama bottoms. He steps into the hole of each leg, ties the waist string.

We'll do Ely first, Mam says. *Then you.* Sprinkling powder over Ely's bum.

Me too, Des yells. But before I can get my hands on the powder, Des snatches the plastic box, pumps a blast of white into his eyes and he's crying.

Fee takes him to the toilet to clear his eyes, so I have the baby powder all to myself.

Just a little, Mam says, pinning Ely's nappy snug to his middle, then into his plastic pants for the night.

I sit at Mam's dressing table with the blue tub of cream for under her arms, hairpins laid in a scatter of baby powder snow. In the mirror, I can see me. That is me looking. My me in the glass is looking back at me. Blue eyes, shocky blonde hairs.

Stop playing in the mirror, Mam says. *It'll make you vain.*

I tip the powder onto my palm, pat it on my chest, under my neck. Now, I smell like baby. Take my bugsers—used to be Fee's bugsers, but they're my bugsers now—off the storytelling chair. Force my feets into the feetsies, there's room to grow. Pull on the top part and snap it to the bottoms. Wearing my bugsers, I feel like Bugs Bunny. Alls I need is ears.

Mam settles Ely in his cot at the foot of the bed in the MamDad room. Ely sleeps in here with them. I rush to Ely bundled in his cot. Rush to hug, to love, to kiss him. I love my round brother Ely. Love the two holes in his nose. I look up his noseholes into the black of his mind. Wonder what's going on in there. What he thinks, what he sees.

Love you lots and lots of jelly tots, tons and tons of jammy buns. Ely smiles so wide. He's mouth, he's all smile.

When Des and Fee come back, we crawl under the covers, ready for Mam's story.

Mam rocks in her chair next to Ely in his cot.

Story! Ely orders. It's the third word he ever learned. Mam first, Daddy, then story. His fourth word was Yeeny, that's me.

Ely wants a story, Mam says. *Shall I read you a book?*

No, I say. *Tell us a story from out of your brain.* 'Cause those are the best of the best-best stories. Mam tells us her young years before she met our daddy. She tells us about sledding down hills in snow. Spitting watermelon pips in summer. Running the soybean fields on the fambilly farm and eating beans-beans-beans 'til she could never eat 'em again. My mam lived through Depression. That's when America had no money. Her family had no money 'cause her daddy died when she was seven years of age and left her mam to rear six kids alone. So her brothers got sent to stay on a chocolate farm. They were banished to live away and go to school in Hershey, Penn-sly-vania.

Here in the MamDad bed, it's warmworld. Mam's rocking into starting, thinking over what she'll tell us. Thinking how she'll take us off to storyland.

When I first came to Ireland, people were singing in the street. Buskers, they're called. There was a lady in an emerald evening gown playing a golden concert harp outside. Dublin was heaven. So different from German-Pennsylvania.

Inside the flow of Mam's American words, inside that hum, I can see her. Tall. My very gentle-going mammy, walking into Dublintown.

Ely turns in his cot. His tummy wambles.

He's starving. Fee scoops him up, gives him to Mam.

There's a good Ely. Mam opens her blouse, backs into the rocking chair.

Ely hungers at my mam. He's pressed against her shirt-front, toes wiggly in his happy.

Did you feed me with them things? I ask her.

Yes, Fee says. *I saw Mam feed you.*

Wouldn't want them fat things in my mouth, says Des.

Mam lies Ely in his cot. She fusses over him, gives him a kiss middle of his forehead. It's not fair—getting big. Once you get big, Mam kisses you no more.

All right, kids. Time for B-E-D.

I shut my eyes lightly, like I'm sleeping.

Come on, Des, Fee says, pushing him off the bed with her feets.

Noleeny. Mam gently nudges my shoulder. *Time for beddy-bye.*

I snuggle in the pillow, hoping she'll believe that I'm truly asleep so I can stay in the bed with Mam 'til Daddy comes home.

Wake up, Noleen. You're too big for me to carry.

Jammy buns. I mutter, pretending to be lost in the words of dreams. *Bradley sandals.*

I can't lift you because of the baby.

Everyone's on about that new baby, six more weeks it'll be here. I squeeze my eyes tight.

Up you go, jump into bed.

I turn over, ignore her.

I am a lucky, 'cause Mam believes I'm soporific as Peee-turrr Rabbit. She takes me in her arms and shuffles to the kidsroom. Then I pretend to wake up so we can say our prayers. Daddy never does prayers, he never does stories. He just tells jokes to his pals when they pay a call.

I know God, Des is boasting.

God is in the wind, I say to better him.

He made the world Himself.

Up in heaven He is. And I can see God up there in his grand heaven. Smiling away at how good we're being down here, going to sleep so easy for our mam.

Lie down now, lie down now. Ye small birds. Mam's whisper-words at the kidsroom door. *Ye small birds.*

Soon I'm falling-sliding-falling into dizzy-dazzle dreams.

Go to sleep now, O sleep now. Bird-eenees, bird-eenees. Mam sings in Irish this time. *Sho-ho-een. Ein-een-ee, ein-een-ee.*

Boots, the day barman from O'Donoghue's, sticks his head into the arched doorway of O Dearest Mattress, a bedshop on O'Connell Street. It's a rain-slutting night. Spitty flicks of annoyance in yer face. O'Feeney hunches to the door-frame, making room. It's nine fifty-five on Clery's clock. Early. What do you know.

Heyeh, Head, Boots says. *Gorra smoke?*

Just the one, Olly says, slipping easy into the Northside accent the way he does when he and Boots scheme together. He plucks a fag from over his ear. *Gorra match?*

Gorra mouth?

Gorra lung?

Do I fuck. Actually, em. Boots jokes him. *I've two.*

Lucky you, Olly says. *Got that match, or what?*

That I have, Mister O'Feeney. That I have. Boots pulls a matchstick from his shirt pocket. Sparks it, and they share.

I know an architect. Olly jumps straight to the business at hand. *This architect thinks we*—Neglecting to mention the word *naval,* as in naval architect. His brother Nick, the Royal Navyman, designer of sludge boats for her Majesty the Queen. *The way to do it. Do it complete,* he says, *is lay the charge at the point of breach. That would be in the cage, on the lookout platform.*

There they are, the pair of them, squinting through the misty rain at Lord Nelson up his pillar. Olly thinks to Christmas Day. After the porter, the dinner ham, him and his brother Dominick came up O'Connell Street to get the lowdown on Nelson. Bloody pest of a thing middle of town. Christ, he was there during the famine. Doing nothing, looking out over the Irish Sea. Sure, he's a chunk of granite only. It's time we brung him to ground.

The brothers worked the operation out between them. There's the column, the platform, the statue above. Lace the platform with a necklace of bombs, and *ba-boom bam-ba-damn,* topple him. This is the perfect time leading up to the jubilee, the fiftieth anniversary. But not on Easter, no. Some other day they'd not expect. And careful, so no one's caught in the fall.

After five minutes muttering out the side of their mouths, Boots and O'Feeney head up the road to the boozer at Dreams Hotel so's to further discuss their little prank on Nelsey. If they were to do it. If it was to happen...

At the backa Tolka Row, down our lane, there's a flash and a flood of light. Light stretching up the kidsroom walls, splitting my brain into a zilly-unn tinsel bits. The filaments. O, the filaments is in me eyes and blinding me. Turn off that light, go way.

Wait-but, it's a car on the lane. Someone's come home to visit us. I climb outta bed, step into the window well, look down. There's Paddy in his squeaky black cab. And Daddy. Pals tumbling out like circus clowns. They've bags and banjos. Music's in their cases with the mandolin and guitar.

More blokes, now, more. Blokes rushing over the cobbleding stones, into the courtyard below. Tonight is joyworld, 'cause Daddy's brought a party home.

It's the Cornerboys. Just in off the road, home from their first ballad tour of Ireland.

I creep from the kidsroom, perch at the stairtip to watch the goings-on in our one-big downstairs room. Downstairs we have two fireplaces made of gleaming Wicklow granitestone. One works and one does not. Mam's got something going in the fire that works—hot turf packed round a cast iron pot that sits in the flames on three pointy feet.

Welcome back, Lumps, Mam says. It's Daddy calls them the Lumps, and great lumps they are. Lumps of men, with lumping boys still inside 'em. Plunking their instruments everywhere flat. Table, landing stair, floor. *How was the tour?*

Mighty, says Growler, the band daddy. He runs the band. *But next time? We bring Boots along. Stead of him staying home and minding Mammy.*

Shurrup. Boots stomps in Growler's general direction.

Me ma is a cripple. So you, don't be on me. Boots is a Mod. Black suit, white socks, and them pointy spank-shoes. He is just a tumble-runk of curly red hair.

Have youse anything in the house? Growler asks Mam, speaking in his deep-dark throaty Dublin. *We're only starving.*

You may have anything in this house. There's the sharp clang of the fire tongs and Mam carries her pot oven to the kitchen counter. She takes a tea cozy to the heavy lid, there's spuds and a pair of roasting chickens.

Ah, Queenie, Growler says, nose in the pot. *Youse are my queen.* Growler's voice is rough, black, bitter. But when Growler goes to laughing, he's my age in his face.

Mam's turning up the cuffs of her *baínín* Aran sweater. Rolling one sleeve, then the other along the full of her arms. My mam, my daddy are tall. They are tall-so-tall together. There's no one else like them-togetherly in the world. And right now they're winking at each other in the squashy kitchen, cooking food for their friends.

Mam slides jam buns and cold scones into the oven for a heat. She pulls the kettle from the cooker, slices bread and sets the crockery. The left sleeve of her Aran flops down her arm catching on the butter in the dish. Mam shoves the sleeve far up her arm. And I see the top of her arm is purply blue. Above her elbow is solid bruise.

Daddy dips his head in the small fridge under the kitchen counter. *Give us a look.* Finds ham and cheese wrapped in butcher paper.

Would you ere have a bead of mustard for that? Growler asks with a funning smile. Growler has saucer eyes. He is hairy and beardy like all the Cornerboys. They live in a boarding house on the Liffey's Northside. 'Cept Boots, he lives at home.

Easy on that mustard, Growler, Daddy warns.

Hump aisy, go slather. Growler lathers up his sangitch, chomps down his yellow teefs and—*Hey-haw, God, give me breath.* Shaking his jaw, a throaty laugh. *This mustard is bestial.* Growler flicks a blob of mustard from the jar, pops it in his mouth. *Tis marvelous nosh, youse've got.*

Them Lumps, their clothes is shabby from tramping the roads, riding in vans, digging in dirty lodgings with no baths. And the one? Stilly Dunn removes his shoes. There's twine in place of shoelace bows. *These schtockins. Me feets is only scootrified.* Stilly's socks is more hole than sock. He's on the couch scratching himself out of one itch and into the next.

Wouldja fuck off, Dunn, with yer smelly feet? Growler's roaring. *Yer one pair a socks. Stenching up our digs something loathsome. Do something about them socks, or I'll murder youse all.*

If the band splits over a pair of socks, nobody-but-nobody'll hear you play outside of Kilrush, Kilkee, Killala, Daddy says. *Stilly, pay us some mind.*

Gina, would youse ever mind scrubbing these in your sink? Stilly picks his way over to Mam. Socks ahead of him, socks far as his arms can go.

Hand me down that saucepot, pet, Daddy says to Mam, while running the hot tap. He squirts Fairy Soap into the pan and Stilly drops his stockings down.

How 'bout a rosiner? Boots asks.

I've an awful longing on me for a pint, Growler says.

Name your elixir.

How's about? A bockle of stout, the flask of song.

To the most killing ballad tour this country's ever seen. Daddy's passing out the bottles.

To our next ballad tour. We'll be the world-known. Growler taps the neck of his bockle to Daddy's.

Borry your fiddle, Queenie-Eye-O? Aonghus is a titch of a fella. His shy, his small, lives in his broken-hearted looking eyes. *Can I borry your gutbox?*

"Violin, it's a violin," I want to shout. But I don't say nothing, 'cause they'd find me at the top of the stairs. And it's off to bed like a sack of taytoes. Over my daddy's back, packed away.

Mam ducks under the steps just beneath me, don't find me out. Next to our piano, beneath the open-backed stairs is Mam's violin. She lifts the lid to red velvet softings. Rosin in a clever box under the violin's thin dark neck. O, welcome yon rosin the bow. Mam twists the brass knob, tightens the horse hairs, lightly scrubs the bow with a golden rosin block.

Mam swings her violin over the counter. Aonghus catches it by the black scroll, flips it under his chin and bops out a quick-tune.

Magic. There's elegance in this gutbox. Aonghus sighs. *Ellygance and dripping hooredom. It's... Ecclesiasticals is what.*

Growler and Battling Jake pluck their banjos. Growler uses a silver thimble for a pick. Boots takes a recorder from his coat pocket—it's a woodener. Trips of song toot through the holes.

From nowhere, them Cornerboys has got their instruments going.

Irishmen, Growler announces. *Attention.*

But the peat drops in the hearth.

We're outta turf, Stilly says. *But I've some in me bag.*

At the foot of the stairs, Stilly digs about in a wore-out leather satchel, finds three or four clogs of hairy bog turf.

Where'd you get that? Daddy says.

Nicked it from our digs in Carlow. Fingers thin on the chimbelly stones, feet-bare on the granite flags, Stilly rests Carlow peat in the ash.

The lads tuck them pints away. Growler and Daddy're one bockle ahead, 'til Boots reaches for the Paddy's. *By the Janey, here's to.* Boots shakes back his roaring red, bubbly hair and takes three deep swallows. *Hup-hahhh.* From way down his throat. *Now, that's whiskey.*

What'll we do, what'll we? Jake asks.

We'll do the Dartinne—*Virgin queen of Wicklowtown.* Growler says.

Spald it, yeh lunkards. Daddy braps the *bodhrán. Split open the song.*

Pete-Pete come home, Pete-Pete home-home
To thin gray slate, our fireside's floor
Flakes spark-n-fly, dartinning up with the roar
Ah, Pete, my dear Pete, come on home

Stilly's peat in our fireplace, a smoky wild-smell. Farmstalls, bog rats, chicken poo and sheeps. Smells ashcanny, like woods burning at the ragends of time.

Serving your tender over the sea
Follow blue flames up the chimbelly
Fly off with the sparks, on home to me
Pete, my heart, Pete, come home

Just then, a knock comes at the window. *Tip-tap.* There's a girl out there calling.

Sweet Fern. Growler pushes the window up along the frame. *Get in here and give us the proper kiss.*

You stag, Sweet Fern murmurs.

'Mere to me, my lovely bird. Growler's got her now. She walks into the house over the window ledge. Fern blinks in the broad light of the crowdy room. Lamplight spills on her rain-wet skin. Sweet Fern swats drizzle from her delicate frock. That frock is a party in itself. It's got drawings of tiny Eiffel Towers and blue poodles.

Even in heels, she's teensy-so, though her monster black hairdo makes her giant. Tossing her arms in an upwards V, she flops down. Up ploofs her frock, poodles leaping. Then I see, Ferny's got no knickers on.

I've been searching the pubs round Parnell Square and my wild boys is here with you. How-ya, Gina-n-Olly?

We are having one riotous session, Mam says, setting a plate of warm scones and jam buns on the dinner table for the lads to devour.

The most important world-in-the-thing is you, Growler says, nudging Ferny with his bockle of stout. *Youse are The Treat.*

Tambourine? Which of you rascals has a tambourine? Sweet Fern's already cross the room, foxing in their clutter of bags, searching out a ratta-tat tambourine.

And *clap*, Growler cracks his hands together with a mightly clout. *Now for something more rumbustious.*

Will youse wait? says Aonghus, sunk in a boozy veil of smoke. *I've a half-ciggy left.*

Yeh know what fucking-girl? Growler urges. *Let's youse and me have our own party, 'cause these slinky pissers? Don't know pipes.*

Leave off the pipes, let's get dancing. Sweet Fern hooves off her high-heeled sandals. *My dear laddies, all we need is this.* She tats her tambourine. *'Cause this is how to live. No matter that you're a band scratching to make a living here in Holy Ireland—where the whingers don't expect to pay for it. Take no matter from that at all.*

Sweet Fern sounds the beat.

Leave off your words and melodies.
It's this. Only this.
This-**this**.

And *hooo*! Them chaps leap up to join her. No words on this song, it's a jig, it's a reel, a kickabout jump number.

Yahhhhh feckboys. Sweet Fern snatches her dress up, so's to better the dance. That Ferny's a gas ticket. She is a song, like. Whap-riding the slamming notes, she sails, striding the boards.

Let's get you dancing. Fern drives Mam from the kitchen.

But, I can't—I can't dance. Mam sputters. Mam is right 'cause she's looking herky, dancing jerky next to Sweet Fern.

Come up, yeh. Sweet Fern coaxes Mam. *Take my hand, look in the eyes.*

Sweet Fern takes Mam's hand. Elbow to elbow in a small box of space on the floor, they lock eyes, pivot and spin. And spin. Mam tips her head back, looks to up.

Her mother, Gina Volk O'Feeney, Ideas Girl, is in her prime and spinning. She is inside the music, the beat, and is free. Round the room goes, round the ceiling.

Deep in the spin, ideas come in a bright flash, she's already typing:

Olly O'Feeney Productions present...
The Cornerboys at the Gate

Ferny releases her grip and Mam bursts into laughter.

Stilly runs to his leather satchel, brings out steel-tipped dancing shoes.

Here's Mister Stilly Dunn on the feets, Growler announces. *Take-it-up, take-it-up, take-it-up.*

Stilly skids pell-mell into the hurling-hurling-hurling zoom. Lepping 'bout the lino, chasing pandemonium 'til alls Stilly *is* is a leggy boy, kicking inside the reel.

The Cornerboys let Stilly carry the beat. Tramping faster than *than. Rip-rap* in a blizz of beats, knocking sparks outta the granite hearth. Steel sparks fly out at heel and toe. Lost in the beat, he's a reel in the house. He is heat in the slap of his bappitting, sparky shoes.

Never seen feet move that fast in all my life. 'Cept when there's a bill. Ferny's laugh tumbles. She takes a half-turn in. Onto Growler now.

Growler's shaking notes out of his thumb-pick. He's toughed-out on the banjar. Bearing down and *zang.* The thimble spills from his thumb, bouncing silvery, dizzing into the fire's blaze.

Look what Ferny's after making me do, Growler wails.

Take-it-up, take-it-up, take-it-up. Boots calls and Banjey Jake is picking, battling lone on his round banjo. Jake is fine and well away.

Once again, Fern turns to Growler, hips thrusting the beat.

You wicked tormenting girl. Growler's breathing hard, shirt slickwet. He licks Fern's neck, takes a vicious bite of her trolloping hair. *Sweet Fern, youse've got sugar in your hair.*

Must be Gina's jam buns.

Music-the-music, a ripple in Fern's body. Her painty toenails stroke the floor.

Stop to kiss, they do. Sweet Fern and Growler do. They kiss and they kiss with the beat 'til Growler gets all grabby bum and Ferny bats him away.

Wow-whee, Mam says to Daddy all American-like, and the spell is broke.

Shyly, so shyly, Sweet Fern brings both hands together front of her heart, in prayer. *Pay for us singers, now and at the hour of our debts, ahhh-men.*

With the dancing over, Mam and Daddy hang at the wall. Tight together—full up on jigsongs, gladshouting and friends.

Himmel, Mam says when she's amazed. *Himmel-bimmel.* She's more than amazed.

That session was demanic, Daddy says.

That was sixteen concerts in one reel. Mam is giddy. *Oliver, put them in your show at the Gate. You'll pack the mobs in.*

I'll stop round tomorrow, Daddy says.

Chuhh—the Gate. Aonghus scoffs, already smoking a rollup.

Growler paces, aimless at the fire. *Do it. Don't do it. I don't give a monkey.*

Yeh git. Daddy shouts at him, clearly cross. *Don't pretend you don't care.*

If we go in the Gate Theatre with Olly, I could actually, em—Boots nervously taps the holes of his recorder—*Be in the band.*

You'll have thousands clapping you of a night, Daddy says.

Growler looks trapped. Afraid 'cause they've only played the back bar of O'Donoghue's and Grafton Street Cinema once or twice. Dublin doesn't yet know them. *Give us a shout only if they say yes. Now, how 'bout one more from way-backs.*

Athenry? Mam says.

No, I mean a real farback one. Do youse know Goosetown?

Sure.

I am completely quelled by that, Growler says. *'Cause Goosetown is a rare ould ancient song. The odd balladeer, if he's any good, might have it in his ear.*

Know it by heart, Mam says. *"Out of Goosetown." An island woman taught it to me. Out in the* Gaeltacht, *one Christmas with Olly, twelve ruby years ago.*

Wouldja ere give us the chorus on piano then?

Mam turns the piano lid, flicks a smudge of chockie off middle C. Oops, a bit of my Flake bar from when I was practicing after tea.

It's long after midnights. Ferny holds in the doorframe, like she needs a word from Growler that he wants her here. *Must be getting on.*

No, stay with me, stay. Growler tests the tune, head tilted in to his Spanish guitar.

Stilly dumps more country turf on the fire, takes up poker and tongs, gives it a quick stir. Embers crack and jump to flame, the fire is on.

And-so, the geese, Boots says, switching to the tin whistle for this song.

Ahhhh, the geese, Aonghus whinges. *And them leaving.*

Sweet Fern goes around snicking off every light in our downstairs house, save for the flicker of firelight on the ceiling.

There's a lonely last bun on the dinner table. Slow, thiefing sneaky down the steps, keeping my eye on that last lonely bun, 'cause that last jammy bun is for me.

Hidden in their tumble of bags, crouched in the dark, licking jam from the bun. I lick, listen-lick in the listening now.

Arrraw. Aonghus bounces Mam's bow on the strings.

Growler calls the Lumps to song. *'Cause we belong to proud races, and we belong to proud rages, we dip this song in the scream.*

Stilly clashes poker and tongs with a mortifying *patang.*

This is for the six missing counties.
Antrim, Armagh, Fermanagh, Tyrone
Derry, Down, County Down

The Lumps go to music front the fire.

At the start of November, year after year after year,
Graylags swarm in by the meelas
To feast on our meadows and hills

Feeding and roosting in Dear Ould Goosetown
Long the lush floodmeadows and loughs
Meelas-O, meelas-O means God's thousands
Meelas-O, meelas-O have come home

Battling Jake takes up the next bit.

'Til the one late October
When wildfowl turned home from the sky
Their wetlands, their coastlines ripped bald
And all proud tenantry gone

Off so, go the geese, the flying ganders
Miles high in the mackerel sky…

Suddenly I see, each Lump is a youngboy only. I see into their homes. Brothers, sisters, daddies and mams. Living slim in Kilrush, Kilkee, Killala. I see into Ireland's all. Farback-far and far's ahead. Can feel feathers beating when the geese flew away one Octobersoft day.

Flying up, flying off, outta Goosetown
Broken fields, stolen crops, way-far-way

Fla-fla-fla, into fla, far from Goosetown
Fla-fla-fla, into fla, they're away

One by one the players stop 'til Boots has got the tune alone, his piping tin whistle. And the notes slip to a close, sending the geese out and on, to the wishing realms.

"Antrim, Armagh, Fermanagh, Tyrone. Derry, Down, County Down." A silent anthem in my mind. Scored into me, never to leave.

Stilly stirs the fire, sparks *splink* and—Turn to geese. The sparks is geese now. Graylags, small as pocket pennies. 'Cept for one weeshy goose behind. She is small as a thrupenny bit.

Our house is aswarm with geese. There's ganders beating the windows. Can't get out, 'cause I won't let them.

Must stay and live here now
Where we shall ever keep them, keep them
It's here they'll fly forevers
Peacedeep, in the heart of our home-home-home

the deadevens

Three more weeks and Mam's gonta have a new baby. I'm singing my Baby Song into the air. *Three more weeks, only three more weeks...*

I'm walking a circle on the floor, round the circle round. On the floor of the Rotunda Waiting Room is a circle in tiling. Sandal one and sandal two, round the circle round. Sandal-sandal-sandal-sandal, sandal slap, and sandal slap. *Mam's gonta have the new, have the new baby.*

Inside my mammy is a babby growing. The whole fambilly put bets on what's in there. If it's a boy, we'll name him Rowan. If it's a girl? We'll call her Annie after Gran. Daddy and Des want another boy, but me and Fee want a sister. Mam says she doesn't care what we get, she'll be happy when it's over, 'cause all through her pa-reggy-nancy, Mam's poor oul pegs. They ail her. She has aches and pains and pakes and ains in her legs. She's in with the doctor and he's sticking her with horrible needles. Into her veins. The veins in her legs is blue. She's got purpling knots of vines in her pegs. And ballybunions.

My pegs, they ail me too from walking this circle. And my ballybunions is killing me.

Sandal slap and sandal slap, slapdee-slappedy slap.

This is the Rotunda. I was born in the Rotunda. All us O'Feeneys was born in the Roto. It's the hospital where the new babby will come. Round the corner is the Gate Theatre and my daddy. He's doing a show there tonight and every night these days now. It's a show with the Cornerboys. It's packing 'em in.

Three more weeks and three more weeks and—

There's a granny over there with gray spaggy moustaches. *Oofff.* Why doesn't she pay a visit to the barber? What's she doing sitting here with all the mammies waiting to go into the doctor and get their babies?

Mammy's gonta have the new baby.

'Mere to me, lovedy.

There's a lady calling me over. Don't know if I like her. Round her front is a tweed blanket and in the tweed blanket is a wee babby with one hand fisting and the one foot kicking, sticking out filthy, battling the air.

Come on you little chatbox. Would you like a chockie bar?

Ummm, an Aero Bar. "It's bubbles of air caught inside chocolate. Buy an Aero Bar today." *I'd love that Aero Bar.*

You can have it all to yourself, if you stop singing that stinking song.

In three weeks my mam's coming here and bringing home a new baby.

All of us here, waiting in the waiting room, we know.

How do you know?

On account of your song.

She's looking at me, right into my face. Her eyes are leaping blue. I'm standing, she's sitting on the wooden bench rounding the roundy walls of the Roto's waiting room. She's got the ruddy face of living outside. She's a roadwoman, going the roads with her babby wrapped in a blanket on her back.

It's my song and I'm singing it. Back on the circle, going round. *Three more weeks, only three more weeks and Mam's gonta have the new babby. Haaa-ha ha.*

She flings back and laughs a gallon of laughter. *Don't want my Aero Bar? More for me.* She pops half the bar into her mouth.

No, I'd like some. I'd like some, please. And she gives me the other bit. So I spunch in on the bench beside her, wagging my sandals in the air.

If you put your tongue into the bubbly hole of an Aero Bar, it sinks into another bubbly hole and another bubbly hole 'til your tongue turns into chocolatey, melty-more chocolate. Aero Bars are only lovely.

Are you collecting a babby from the doctor today?

You don't get babbies from doctors.

My mam is here for one. First he looks at the babby, then he pokes injections in her legs and wraps 'em with bandages.

Everyone knows you fetch babbies from the cabbage.

Babbies come from mammies. They live in your big fat tum before they get born.

Round the back of this place, they're building a garden of rememberies. It's for them who gave their lives in the Rebel Rising. They're working hard to get it done in time for Easter. That's where, in the garden there, they've got the cabbage, and in the cabbage comes the new lickle squaggelly ba. Bet your ma is out there seeing if your ba is ready.

I squinch my fists and think. Mam told me the baby is in her tummy. But that lady doesn't have the fat-tum of a baby inside her. Maybe her babby came from cabbage, 'cause her ba has three fingers in her mouth. She's sleeping and sucking them fingers. All the toes of her naked foot is curled down over the bottom-sole like an impy chimpy.

Do you have any other babbies 'sides her?

No, she's my little savage. The lady nibbles the babby's cheek. *Take a bite of my Nuala.*

That's her name, Nuala? Like the ballet.

Yeh, Nuala. She smells the babby's head. *Me wee* girsha.

What's girsha*?*

Girsha *is Irish for little girl,* she says. *My wee* girsha *Nuala has a story in her name.*

Is there a story in my name?

Depends on your name.

I'm Noleen O'Feeney.

Nuala Ní Fearna *is your Irish name.*

Not Nuala, I'm Noleen.

Noleen means little Nuala.

That's the English name for Nuala?

Yes, Wee Nuala.

We've a story in our name?

Right-so, story-the-story. She nods knowingly. *The first Nuala was Nuala of the Dagger.*

I know Nuala and the Apples.

This is the Dagger-Nuala, will yeh listen. The lady cradles Wee Nuala close to her heart, settling in to tell the story.

Hundreds of year ago, in the time of the Old Gods and the Finnii of Erin, there was a castle in the West. This High King had the handsome wife, hair thrilling down, all the way down to the down of her back-knees.

Nuala was a warrior, rode by her fellah's side straight into battle. They carried shields and swords heavy as pianos. Together, they battled, kept their enemies at bay.

'Til came the day, there was a whispering and a singing from her castle's garden. And she knew. Quick, quick-quick. Tis time to go round back and pick out a baba from the cabbage. Her fighting days were done. Now it's nappies and gruel all life long.

Bing-bing-bing, she kept going round the back garden and snatching up the kiddos. 'Til bing and a bing and bing-bing again, she had a dead even dozen. All boys. With the curled-out, tussled hair so snaggy she couldn't pull a comb through. Though they were savagers and wasters, Nuala only loved them, loved them to bits.

Everything was glorious-glorious altogether. The lady runs her words togethers in a rush. *'Til the one morning, Nuala had the dream and in the dream, all her fambilly's possessions, all her darling sons stood out in the front fields of the castle.*

Nuala leapt from sleep, out of her feathered bed, fled down the stair, into the courtyard. And there on the stones lay her husband with the throat sliced deep-so-deep his head was cut clear off him.

The wail then, her wail. It's a wonder her castle still is standing.

Cromwell and his men—I think Cromwell. Or could it be the Anglo-Normans? Roman-Britons? No, I'm telling a lie, 'cause this happened and happened to us so many times through the length of days, I don't know, do you know. But-anyway, Cromwell's men had slaughtered Nuala's serving people, her cattlejobbers, stableboys. Only people left was her twelve sons. In a line. Tall to small and tall to small.

Well. She knew their plan. First, they'd have at her and have at her 'til she was blood on the drumlins. O, they'd have at her straight off right there in front of her boys.

Next? They'd slay her sons. Or take them capture, turn them into enemies.

In a flash, she had her silver dagger out, and up, and stabbing.

Bing-bing-bing, 'til bing and a-bing, and bing-bing again, she had a dead even dozen. All her lads, the full twelve, toppled to ground. Their curled-out, tussle-snagged hair. Their hair, she couldn't pull a comb through.

She struck them down to keep them hers.

The knife and the knife. Up again, it's up again and striking. Nuala striking her own neck. Gone now, she's gone. She's done on the drumlins. Nuala's lying on the stones.

On Upper O'Connell Street, Gina O'Feeney grips her daughter's hand. She is in agony. Under her thick nylons, the support hose her mother sends from America, are the doctor's tightly wrapped bandages. With each shriek of pain through her veins, she is forced to stop.

Mam? Noleen asks, her voice a rusty squawk.

What? Gina says curtly, biting her lips. The lipstick she wears whenever she leaves the house is long since worried away.

Did you and the doctor go round to the back garden?

What garden?

The Garden of Rememberies. Noleen points to the worksite on Parnell Square where gardeners are rolling wheelbarrows and lugging buckets of geraniums.

Oh, isn't that fan—Gina gasps.—*tastic. They're building a garden.* She struggles forward best she can. A workman spreads pebbles around the base of a bush. She remembers tending her mother's victory garden in Reading all those years ago, during the war, with three of her brothers off in Europe—Donald, Dutch and Ely. The horror, the ongoing terror, really, of never knowing would they come home.

Where's the cabbage? Noleen asks.

Cabbage?

For the babbies.

What?

Doesn't the doctor help you pick out the baby? In the cabbage?

No. Gina's exhausted.

Didja get me from the cabbage?

Babies come from people, you know that. If I could pluck it from a cabbage patch, I would, and avoid all this leg pain.

Is your legs banjaxed from having a babby?

Just stop, Noleen. We'll chat when we get to Bewley's. After every visit to the Rotunda, Gina takes Noleen to Bewley's on Grafton for a curer. *What will we have? When we get to Bewley's?* Gina's walking again, though she's hobbledy.

I want a chelly bun and tea with lashings of milk, four cubes of sugar. You will have an almond bun, 'cause you always have the almond bun, and coffee. And, Mam? Do I have a story in my name?

I named you Noleen 'cause you looked like a Noleen with your periwinkle eyes taking over your face. Gina thinks of Noleen, her born-early kid. So excited to see what life is, she couldn't wait to get into the world. Arrived six weeks early, no toenails on her baby feet. Desperately ill with pleurisy, same as Gina. It's a wonder Noleen arrived at all. And Ely her next one, born so healthy—nine pounds—came backwards, like he was loathe to leave his mammy. Though she marvels at this coming ba, she wants the pain over and gone.

Screeping down O'Connell Street, the city swoops around: delivery boys on bikes too big for 'em *brrr-ing brrr-ing*-ing their bells. News lads howling *Hurr-uld 'n Press, Eeev-nin Hurr-uld 'n Press.*

Double-decker buses with *Baile Átha Cliath* and *Colún Nelson* on their destination blinds spit gusts of thick black soot. A conductor, leather pouch slung low on his hips like a cowboy's gun, lets go of the pole at the back of the bus, drops to the street, trots to the front as the bus brakes, squeals, sags to a stop. Passengers step aground at the Nelson Column.

Mam sucks her teeth, holds her breath, freezes. She'd better mind, someone could bash her rickety legs. We're caught in the hustle of the Nile Siders, them flower sellers trading in the dark shadow of Lord Nelly's bum.

Sixpence, the daffies. The dealers call, singing out their flower selling songs.

Shamma-rocks and violets. It smells like we're inside a perfume bockle. *Get your shamma-rocks for Patrick's Day.*

The pillar shawlies are selling bunches of real-true shamrocks for Saint Pat's. Every morning 'til next Thursday, they'll send their kids to the Green. Soon as the gates is opened, them kids'll pour into the People's Acre and pluck shamrocks from the grass.

Shamma-rocks or violets, their mammies bawl. There in the well of a bockety pram is clusters of purple and bunches of green.

Howya, Noleen. Youse ready for Patrick's day? It's Jacintha, the fir tree shawlie from Moore Street. She twirls a single shamrock 'tween finger and thumb.

Can I've sixpence, Mam?

Mam can't think for the P-A-I-N, so she taps my shoulder with her shiny green bag. Meaning I should help myself.

Jacintha takes one look at Mam. *Sit down, Queenie O'Feeney. Youse look trollied.*

Sorry, I can't, Mam explains. *Doctor's orders.*

Brutal. Jacintha clicks her teeth in sympathy. *The very-close veins is murder.*

Won't be long now, Mam says, meaning the baby, that baby, getting all the attention while banging up Mam's legs.

They have a bit of a chinwag as I root through Mam's bag for the spondoolahs. I could pay a visit to Lord Nelson, upstairs. Only sixpence a go for "a splendid view," the sign says. Going up Nelson is better than shamma-rocks, better than bumper cars, better-even than the zoo. 'Cause Lord Nelly stands in his magic kingdom in the sky. He's higher than five double-deckers stacked tall. Inside the column is a thrilly mystery carnival ride. At the drop of a sixpence, *click,* you run your way up the spirally stairs to a lookout platform fenced in steel.

Locked up in a cage in the sky, you can't see ould Nelson above. But press your nose to the grill and Dublin City spreads below. Gulls loop and glide on Liffey breezes, and the peoples on O'Connell Bridge look like grubs. There's the Happy Ring House bride and groom, Clery's, the O Dearest Mattress shop. I wish Mam could have a lie-down in the mattress shop and rest her banjaxed legs.

Do you want your shamrocks, Nolee? Mam asks me.

Piggers. It's a minute past three on Clery's clock, too late to be shooting up the pillar. *'Course I want my shamrocks.*

Jacintha hands me two bunches. *That's for minding your ma.*

Southside of the Pillar, TRAFALGAR is stamped in the granite base. At the double gates, the Pillar man is stamping, shifting foot to foot. Folding his long overcoat about himself in the March cold. Lorries pound and engines gun. *Hoot-hoot. Parp-parp.* A motorbike screams to a stop at the Pillar's gates. The rider's got drainpipe trousers like a Teddy Boy. When he removes his crash helmet, out springs a mop of jumpy orange hair. It's Boots from the Cornerboys. His eyes is slicking side-to-side, he's on the lookout all the time.

At the taxi rank, there's Paddy the Cabby parked in his cab.

Paddy, I scream, bolting towards him. *Can you run us home?*

We can't take a cab, Mam calls, plodding after.

By the time I reach Paddy's cab, Boots is heaving a pair of plaid carry-alls from the back seat.

Paddy hands the Pillar keeper an envelope thick with bills. *Here's some money. For sweets.*

Ta, the keeper says, locking Boots inside the cast iron gates.

Boots plunks down the heavy carry-alls. One tips to the side, a burglar's torch strikes the granite and rolls.

Do all the divilments you want. The Pillar man pushes a brass key through the bars. *But lock it on your way.*

Boots takes the Pillar man's key. *Gunna sling it up his lordship's hole.* At the door leading to the Pillar's stairs, Boots hauls his carry-cases over the turnstile and goes in for free.

The Pillar keeper lights a ciggie, ambles straight up the city center, past the Nile Siders, Jacintha and her shamrocks, toward the Garden of Rememberies.

Hiya Noleen, Paddy says.

Can you give us a ride? I ask, just as Mam comes lumbering, finally-finally catching up.

Jayzus, Gina, are yeh perished? Paddy presents her with his arm. *Like a lift?*

I'm supposed to walk.

Doctor's orders, I shout.

Deadly. Paddy shakes his head.

But thanks, Mam says and on we go.

Middle of O'Connell Bridge, we take another rest.

What? Will we get—When we get to Bewley's? Mam chants it like a prayer.

Chelly bun, tea. Almond bun, coffee. Chelly bun, tea. Almond bun, coffee. That's what I sing to Mam, but in my head is "Nuala-the-dagger, the dagger-dagger-dagger. Nuala of the silvery dagger."

It's all about. A pint of stout. There's Olly O'F in the pub of Dreams Hotel. He's sitting in a snug jampacked with mentallers. Some are hacktors from his show at the Gate and some are Paddy the Cabby's cabby friends. Olly and his showcrowd is fulla slick-shiny excitements. Everyone's yapping on top of each other and all at once.

At the rail, Paddy calls in their order to yer man on the tap. *Eight pints of happiness. Keep the heads high.*

Olly, you're after smoking the last of me fags, says Jimmy Downs, worthless sponger. A black Guinness stain rings his mouth.

I'll buy yeh the new pack then. Olly throws Jimmy a ten pound note. Keep yer eye out for Downs. He'd down your drink when yer back is turned. Up to no good, Downs.

Olly's paying for the smokes and for all the drinks they do be drinking. He has always—always, always—these moochers and hangers-on-ers. All these broken people needing to be fixed, leeching him. There goes his money in booze, brimming up and foaming over, streaming down the frosted sides of the mug. Money and booze and money. Pooling on the counter, leaking out the door.

"Live life to the power of Guinness." The barman slams down eight mugs, thick-foamy with cream. The moochers rush the bar like pigs to the trough.

Ah, there-Jeezuz, there's that one, that Stacia-one. Chorus girl from the Black & White Dancers, an act in Olly's show. "O'Feeney and the Cornerboys" now playing at the Gate.

Stacia and her bumswagger, her eyes slice the room. Lookit that hair, wouldja. Piled high and teasy-teasy, a tangled-rude bowl of hair.

Stacia's gotta ladder in her stockings, the left knee.

You buying, Missus-Woman? Olly says to her.

Haven't two wax farthings.

Come sit with me, sit.

Leave off me. Stacia fist to her nose, holding her breath like she doesn't want to breathe his air, like she doesn't want to be suckered back into his life.

There's a band taking over the place, marking off a bit of stage. A fiddler, piper, the son of a piper, one or two of the Cornerboys tuning up. Stilly Dunn, Battling Jake.

There's a great pack a hoores in here tonight. Stilly roars the crowd down. *I'm excirah, delirah and sweating. For tonight? Is capguns, fellaheens.*

Tonight is the best St. Paddy's prezzy in years, Jake yells. *For tonight? Is jelly-ga-nite and ammonias.*

Jake steps to the mike. *Right-so, away we go now with Humpty Dumpty. He had a great what for himself?* Banjey Jake cues the audience, lifting his round banjo. *Humpty Dumpty had a great...*

Fallll. They split the rafters with the most raucous tale of Humpty Dumpty ever told.

When Olly O'Feeney steps upon the bar-top, his right arm is rigged behind him, with the flap of his sleeve tucked into his suit. There's bottle caps sellotaped to his breast like brass medals. He carries a broom handle for a sword.

I say-I say-I say, I am in need of a bevvie—Nay, four. He announces like a posh British toff. *And a pig chop.* He sketches along the counter, a showman *in excelcis. I've not supped nor victualed in one hundred and fifty year.*

Hey, the barman shouts. *You can't walk here.*

I, my good man, can walk where I like, Olly says. Face pleated with the begrudge, the sneer, the snides. *For I am the illustrious Duke of Brontosaurus Hoore-atio, Lord Nelson, Vice Admiral of the White, the Blue, the Orange and the Yellah. But you can call me the Nelse.*

Off me counter. The barman swats Olly's shoes with a wet serviette.

The whole pub is slaughtered laughing, it is bedlam.

Don't encourage him, Barman says. *He's a rattle.*

Can't you pour me a pint? After the bottles I've—Battles. After the battles I've been through—

I've gorra hand it to you, Nelsey—

You're going to have to. Olly's voice slips back to Dublin. *For I've the one arm only.* Trembling his bottom lip with self-pity. *Lost me arr-um in the Nile, the willy in Leghorn, me upper teefs in Trafalgar. And fifty year ago?* Accusing the crowd with his broomstick sword. *Fifty bloody year ago, youse thricky, treacherous drunkards and knaves shot orf me nostril in your Easter Rebellion.*

Shut up, the barman says. *And get down.*

Olly points the broom handle at the barman's throat. *Just pull me a pint.*

Never, the barman roars.

You and your vile crew can go to blazes. Olly mock-trips over a mug on the counter. He pivots and kicks into a one-armed front handspring, then a thripple-tucked trammelsalter. Landing on the sawdusted floor with a wee *plié,* he dips his head, a modest bow.

If yer man can't do that—Olly deadpans. *Leave him.*

And the crowd goes to mayhem.

You should go on the RTÉ, *Olly.* Paddy the Cabby passes him a dinted flask. *I was falling in the toilet laughing.* Just then, Paddy catches sight of Boots groping toward the bar. *By the morto,* Paddy says. *He looks very shook.*

Howya Boots, Olly calls. *Get in here and tell us.*

It's done, Boots manages.

Right. Paddy notes the time on his wristwatch. *Look after him.* Paddy signals the cabbies with a sharp whistle. *It's time.* The taxi-men file out of the door.

On the bar top, a pint waits for Boots. He downs it in one greedy pull. The barman sets a second pint before him and it's a doner in three hungry slugs.

Me nerves. His voice dusky with fear. *Me bloody bared, baldy-bottomed nerves.*

Well, yeh did it, Head. Olly plucks the bottle caps off his suit jacket, lines 'em on the counter. *That's what matters.*

The Pillar at night is a haunted tomb. T'would wring the heart of a demon. I mean—I'd no trouble laying the charge, it was just—In the cage when the job was set, the notion came: I am the last man ever to climb Lord Nelson's Pillar.

Olly tats two caps together like mini cymbals. He has his eye on Stacia in the corner, sipping a double rum, tuttering on her stilettos.

Didn't the batteries on my torch run out. Boots goes on. *I'd to go down in the dark alone. There was a sudden clapping of hands, the stench of water and dirt. A shrill moan coiled the length of column and there in the shadows of the window ledge, two gleaming golden eyes. I took breath and flogged it. But on each window ledge all the way, a pair of goldy-yellah eyes. Ghosty beasts watching me all the way down. Though I had a definite feeling they were urging me on, urging us into this night, this night-this—Historical Night, never was I so happy to see the Pillar man's teapot on the bottom sill.*

Boots, nose in his third pint and draining, has aged twenty year this night, this night, this Historical Night.

Let's go, let's go. Olly steers Stacia to the lift. *You never told me, Stacia, why we aren't an item any more.*

You hit me.

Did not. Olly looks truly shocked.

Yeh bloody did. I was yer Black & White dancer with the matching black eye.

Don't exaggerate.

'Sides, you are married. Stacia stands inside a long moment, picks at the ladder in her stocking, pulling the snag 'til the ladder rolls up her leg. Her plumpskin bulges out in square cobbles all the way up, under her mini.

Feh, tore me nylons.

No matter. Olly reaches out and tears the stockings pure off her. The rip, the animal-rip of them. To her waist and—Now gone.

Kissing in the lift, they're kissing into each other. Olly climbs clear inside the mouth of her 'til the lift clunks to a stop on the rooftop. They pick their way past a jumble of cracked chimbelly pots and Guinness barrels to the building front. Olly places a hand on a waist-high brickwall. He looks out over Dublin.

Far below, Anna Liffey snaking under the Butt Bridge, the Ha'Penny. Taximen in their cabs at the ranks by the

Pillar. Mods drifting from the ballrooms of Clery's and the Metropole, dances long over. A pair of girls, arm in arm, giggle and sploother. When doesn't Paddy swing his cab to a stop at Clery's clock and beg them in. Their skirts, their legs, their high heels pull into the back seat. Car door slams, they zoom away.

Olly looks at the Pillar in its last moments and members asking Gina. "Marry me, will yeh? Make an honest fool of me." They were on the lookout platform in the cage. All their tomorrows lay ahead. "Yes," she said. That simple.

And-so, they married.

A gull streaks up past Stacia and Olly standing in the rook of Dreams Hotel. It's a clear arch of night, fair weathery. Moon at the last quarter. Sky, a goldy stutter of light, stars.

Lookit, woudja, Olly says, in perplexity. *The stars is not in place. The plough—Is plowing the wrong star-field tonight.* Looking at the stars, Olly seems scared, so young.

Stacia melts a little. *The girls miss their new da,* she says. *They ask for you every day. "When's Olly coming, Ma? He's so funny." They only adore you.*

Olly looks at her. Face fulla makeup from his show. Eyeliner blotty, one false lash bent upwards. He loves this broken doll. *I want the life of you, of us.*

You've a wife, a life, other side the city. One foot in her life, one foot a root up me arse.

This is my real life. And for the moment Olly believes it. *You.*

He gives her a dancey twirl, wraps both arms round her, pulling her back in once again.

Life is here. In your arms, she says.

Life is here. In me arms, says he.

Life is here, they say.

He breathes in the dim, the pitch, the never and steps to behind her. Tugging her skirt. *Give us some* croí.

He's into her now, their slap and squabble. Rocking her forward, taking her round the side, ride the sound, round rover. He's riding her over that sap moon. He's coming, yeh. Coming, yeh, come onnnnn—

Stacia's bracing herself, hands on the brickwall while Olly has at her. She's studying yer man Nelson, his boots, trousers tight to the calves, up the length of his thighs. When out on the end of her eyelash, the flash, and bang-shot, bang-bang shot out of the clear blue middle, an orange flame spurts, burrr-looms, punches skyward.

Then the bombscream after, awfully tremenderous. Sound-the-sound that's no other. Sound-the-sound pulling all sound to inside that scorching roar.

Sound that's a fastkick. Godslam. A God-slamming-down bomb.

Bomb, the-bomb, a rush a-raging—*Ruirteach* raging over Carlisle Bridge, Winetavern, the Midden piles. Past-and-past Trinity, up Kildare—the museum's bogman, the Gallagh Man's mudsleeping leather-ud bones. By the Green, on into through: flats, shops, houses, all our homes.

Amliffy, Amplifee, Ampnlyffy.

A deluge of clashing-shitters, tumbling granite, Portland stone. Dublin's toppling home to hell.

And Lord Nelly? Lord Nelly could fall.

He's leaning into the tick-half of tock just after the hellslap, just 'fore the before. He's listening, looks like, putting his ear nearer to near, when he goes wibble-wobble and Nelsey's tossed head-down into the black.

There's a second *blam* when his body hits the ground. That's Nelson vanquished and the Pillar gone.

On the roof, Stacia's rushing to the stairwell, heart racing, down all the flights to the ground.

Olly's behind her, jigging with glee. *He's well away, the yellow beggar.*

That was a bomb, Oliver. A bomb.

That was the spanker he deserved.

If you'd anything to do—Stacia's face shudders, breaks into itself—*Anything to do with this—Didja?*

Olly meets her eyes, says nothing. She holds his gaze waiting on an answer.

Olly looks away.

I'm going, you coming? Stacia asks. *I've home to get to my girls.* And Stacia, high heels in her hands, runs barefoot up Parnell Square, off home.

O'Feeney stalks O'Connell Street, through clouds of gas and bomb mist. Pillar a stump, smoke snarling. There's broke stone everywheres, inches deep in snow-white dust.

There's a lifeless head, a lifeless arm sticking out of the mound.

Death alive, Olly mutters. Is that a body? Paddy and his cabmen was keeping things clear.

That is a man mid the road. Olly claws the masonry, kicks it, screams at it. When it suddenly stirs.

It's a gray-haired, oldy fella clotted in blood. He's cut and gashed in every part. His nose is gone. One eye, one arm—

not there. His chest is shot through, there's the spine of him hanging, blue knobs of bone.

The Ould Fella is coughing out life, but the wounds on his chest are mending. His empty eye bulks blue. He has clothes now, not rags but peg-tucked trousers and a waistcoat glinting with medals big as stars. His hair's gone yellow, he's come young.

What's this now, two hands? I lost an arm—In the Nile? So long ago—But now I've two hands, two arms, two lips, two nostrils.

When he reaches into the cinders, pulls out a cap in the shape of a ship sailing away on the ocean waves, it is clear. This is Lord Horatio Nelson, Vice Admiral of the Blue.

A red flush sweeps his face, life flows in the granite once again.

Halloah, Nelly calls. He's on his knees and crawling down the stonecrop. *I say, fellow,* he says to Olly. *Can you give me a hand?*

But—You're dead, been dead for a hungerud and fifty year.

Tell me, dear boy. Nelsey swats dust from his medals, voice booming. *Where can I find a Wimpy's Snackery? I need a square meal in a round bun. And a brandy.*

Tis the drink, the drink it do be talking. Olly stumbles upon a cumbrance on the ground. There by his shoes is Nelson's sword, the brass bent in the blast. Olly heaves up the blade and clocks Nelson on the crown.

But Nelsey just keeps walking. Olly cracks him and cracks him, but he's a dragoon. He's hell come up to strut the streets. He's a monster loosed at the verge of day.

O'Feeney bursts him and bursts him, but nothing stops Old Lord Nelson. Fact, he gets bigger from each blackstab.

Strike me again. Lord Nelsey's breathing in the warm air of this world. *For releasing me this night, I will be the making of you forever.*

And no sound, save Nelson's bootstrike on the drumlins, the troop of horse and four thousand feets. He goes and goes, swanks out of the skirling smoke, mounts O'Connell Bridge, past Nunnery Lane, the Croppy Hole. Over the living roads. Straight into, on into Ireland.

Back at the mound of stones, piled high in a ghosty light. Olly grasps the sword belonging to Lord Nelson, Vice Admiral of the Blue. It's burnie-burnie in his hands. It's power, it's love, it's all things good.

Just then Paddy swings by in his cab. *Git in. 'Fore the Garda grab yeh.* And Paddy runs him home to Tolka Row.

Dawn patters up the windowpane. Nuala the Dagger has me awake. She's stealing my dreams. Down the stairs is my Peter Rabbit bowl and Wheetabix in the kitchen cupboard. There's six bockles of milk on the doorstep—our daily delivery. Alls I have to do is git up and go. O, but—Nuala might get me, stab me down.

Fat bladder-bags, I've to wee.

Out in our yard, Ely's nappies flap on the line. The sweet low notes of morning coming. It's lavender, the sky. There's clouds and laughing birds *chirr-chirring.* I gather the milk bockles in me arms like childer. They clunk against me front, cold shiverdy thrill.

Them birds pecked holes in the silver caps. Them birds is after supping the cream from top our milk.

Back in the house, there's Daddy squandered on the couch. What's he doing down here? He should be upstairs in bed with Mam. Instead, here he is snoring, snorting out a snot of breath, wrist limp on his leg. He's in his suit and shoes still. Dust on his shoes and dust on the knees of his trousers. There's glinty ash on his blick-black divils-the-hair.

I plunk the bockles on the dinner table. Me plunking the bockles was loud but it doesn't wake him.

Holy Jacob, look at that thing Daddy left by the fire. Like a bit of bent train track. Or it could be a sword? It is a sword, a bent sword. Betcha five pounds I could lift that sword. I am the strongest *girsha* born in histories. I could lift up America, like that man on the telly carries the world on his back. I have muscles. I can lift Desmond off the floor and he's just about eight. The one time I picked up Daddy, wrapped my arms round his bony legs, and a huff and a puff, he raised off the ground.

The sword is bigger than me. It touches the mantelpiece, almost reaches the clock. I'll give it a go, cast it with all the force I can mustard.

Ehhh—That really smells, can't lift it at all.

Nuala-the-Dagger. I chant like a spell. An electricky *zlick* sparks through me rushing with the strength of one thousand men. I lift the sword easy-peasy.

Nuala-the-Dagger. There's the clash of steel, the troop of horse and four thousand feets. A cold bell peals. Everything bursts and whirls afore me. There's an abrupt *flick* like a telly smapping on in my head, a magic window. Wherever I aim the sword I can see inside things. See through the kettle on the kitchen range, to the ring of rust on the bottom plate. Out the window to the bones of a bird perched on the clothesline. There's our house, the inside of it. The chimbelly, a peat-stained passage of Wicklow stone. I point the sword at the clock. There's the mechanicals clicking the circles of time—on earth, beneaths, the sky.

This is some kind of queer magic, something strange coming off the sword. It's burnie-burnie in my hands. I'm too little for it. It hurts to be small. So, I drop it, drop the very sword I'm holding. When it clatters to the lino, the pictures in my head fold to a stop.

On the couch, Daddy doesn't flinch.

I turn, run up the stairs, tear up the stairs. I go.

in breakfast's bed

The morning is well along into itself, but her da, the actor, producer, is still abed. He's roosting in the covers, perusing the news, reading everything he can about his little jape that got away from him. It's been two days of the papers going on about "The Pillar Outrage." Nothing less than "rebellion loose in the land." What to hell are they taking it so seriously for? It was a bit of comedy, a theatrical act. If anyone finds out he'll be ruined, put in prison for the best of his life.

The IRA Publicity Bureau denies they'd anything to do with it. Grand, that's grand. Olly swallows some spit, nervously tapping the back of the paper as he reads. Intense Garda activity. Visits to men connected with extremist republican organizations. Some taken to the Bridewell—huh. Four of 'em released this morning. Builders' laborers. Official view is the explosion was a fool stunt carried out by a fringe group with the simple aim to demolish the pillar. Very good. *Providential* no one was killed. Thank the Lord, thank the Lord, yeh-yeh.

What else?

Here's something. Thundering Jayze, his heart'll throbble him if he doesn't calm down. Don't tell me. That bastard-knacker Jimmy Downs—*fuhhh.*

THOUGHT IT WAS PART OF 1916 FILM

Dublin actor, Jimmy Downs, who witnessed the explosion which destroyed Nelson Pillar, at first thought it was part of the 1916 Teilefís Éireann film currently in production.

Downs was in Upper O'Connell St. when a vivid flash lit the column. "Couldn't think, I couldn't hear," he said, "I saw only bright, white light."

"VERY REALISTIC"

"My first notion," said Mr. Downs, "was that Brinsley Pidcock, the telly producer, was being very realistic with the details of 1916. But seconds later I saw masonry falling round the stump of the Pillar."He said he ran to the scene to see if he could help in rescuing victims but there were none. He discounted rumours that he had taken Nelson's sword as a souvenir—

First of all, Downs is no actor. And two, why doesn't Olly have a part in that fil-um? He flings the paper into the dressing table, knocking over a tub of cream for nappy bum itch.

Gina. He roars. Bringing his wife to the doorsill, with a smile and a breakfast tray.

Gina's out like a balloon, babby ready to go any minute. She waddles through the door, eager for their morning script session. Every day, with Lily the housekeeper downstairs and the gang off to school, they breakfast together and work on their latest sketch. So nice, just the two of them hard at work in the day. Gina sets the tray on the bed beside him: scrambled uggs, as Gina calls 'em, a mad gang of rashers, three toasts, and jazzer ram. O, the Dubberlinnn mally-props and pooner-spizzums have him in their grips this morning. A sprig of shamrocks jollies the tray. There's a copy of the *Irish Press*. Splashed cross the front page is: MYSTERY MAN HAS NELSON'S SWORRRRR— Fuck-fuck, to-*fuck*. I'm going to jail.

Olly rears back and leaps from bed, spilling his breakfast to the rug. Curls to a ball and wails.

Can't-I don't-I won't. Can't-can't, I can't. He wimpers. Retreating under the bed, crying like a boy.

Olly, come on, Gina says, collecting the breakfast things on the tray as best she can. She's seen this before. When he's convinced the world is after him, he flies into a sadboy tantrum. All the worst things in the world will happen, *are* happening right now to him. Things were done on him. Wicked things. *Come on out*, she murmurs. *Can't climb down to the floor in this condition. I'd never get up again.*

Nooooo. It hurts—

No one's hurting you, Weeshy Boy. Reverting to the baby-language she uses when he gets like this.

I'm bad.

You're grand.

I'm horrid.

I'm here, you'll be fine. She hopes he doesn't snap to the vivid rage that often follows this little boy act. But it's not an act, she knows that. It's very real for him even though it's inexplicable to her. Reason means nothing when he's in these episodes of—

Nobody loves me.

This boy, she loves this boy.

You don't love me. He accuses.

Yes I do—

Kill me, kill me, kill me **now**. *I want you to. Kill me—*

His words so rapid she must stop them. Come off it. She has the sudden urge to slap him hard.

Instead, she says, *I love my love, my Oliver.* She sinks to the storytelling rocking chair. Tummy so round, just bursting with the new baby. *My-love, my-love, my Oliver.*

Would somebody just kill me. But he's slowing down, which is progress. He has no direct memories, she's asked him. He describes it as a glimpse of something at the end of a long-long corridor. Nothing solid, only dodging under a table, the bed. Diving, flipping, soaring. Running to escape.

I love my love, my Oliver. Rocking to soothe him. *I love my love, my Oliver. My-love, my-love, my Oliver.*

Under the bed Olly sees her feet, bare. The hammer toes, the bunions—monstrous. Her tipping toes, rocking back. Heels to floor and rocking forward. Tipping toes, rocking back.

Don't go back.

Under the bed, under the bush, under the table. Hide-hide, he's coming—hide. Run for dark corners. Heart pounding so loud he'll be found. Under the bush, under the bed, under the tools in the shed. Hide-hide, for he's coming, he's here.

First the beating, then the kiss, his father's groping.

Blood, it's in his spit, it's in his kiss, it's in his kissings.

Bloody spittle every morning. His bloody spittle, bloody spit.

Blood in the sink, blood down the wall.

Under the bed, under the bush, under the table. He'll be hit, kissed, put in hospital. Forgotten and left for years.

Shall I tell Weeshy Boy a story? Gina asks. *Or, will you tell me?*

Let me, Olly says from under the bed, like a boy. *Let me.*

What story will he tell her? What lie?

Olly grazes the sword he's stashed 'neath the bed.

Nelson's sword.

And when, and when, and when-when-when Olly grasps it, it's burnie-burnie in his hands. It's power. It's all things good and wishes answered.

What story will he tell her? What lie?

When Olly snakes out from under the bed, his tartan bathrobe rootches up over his gaunt ribs, revealing ghastly scars. Her Weeshy Boy. So singular, so funny. How they lie in bed, hold hands, dream and scheme and break their hearts laughing over the scripts they write together. Here he is in this filthy mood again. What can she do to turn this around? And just what is this dusty ould thing he's dragging from under their marriage bed?

What's that? she demands.

Here's-the, here's-the, here's-the story, Olly says. All the past is in his voice, his trembling confession. Jayze, she'll kick up murder. *It's eh—Nelly's sword.*

Gina stops rocking. *What's it doing under our bed?*

Coming home after the show Tuesday morning. The skillar plew—The Pillar. Emphasizing each syllable slowly. *Blew sky high.*

She can't believe they blew up the Pillar. Such an

adolescent act. She has a queer place for it in her life, 'cause one June day, Olly surprised her with a visit to yer man. The damp, twisting stairs of black stone.

Dublin lay beyond the cage.

He asked her to make a life with him.

She didn't answer at first, she didn't answer.

If she marries Olly, children will come. But her career? What will happen to her life in the theatre?

Baile Átha Cliath spread below, the Wicklow Mountains, Dublin Bay. She could see to the sea and the wide world beyond.

She believes in him. She believes in them.

"Yes," she said. "Let's marry."

I—Olly's floundering, words lost in his mouth. *I found the sword in the rubble, would you believe?*

It's in all the papers. They're looking for it. They're looking for you.

They'll think I'm the IRA. I'll be put in jail.

Olly blubbers and whines. Pathetic wreck. How did she land in this? What will she do with him?

Gina, his genius wife, the girl who one day took notion she'd like a job on *Radió Éireann*, two weeks later she's in the studio recording. Bit parts, but parts no less. *Tell me,* Gina says before an idea has fully formed in her head. She has got to divert him. *How're the bookings?*

What bookings?

You and the Cornerboys.

Last night we had an audience of three hundred nine. Took in twelve hundred fifty-four pounds—middling.

Lucky-kid O'Feeney. Gina's rolling-rolling-rolling with

American optimism. *Take the sword in to the* Irish Times. *As publicity. Wouldn't that be neat? Tell them you rescued it. Put a new sketch in the show—*

An act about the Pillar bombing—Olly says.

Invaluable publicity.

We'll pack the mobs in. Olly, his eyes over-brilliant, undoes his tartan bathrobe. He re-ties the sash in a jaunty bow, excited again. Full of go, not full of fright. Just like Ely, so easily delighted, his childish tantrum over for the moment.

Take an Aspro and get dressed. Gina snaps her fingers—all business, like the director she is. This needs quick, confident planning. *We gotta get on the stick.*

Her mother, her father—Gina and Olly—hold hands and flash their teefs at each other. They're waiting on a soundstage at *RTÉ*, ready-to-bursting with the short telly sketch they've written, rehearsed, blocked and re-blocked over the past two days. Three cameras big as tanks focus on the action 'cause this weekly show goes out...

Live from Radió Teilifís Éireann*, it's the Late-Late Show with Gay Byrne.*

Gay peacocks into view and the girls in the front row with the poofed hair go crazy, screeching like Gay is the Beatles. Get a grip, this is Ireland, Gina thinks. Olly's palm is slick with worry. Though he'll be fine. He loves attention, can't ever get enough.

You must have all lost your minds. Gay flicks his microphone wire, flirting with the chrissies down front. He wanders up the rickety risers and into the crowd of about—eighty people, she'd say. Not a bad audience for a studio this small.

Now's Olly's chance, while Gay is keeping the audience busy. Gina squeezes Olly's hand. *Have fun.*

Olly rushes to take his place on set. Charming, radiant, a roving and dashing blade. Dressed in a parody of Lord Nelson's finery, he's wearing a waistcoat, topboots, and bull fighting kneepants.

I beg your pardon, don't mind me asking. Gay sticks a long thin microphone under the nose of an Old Bat. *But has Ireland gone mad? To blow down Nelson's Pillar?*

I tink it's dire. I tink it's atrocious. The Old Bat is suitably disgusted.

Hilarious. The man next to her elbows in. *What he deserved.*

And it's rocks forever on O'Connell Street. The Old Bat goes on. *Dublin's left blank without Nelson.*

We are left with questions, Gay says seriously, holding still for a close up. He's worked his way back to the stage with no one noticing, not even Gina. *Who dared bring it to dust? What about the sword? Who is the mystery man seen with the sword in the mishht on the night of the fall? I have him here tonight, ladies and gents, to tell us all about it.*

A monster camera moves slowly around Olly who's standing under a miniature replica of Clery's Clock. Looming behind him is the backdrop Olly made yesterday. Laid it on the cobbles of their yard and painted it to look like the double gates of the Pillar entrance.

Olly's holding a copy of the *Irish Press* in front of his face. The headline reads: "Mystery Man Has Nelson's Sword".

Olly lowers the paper, revealing one shut eye and a limp sleeve tucked into Nelson's fine waistcoat.

Chuckles ripple through the crowd as they recognize O'Feeney, funniest man in Ireland.

Hence, fellow. He shouts at Gay, tossing the news over his shoulder, and Gay Byrne steps aside.

Monday night—No, I'm after telling a lie—Tuesday. Olly points his index finger skyward, deathly serious. *Morning.* He sways, recovers. Widens his eyes, shakes his jowls. *Sauntering down O'Connell Street when I look to the 'bove.* Olly trips on his topboots, almost falls, but catches himself by sweeping his free arm expansively. *And it's a clear arch of night, fair weathery, moon at the last quarter. Sky a goldy scatter of light, scars. O, the scars in the sty—Sty? Scars?* Olly lurches to attention like he's been doused with ice water. *Stars, the stars, I'm saying. Stars. In the sky.* Olly staggers to the side like a drunkard. The Old Bat is slapping her kneezey bones, cackling.

Don't mind tellin' yeh. Olly winks at the cameras. *I was halfway to Bally-Fluthered. Sauntering towards Lord Nelson, the philanderer himself. Filthy oul fellah full of his own importances, up there on his pedestal, overlooking the city. When I say to him, I say: "Nelly?"*

"Yuh-esss," Lord Nelson answers.

"Blow yerself up."

And ba-boom-bam-ba-dam, he does it. Blows himself up.

At these words, Olly does an astounding back-flip, a forward thripple-thropple, pitching onto his face, rump in the air.

Gay enters the frame, looks at Olly playing Nelson on

the studio floor. The perfect straight man, he says, *At his feet . . . lay Lord Nelson.*

Olly throws a fist of baby powder into the air like a puff of stonedust.

The audience tumbles into Gaels of laughter.

Paving stones beneath my teeths. Olly lisps in a British accent. *My famous grin chipped toothless.*

Astonishing, Gay says to the camera, resuming control. *And that's the truth about Nelson, he blew himself up. Can I have a big round of applause for Oliver O'Feeney? This is only a taste of his smash hit, "O'Feeney's Round the Corner with the Cornerboys." Now playing at the Dublin Gate Theatre.*

Next on deck . . . the Cornerboys.

My little Granny O'Feeney doesn't laugh one jot. Aunty Mara says "that's funny" once or twice, but Des and Fee are in fits of giggles. Janey, I've a pain from laughing.

The bowsie, Gran says, after Daddy's act is done. She raises her eyebrows to heaven. *The scandal.* Gran's sitting in Mam's storytelling rocking chair by the fireside. She's just about in the fire 'cause she's always cold.

Granny pats her shining, white permed hair. She has flashy red nails. *Putting that round the town about himself. "Halfway to Bally-Fluthered." Has he no shame?*

Mam, Mara says, topping up Granny's milky tea. She and Gran are over from their house 'cause they don't have a telly. *Shhh. The Cornerboys—*

Shush yourself, Gran snaps.

The kids hunker down on the lino front of the set. We

don't want Granny to send us to bed. We're up for *The Late-Late Show* for the first time in our lives.

Doesn't a roar go up when they come onstage, five beardies in sharp black suits. Mam made Daddy buy each of them a suit for their show at the Gate. New socks for Stilly and new shoes.

Who's this packet of slummers? Granny scowls. She's got crinkly skin under her face powder. She's all length and slenders, smells of Yardley's lavender. That's to cover the whiskey, 'cause she drinks all day from an ould perfume bockle hidden in her bag.

They're not civilized, Gran says, burning with the bitters. Granny is sour on everything.

Growler steps to the mike like he runs the place, opens his mouth and out comes his voice, a raucous sawmill. *As Padraig Pearse says, "There is only one way to appease a ghost."* Growler's strumming his goldy guitar. He looks into the eye of the camera. *"You must do . . ."*

"The thing it asks yeh." The telly audience answers.

Glad to see you know yer Irish history. He growls and the country falls in love with him. Growler raises his chin. *And this is for . . . the six missing counties.*

Antrim, Armagh, Fermanagh, Tyrone
Derry, Down, County Down

The studio audience takes it up, solemnly chanting.

Antrim, Armagh, Fermanagh, Tyrone
Derry, Down, County Down

Growler and the Cornerboys go to *Goosetown* front of Ireland.

We fly up, they fly up, out of Goosetown
They fly off, we fly off, and away…

Down the backlane on Tolka Row, Noleen and the kids and Aunty Mara sing along. Not Gran, though. She never went to Olly's shows. Never heard of the Cornerboys, nor Goosetown. She was only there that night 'cause it was her son's debut on *The Late-Late Show.* And by some shake of fate, dumb justice, *Outta Goosetown* goes on *Top of the Pops.* Hits the charts at number two and the Cornerboys step forward into histories on the wings of an ancient ould Fenian song. Them Lumps fly around the globe and get the world-known. Leaving Olly O'Feeney far behind.

Later he would say it was due to the kids, his wife, the fambilly that he couldn't grab the brass when it was his alone, that he had to share in his fame. But at the time, he was thrilled to the gills to be offered a show of his own on *RTÉ.* Called *Our City*, it had a solid run for a short bit of wild.

Into the Weirds

1967

a smarty girl

One Saturday, Lily the housekeeper lets me take Daddy's lunch in a bag to the Gaiety at the top of Grafton Street where he's rehearsing his new show. I stop at the crosswalk, wait for the light to go green. Look right, look left, look right again. Then run, run cross the road, run for my life. Through the stagedoor, past Crying Eyes—he's called Crying Eyes 'cause he's a porter-y ould doorman with weepy eyes—and into the theatre.

I do love the quiet in theatres when rehearsals is done. The velvet tip-up seats, purple walls and plaster moldings with naked cheroobs. Plaster vines cover their nippy boobers and langeroos.

Backstage, under the fly loft, through the shadows of the wings, and cross the stage. I pat the lowered front curtain, a goldy fringe brushes the floor. That's a good job, running the curtain up and down. I want to be a curtain lifter when I grow up.

I find Daddy chatting with the girls in the girls' dressing room. He's got the heel of his boot hooked on the rail of a high stool. When I hand him his lunch, he tears into his sangitch like a heathen and tosses the plum to me.

I'd eat the plum but for the smell of the makeup—

chokey wax would make you boak. The grownup girls rush about in their bras and slips. Look at the girls. So glam, with the green eye shadow and the long lashes they buy at Woolworth's. They're Daddy's Black & White Dancers. "Black & White—the whiskey with the smoother flavor."

That one. Daddy points at Stacia, a waddly fatty blubbering into her hands. *Has had more fellas than dinners.*

Stacia drags her fingernails down her face, streaking her cheeks with brown eyeliner. She breathes in and out through her snotstrils, pouts her bottom lip and rages. *Yeh son of a fuck.*

Yeh mad hoore. Daddy pops the last of his rasher sangitch into his mouth, taps the corners of his lips with his knuckle like he could care less. *There is nothing like a rasher.*

Yeh have me nerves in tatters. Stacia hurls a hairbrush at him and flits from the room.

Daddy laughs and laughs. The rest of his dancers laugh at her, too. Then he's being cheeky, making the girls go red-faced. Is he s'posed to be looking at them in their underpants? I sneak out my finger, touch the spikes of an eyelash, dead caterpillar on the dressing table.

Get your filthy hands outta that. Cynthia scorches into the room. *That goes in my eye.*

There she is, that actor-essy one in all silver stuff. She has sparkles up her arms and on her neck. She's got legs to her ears. What a dancer.

Hiya, Cynthia, Daddy says. *Was waiting for you.*

Wouldja you shite-shutup with yourself, she yells. *And arse off.*

The other dancers fade from the room.

If that bloody bitch, Stacia, doesn't learn her bit, I'll unhair her head, Cynthia says. *Why doncha give her the boot?*

Yeh, Daddy says, but I know that yeh. It means no. Daddy's tongue is twisted 'hind his bottom teefs with worry.

I am spun out, Cynthia says. *The feck of annoyances. Me costume doesn't fit—Sorry for talking this way in front of your chiseler, but—*

I know feck, flip, eff off and fuck. Ticking the words on my fingers.

Isn't she a roar, Cynthia says, dead deadpan. *You should go on the stage like your dear ould da.* She's wriggling to reach the back of her super-short Heidi frock. *This belly grinder's murrrdering me.*

O, the huff and the puff as Daddy tugs at her zipper. Then she's standing there in her sausage squasher—that elastic thing that mashes her front up and her bum in. I squeeze in to help.

G'wan home, Daddy says. *We're on lunch.*

They push me out the door and *slam*. When Cynthia starts giggling, I fold my ears down and run.

Girls in spangles are chatting up and down the corridor. There's a slice of light from the back corner dressing room where a girl named Mahree is brushing out a blonde wig on a stand.

I inch into her room, watch her spread cream on her face. She leans into the mirror, the bright bulbs. On her dressing table is a rainbow of lipper tubes. Mahree goes behind a screen and over comes her stocking one, her stocking two, her garter with clips.

I pull the garter over my bare legs. Snaps like mouths

open and close, saying: *Wah-wah. My daddy's in the dressing room with Cynthia. They thrung me out.*

Around the screen comes Mahree. *Hell-loh, lovey-doh.*

Mahree says her name all French-like. Mahree with the accent on the Mah, not Mary or Marie like she's common. She's wearing trousers that come to just below her knees, a round necked shirt, and her front is gone.

Where's your badongers?

Here in my bra, see? In her bra is a pair of springy lumps that make her gazongeroos. *They're pretend. They're for on the stage.*

"What a pair of gazongeroos," my daddy would say. In her really clothes she looks like a boy and I like her. She's all soaps and glamour, too. She's perfume—sweet lavender of my Granny's garden.

Open up. She rolls lippers top my mouth. *Annnnnd bottom.*

Now I've the reddest lips ever. Then she takes these scissors, weensy scissors, not scissors for cutting. They've a spongy thing on the bottom and—

Shut your eyes, love. Mahree blows on my lashes, then the press of spongy scissors tugging my lashes, and I feel—

Gorgia, you are pure gorgia, she says. *Open your eyes and see.*

My lashes are sprung like daddy-long-legs broken upwards. I look and look in the mirror. Can't believe my curled-up lashes and red-red lips. I am a girl near the girl I want to be. I am pure gorgia. *I'm a girl.*

You're a girsha, Mahree says.

That's Irish for little girl, I say.

I know. She's packing her things.

I like that, I do, the word *girsha.* It's far better than girls. Guh-guh-guhrrrrllll. The way it comes out the jaw is a dark thing. A growl of a thing is a girl. Gurrrls are dollies in shops. Girls are Lily the housekeeper scrubbing pots in the sink. Mams wheeling prams, bending into the mist whisting down in the rain. And my mam is a girl having babbies, filling the tall bin in the toilet with nappies from my new sister Poppy. Girls work in shops singing out prices and wrapping up packages. Even them ould wans sitting on orange crates in their little bit of shop, knitting and sucking on plums? Is girls under it all.

Don't wanna be a girl 'cause I hate them.

Sheela steps through the door. *You ready?* she says to Mahree.

Sheela's every way thick, thick round the middle, thick at the brow, thick in the hands. Sheela's slow, she moves slowly. Mahree's lean and boyish, dancey-fast like a moth.

Whose kid? Sheela asks.

Olly's.

Say no more. Sheela takes my hand. *Come on.*

She has a big hairy shirt goes over a pair of man's trousers. Sheela runs lights for the show.

We walk through a hall with a wheely rack of costumes, shoes in a jumble on the musty boards.

Knock-knock, Sheela calls when we reach the girls' dressing room.

I rush through the door and there's Cynthia, bare. I can see her all. Though silver dazzles on her neck and arms, her gazongers hang gray. She's shrugged up against the dressing table, wearing nothing but stockings and heels. The black patch tween her legs. Ugly, frightening.

Use the red to girl-up, now. Daddy's sitting on the stool wearing his good suit for the show. His voice is gruff and strange. *Use the red.*

Cynthia brushes rouge from her cheek to her hairline. On one side, the other.

Don't forget yer mouth. Daddy snatches a tube of lipstick and roughly smudges blood red paint over the bow in her lips.

I want the toilet. I'm going to be sick. I bolt for the corridor and ram into Mahree who's too shocked to move.

Does he have to be so brazen? Sheela says.

Let's go to our place for a tea party. Mahree takes my hand and pats it. *Wouldn't that be gas?*

At the stage door Mahree tells Crying Eyes—*if Olly should ask, we're taking Noleen to the flat for lunch.*

Sheela and Mahree live over a Hoover shop, round the corner from the Gaiety. They have one room with the kitchen off it and a loo in the hall. There's bookshelves to the ceiling, a couch that pulls into a bed, and a flowerdy eiderdown.

Flick the kettle on.

I sit on a footstool scrunched into the wall and play with two china birds. One's got pepper. One is salt. I shake salt on my hand.

Throw it over your shoulder for luck.

Sheela won't get cross if I throw salt on the lino, 'cause throwing salt is for luck. *Where's your fridge?*

Don't need one.

We go to the grocers every day. Salt crunches underfoot as Mahree cooks.

We live at the grocers.

Can you get the kettle?

Sheela scurries to the kettle. Stockings soak in a blue bowl on the counter. There's a wire basket of spuds, sprouting eyes.

Are you married? I ask them.

Sheela looks surprised at my question. *To who?* she asks, scooping dry leaves from the tea caddy.

Sheela and Mahree, Mahree and Sheela. They are in themselves happy. It's the way they walk in towards each other and the way the room fills with their happy selves together. The way Sheela stood at the door of the dressing room, looked in and asked, "you ready?" Like she'd wait for her life in the door if Mahree needed her waiting all that time.

Are you and Mahree married in this house?

Mind out, Sheela, Mahree says.

We're not.

Are you sisters?

No.

That's a true answer, 'cause no two girls ever looked so not alike.

But then do you have husbands?

Such questions. Want some milky tea?

Mahree pours me a cup half filled with tea, half filled with milk.

Sugar?

Three spoons, please.

Help yourself.

Little finger out and wagging, I slurp and gulp my milky tea.

What'll we do? Sheela asks me.

At the cooker Mahree swipes carrot bits into the bubbling turnips, onions, and meat. She rinses her hands. *Won't you do a cup tossing?*

Right. Sheela lumbers to the cupboard and searches inside.

Let's make it magic here. Mahree hangs a teatowel over the windowpanes.

Will we do magic? I ask.

It's magic of a sort.

What sort?

Divinations. Mahree sings it like she's a witch over a cauldron. It gives me thah-rills of horror.

Nonsense. Sheela thunks a wine bottle on the table, colory wax dribbles down the neck and over its straw-fat belly. She strikes a matchstick on her boot and lights a cangle. *It's reading yer tea leaves.*

Each hand takes a hand, Sheela, Mahree, me. Round the table hand to hand, round the table three. Hand to hand to hand to hand, Sheela, Mahree, me. Round the table hand to hand, then Sheela reads the tea.

She swills the saucer.

Sifts the leaves.

Circles the saucer.

Stops.

Just as I thought, you're a girsha.

Girsha-girl-*girsha*.

And of the Sheee, Sheela says. *For deep in your veins run the blood-traces of the Sheee.*

The Sheee. I think in my head.

Is the good people that live under the earth. They're always watching, they look out for their own.

Sheela's planting magics in my minds. 'Cause I never said the Sheee out loud.

You'll travel far, Sheela says. *Wish seven times, take seven pebbles, take seven trips round the world. You'll fly, you'll go, to the spindelling world of the Sheee.*

Noleen's mam, Gina O'Feeney, is in the green-lamped reading room of the National Library. She's come in for refuge. She's come in for a scribble on the yellow legal pads her mother sends from America. She's working a script deadline, or trying.

Light, there's light high in the dome of the round reading room. So much heaven it is, not like home with its ironing-board-brain-space for writing. Here in the world of words. Uhmmm, the smell of the old books, the dark green leather bindings, pages edged in gold leaf. Here, she can do anything, sort out her life. She's far above her world.

Fiona and Des're at music school. Lily's working a Saturday so Ely and Noleen are in hand. And Poppy, who'll be two in April. She's really on the hoof these days, tottering round the house. Well-fed, well-loved. *Her* children, not her philandering husband's kids.

She-knows, she-knows. Is not an idiot. Today she found a poem in his trouser pocket. "For Sin-thia." Maudlin ramblings from his sub-conscious, would-be Joycean drivel. A dancer in their current show. A faceless showgirl tart. This tart would wreck a family.

Today, as she was walking Des and Fee to music school, she saw it. Olly kissing Sin-thia outside the Gaiety—grabbing her into him like a consumption. Gina rushed the kids fast as she could. She's sure they didn't catch on.

All that ghastliness made her feel quite inferior and ashamed for him. He is living in his own destruction.

Dublin filth.

Why does he do this? Why does he?

When Olly has everything, it isn't enough. It's only a matter of time before he lands up in a weirdy ward at the pace he's set his frame. It's the booze, the too-much booze. These escapades with motts, smutgirls in their Zhivago coats and mini-skirts fawning all over him. He sometimes has three romances going at once. Staying out night and day. Drinking and eating and feeling legs. He's a rotter. He's a cad.

There's the Gaiety show she's no longer directing. Why didn't he stand up for her? Instead, he stepped aside and let Gus—the squeezy pig eyes—nose his way in. She was shaking when they canned her. Turned red and stupid in front of the cast. In front of him, in front of Sin-thia.

But—Why fired? Why really? It's up to her to guess and flounder. Did Sin-thia ask Olly to sack her? Did Olly oust her all on his own? She'll never know. The bruising shame.

She won't go to the Gaiety party next week. Sin-thia will be there. It cuts her.

She must stop all this thinking. What a waste of her mind.

And that telly show *Arseity.* Beneath him. If they were writing it together, it'd be fine, but—The *RTÉ* has their Irish writers who know funny, not her.

Gina believes in them together, and he just left her behind. He hasn't written or produced anything of note in ages. It's her ideas, the impressions she's always collecting that work well for him. He needs her to keep him on the right road, doing theatre that's worthy of their talent.

He's earning good wages but none is reaching the family. He gives her such meager housekeeping funds. She must get this script scribbled and off. But her radio work isn't enough. She was counting on full pay for the Gaiety show. They're heading for financial calamity.

How will we pay for the new baby? "Never question a new creation," he said thirteen years ago. She didn't know, hadn't a clue. She's up a ladder, hanging lights in the Pike Theatre when she swooned like in a Victorian novel. It was Olly caught her. "Why, we must be having a ba."

"But what will we do?" She asked in pure panic.

"Never question a new creation." Olly assured her. "We do what we do. We make theatre. We make children. We make life happen."

Now all he has for her and their coming child is disinterest and derision.

Mad, tearful mad. Damn him.

There will be no more children. She'll make sure of it. She'll dust off the old diaphragm. Write her sister, Violet, for the cream. An embarrassment to ask, but so crucial.

So what's the plan here?

She must finish her thesis, publish her book. It's almost

1968 and she's nowhere with her Ph.D. How fast life kicks by. This is what happens when you marry into Ireland. You lose your gumption, lose your way, like the girl turned to swan in the mists of myth.

But here in the library, at the desk with the green lamp, among the books. It can't be so hard for her to write one little old book, surely? Next summer after the new O'Feeney's arrival, she'll put the children in swimming lessons. She'll come here every day and write about Synge. Should be finished by Fall. With her doctorate she can teach in University, return to America if she needs to.

She might need to.

He might push her.

She might have to.

Walk out from him.

After another run-through of the show, off we go—Daddy and me. Out the door of the Gaiety.

There y'are, Jackser Molloy. A schoolboy tugs Daddy's jacket. *Aren't you Jackser Molloy from off the telly?*

That kid's seen him on *Our City*—Daddy's very own telly show. A sit-you-down comedy about a slum-man, name of Jackser Molloy who's gotta wife, nine kids and no money. What's so funny about having no money, I ask you.

"Noleen Molloy." The boys on the playground jeer, eejebags. Getting my name mixed up with my telly-daddy on purpose. I punched the one. Got put down in Babies Class for the day.

Are you Jackser Molloy, the-really? The boy asks Daddy.

G'wan, give it a go. Daddy dares him.

"Jackser Molloy, ye're driving me round the bend." The kid says it out his bottom lip, just like Daddy's wife on the telly.

"Driving yeh nowhere, for I haven't gorra car." Daddy's talking like the Jackser.

Jackser Molloy, you're the Jackser.

That I am, indeed I am. Daddy crouches on his haunches, looks at the boy.

Who's she? The boy jabs a finger in my face.

He's my daddy.

Lucky duck-ya, having the Jackser for all your owns.

When Daddy slips him a bright sixpence the boy goes delirious. He whoops and scampers down Grafton Street.

And here y'are, Nolee. He gives me a shining silver half a crown. *That's for being such a good girl for Sheela and Mahree. If you don't tell Mammy you went to their flat, I'll give this to you for all to yourself.*

I won't tell Mammy, I promise.

By the side of the Gaiety is a sweet shop with all these lovely ladies wearing white coats over their skirts. They're standing like polices behind shelves stacked with chocolates, caramels, and mully-cully sweets. I'm turning me half crown over in my palm. What'll I get, what do I want? The marzipan sweeties made in the shape of strawbellies.

How many strawbellies for half a crown?

Straw-bellies, isn't she a dote. Will you go on stage like your da?

I'm going to be an actor-ess. I puff out my chest, bang it with my fist. When I go on the stage, I'll come here every day and buy all the sweets in the shop.

When are you going on the stage? The shop lady hands me a box tied in peppermint striped string.

Soon as they let me.

Let's go home, Daddy says, squeezing my hand as we spring through the black iron gates to the Green.

Come on. He slaps his left leg—our special signal. It's time to practice our act. *Hoopah!*

Left foot on his thigh, upsie-daisey. I step up to stand on his shoulders. Shins hinched to his head, he holds me at the back of the knees. Left hand on left hip, right arm cocked like a circus *girsha*.

All the peoples in the Green applaud as we strut past the flower bed, over the arching bridge.

Every chance we get we work on our show.

Don't break, don't break, he says to me. That means no laughing. 'Cause when you are acting in the theatre, it's the biggest sin to show how you feel.

Don't break, don't break, Daddy says, dangling me by the ankle and wrist in front of an oncoming bus, pulling me to safety at the very last second.

I never break, 'cause I'm not afraid.

It's how his daddy taught him to be an acrobat. Starting from when Daddy was the age of three, Grandda took him to an empty cow stall and learned him tumblesaults and tiger leaps. He stuck Daddy in the hayloft, lifted the ladder away, and dared him to jump. He flung him around and swung him around 'til Daddy became the funniest man in all the worlds.

Daddy taught me how to cross my eyes, make fearsome faces. I can do tiger leaps through hula hoops, cartwheels, handsprings and *jetés*. We have jokes going and our versions of the radio ads Daddy does for Pan Am and Wimpy's Snackery—"a square meal in a round bum."

Thank you, thank you. Hah-hah-hah. I'm the funniest girl in Dublintown.

Back on Tolka row, Daddy doesn't have his big toe in the door before everyone is at him. He grabs my bag of sweets and passes 'em out to everyone, even Lily.

Daddy bought them sweets for me, not the whole flipping fambilly. They're mine 'cause I promised not to tell—

Daddy smacks my bottom. *Greedy gut.*

OW. Ow-ow-ow. *Daddy hit me—*

Stop it, Olly, Mam shouts. *Get up to bed with that language.*

YOU SAID THE SWEETS WERE MINE.

Up I go to the kidsroom, sit in the window well. I lean my head on my knees, look out at the inky blue sky. Night's coming down, night's coming early.

Poppy is bunched on her tummy in my old cot, taking a nap. She has her blanket in her fist, green twist of wool up her nose. Poppy puts the fringey part of her special blanket up her nose and sucks her thumb. Mammy doesn't like it when Poppy sucks her thumb, 'cause it's a weakness to suck your thumb, a disgraceful habit.

We've two sets of bunkbeds in the kidsroom. Girls on the girl-side, boys on the other. There's the lavender wardrobe, the lilac wall and Ely's painting of the Ha'Penny Bridge. His painting is sellotaped over a hole in the wall. Divil-the-divil lives in that hole. Lurking under, under beneaths, is *him*, the voice of him, Da's howl.

One night. One night of shitten shites, Mam and the kids huddle in the bottom bunk on the girls' side. We're all of us in my bed, hiding. Fiona's shushing Poppy. And he's ramping the stairs. He is the divil. Coming for us.

What're we doing laying about, waiting on loads of trouble? Up with you, on with you, GO!

It's all down to me 'cause I'm Quick Draw's Cowboy Girl. I spring to the top bunk, grab the horse reigns and drop a blanket over the bottom bunk to cover the women and childerings. We're in our Conestoga Wagon train. There's heaps of provisions, water canteens.

Gee-awwww, I holler. Flick the reigns and click my teefs at Miss Nellie, our trusty dray mare. Off we go. Over mountains and over trails. Bockety-brockety, our wagon bed clashes 'gainst the wall. *Giddy-yep, giddy-yap. El kabong.* We're roaring. Into the West and roaring.

Faster-faster, for the love of God, Mam calls.

We gallop and gallop, the kidsroom window opens for us. We pass on out into free. We're away from him, we're away.

Yippee-yi-o-ki-ayyy.

Miles back in the kidsroom on Tolka Row, Daddy slams the door so the knob blasts the wall in a circle of O. Daddy's stopped in the doorsill. The girls' bunk is gone. The window is wide. His family's fled. We are well away.

Up and down Dublin streets, I zap into shops and scrounge free sweeties. Dolly's on Baggot Street has everything: Fizz Bags, Trigger Bars, and my favorite, Lucky Numbers. On the telly, there are ads for sweets that are numbers. Each sweet has a number. In the ads, people say their favorite number sweet while they're doing their jobs. The Policeman loves Fourteen. He blows a whistle and cars screech to a stop. *Number Fourteen is grand!* The Policeman whistles again and the cars go whizzing on.

My favorite Lucky Number is Number Seven 'cause that's the sweet number for the Office Girl. The Office Girl wears spike heels and has gorgeous legs.

Gorgeous legs. Daddy hums it, his eyes running the length of them legs. Mammy doesn't like when Daddy looks at them office girls. *Not all rickety blue like you.*

When I grow up I'll be on the stage and go to the sweet shop next to the Gaiety. I'll order a lorry-load of Number Sevens.

But we're out of Lucky Number Seven at the moment. Won't you try the Thirty-Three? I hear it's divine.

I don't eat Thirty-Three. Thirty-Three is the tired old get has a boxer dog face runked up into his brainings. Hate him. And hate Thirty-Three.

I'm afraid you'll have to wait for more Sevens from the factory.

I want a room filled with Lucky Sevens so I never run out. When I'm grown up, in the nights I will work in the theatre. *Bang* the lights go on and everyone will see my gorgeous legs kicking on high spiked heels. In the day I'll wrap my raincoat belt tight to my waist and head for the office. I'll trot down the road, spin on my high spiked heels, wave, pop a sweet in my mouth and...

"Mine's Number Seven." Wink at the camera, kick my

heel. In I go to the office. tap-tap-tap at my type-machine. I pick up the phone and take orders. I peel the blue-blue sello paper of a Lucky Seven sweet, and pop! In my mouth, the luscious-yums. I eat nothing but Lucky Number Sevens. Clackity-clack, the keys on my typewriter're hopping. Fabitty-blabitty words fill the page. I'm writing, I'm writing away. *Mine's Number Seven.*

Noleen O'Feeney, get out of there. Mammy wrenches my arm from the socket. Yanking me from her writing desk. *Mam's typewriter is not a toy.*

Mine's Number Seven, Number Seven, Number Seven. I scarper out the bottom half-door into the lane.

I love Lucky Number Sevens.

And am true to Lucky Sevens 'til…

The Smarties ad comes on.

See, we have a telly, a great box of flashing light. 'Cause my da was studying to be really good for *Our City.* He studied all the shows. I do like the American shows. All Irish ones are dirt, but not Daddy's. It comes on 10 o'clock Friday nights. They don't use the Holy Name or make filthy-body impilla-cations, but it's too late for us, Mam says.

So at night on *Teilifís Éireann* is:

5.30 *Stamps with a Story* (Des likes that one. I don't.)
6.00 *The Angelus* (Boring Catholick krap.)
6.30 *Quick Draw McGraw* and *Bozo the Clown*
7.00 *Hi, Chaparral. How are yeh!*

'Tween them telly shows, the Smarties ad comes on. Smarties is like teeny fairy flying saucers. Smarties is every color you know. Sugar pink, Kelly green, sky blue. In the ad there's an elfin girl wearing a frilly nightie.

Maaaam, can I get a frilly nightie?

Don't you like your bugsers anymore?

My toes are breaking through the feets. I want a frilly nightgown.

Mam takes this as me wanting to be more of a girl. When really, that nightie will bring me Smarties in the night.

In the Smarties ad, that girl nestles in the plumpy down of her pillows. First of all, she has two pillows all to herself when I only have the flat-out squashed one. Her hair is long blonde, thrilling all round like Rapunzel. The Smarties girl puts her two hands under her cheek, sighs, and she's out like plaster. Then the picture goes all wriggly-wraw. Now the telly set is fine, not banjaxed, 'cause the wriggly-wraw means she's in a dream. Then a magic wand touches her nose, and she's in a magic land where a fairy princess grants her every wish.

And it's Smarties all over. There's Smarties in the trees. The branches bend down, offering her sparkly Smarties. The girl scoops a handful into her mouth. Cheeks bulging, she's beaming—delighted with herself and with her Smarties. Then wobble-wobble, spang-spang the picture goes wriggly-wraw 'til she's back in her own bed sleeping. Smile on her face, 'cause in her hand is...

A box of Smarties.

When I go to bed I unfurl my hair—which isn't much with my Dutchboy chop. I sigh, wearing my daddy's white shirt, since my mam didn't buy me a frilly nightie. I wriggle in the sheets, clutching an empty box of Smarties. The

Smarties box is empty 'cause I had to eat 'em. I shut my eyes, beaming like the *girsha* in the ad, waiting on my fairy. Over the end of my bed, she comes to carry me way to Smartyland.

We're off to a world of sweets. There's Smarties in the flowers, Smarties in the bushes, Smarties in the clouds. There's hills and mountain peaks—the Swiss Alps—covered in Smarties and a rushing chocolate river. I'm paddling a canoe over chockie rocks and pebbles made of Smarties. And way down, far downstairs, a chair falls over. There's footfalls near the fireplace. *Crash.* A plate. *Slang.* The coffee-table-milking-stool skreaks with the weight of her. *Smack.* He does it. Hits our mam.

The gang in the kidsroom go freezy.

You're not allowed to hit our mam, Des shouts from the boys' bunk bed cross the room. *Only lousers hit girls.*

Stop, Fee whispers. *He'll get angry and go at her.*

Don't worm your way out of it, Mam shouts. *Oliver.*

Bang goes the door, he's off. Daddy's vanished for a stroll. Mam's in the sink clattering lids, dishes, pots.

But no, I'm not part of that. I'm in my Smarty dream. I snatch fistfuls of Smarties, gobble 'em down, singing the Smarties smart theme song: *Every day it is a party for the girl who eats her Smarties—*

I want to go to Smartyland, I tell Mam the next morning.

Smartyland? Is that a carnival? Mam's all smiley, her fight with Daddy forgotten. Maybe it was a dream? No, a nightmare.

Smartyland, I say. *In the Smarties ad on the telly.*

You mean the land full of Smarties in the little girl's dream?

I don't want to go in the Smarty girl dream. I want to be the girl that acts in the dream. I want to be in the Smarties ad.

They made that ad already.

I want to make the new ad, then. I want to be the Smarties girl, selling Smarties on the telly. I could make a lot of money.

You're a little girl. You don't need money.

Yes, I do.

For what?

Sweets.

Noleen, you're thinking about sugar too much.

Do they give that girl all those Smarties to eat?

They're props, Mam says wearily. *The boxes're empty.*

Did that actor-girl eat them?

Stop thinking about sugar. If you eat too much sugar you'll catch diabetes and they'll cut off your leg.

I won't get diabetes, 'cause all the Smarties are gone.

The following week: The Smarties girl is off to a fairy world with a waterfall of Smarties, sweets raining down in an avalanche of color. So-so many Smarties it would take weeks to eat them all. I'm angry 'cause they're making new Smarties ads without me.

I want a job on the telly. Eating Smarties and dreaming Smarties, 'cause I love Smarties. Get me a job on telly.

Mam really tries. She asks around the *Radió Teilifís Éireann* where she sometimes works, sometimes writing. No luck. So Daddy went to his producers and got me a part on his telly show. Playing his favorite kiddo—Una Molloy, pet of the fambilly. Ahhh, Jayzus Mack. I'm gonna be on the telly for the really-reals. Every goggler at the box will know me. I'll be famous like my da. We'll do our act, and I'll put on a show of my spectakular feats. And all of Dublin will fall in loves and lather with me.

In Studio A at *RTÉ*, there's the outside of a Georgian tenement house. Atop the door is a cracked fanlight with buckling wood. It's not real, though, 'cause this housefront is a flat, shooting up to catwalks at the ceilings. The house is a flat, and behind the flat is hot lights, wire snakes you could trip on, people for makeups and people for costumes. A man pulls me into a frock made from a tayto sack. I've filthy bruised legs and bare feets. I look like a starving girl. The man fusses with a blob of fake blood on my finger.

On cue, I skip over wire snakes and up the steps to the outside of the house. *Mammy, I'm hurted.* Pound on the door. *Mammeeeeee.*

A brass knob turns and the door swings wide. There's my Telly Mam on the doorstep, arms crossed with the begrudge, the sneer, the snides.

Cut me finger, Ma, I whinge.

Do I look like a chemist? Telly Mam snarls, ciggy wagging on her bottom lip. *Stick it in yer gob and suck it.*

LAUGH TRACK.

And cut. That's my scene over. I sit next to Jimmy Downs, that greasy knacker, and we watch 'em make the show. My da's running scene after scene of stewpid jokes.

Our walls are so thin, I can hear the neighbors changing their minds.

When will Daddy and me have a show of our owns?

Do I know her in the carnival sense? Daddy asks my Telly Mam, raising his eyebrows like a Hollywood Slickie.

Ah, Jackser Molloy, yer driving me round the bend.

I'm driving yeh nowhere, the Jackser says. *For we haven't gorra carrrr.*

LAUGH TRACK.

Watching and listening, I realize that Daddy spends far more time with his telly fambilly. I feel a flush of anger for the *RTÉ*. I'll shoot 'em with my blam gun, punch 'em with my fists. I'm full of hate and viciousness. Wish I could go, wish I could leave, but they might need me to do me scene again.

So in my head, I go over our scripts, our jokey ads. First my parts, then his.

DADDY: Did you Maclean your teefs today?

ME: Yeh, aren't they loverly?

Muttering the lines over and over while watching him be the really star and me sitting here being nothing.

ME: How do yeh make a sausage roll?

DADDY: Dunno. How do yeh make a sausage roll?

ME: Give it a push. (Pause for laughs.)

glass in heaven

One day, a day of ecstasy, I open my eyes to Seven Years Old. I do six somersaults and five back-flips on my bed. Singing: *Seven today, I'm seven today. Having my happy birthday today, having my happy birth—*

Des flings his pillow from cross the room. *Shut up.*

It's my birthday, where's my prezz? I toss back his pillow, clash him in the nose. *That's for spoiling my birthday.*

I ratter the underbed above me. *Fee? Fionahhh.* I push my feets against the wire squares, jabbing Fee's back. *Where's my present?*

Go to sleep, she groans. *Get up at a civilized hour.*

Wake up. I rock the girls' bunk from back to front, banging the wall.

Stop shaking the bed or I'll kill you.

It's five in the morning, Daddy shouts from the MamDad room. *Go to sleep this instant or there'll be no party. Want me to cancel your party?*

Noooooo. All my friends in First Class are coming. I dig under my pillow and bring out Judy Littlechap, the most marvelly dolly ever made.

My Granny Volk is so very good, she gives brilliant presents. We never know what we'll find in the wooden crates that sail all the way from Pennsylvania.

For my birthday, she sent me three new dollies. Not the rounding chub of baby dolls, but slender dolls shaped like real people. One's a daddy. One's a mam and the other's their zany-fun teen angel daughter.

Dr. John Littlechap wears a suit and a white overcoat. He carries a black case and round his neck is that snaky thing doctors use to hear your heart. He even has a face mask for surgeries.

The mam's hair is swirled high on her head like a cherry bun. There's a stripe through her hair like a skunk. She has pearly earrings and a string of pearls round her neck. Silver slippers peep out from beneath a long-flowing, shimmering blue gown.

Doctor Daddy is dressed for going to his job, but the mammy is ready for a fancy ball. Every day after work Doctor Daddy takes Posh Mam out waltzing. Today they're at a huge summer party, outside on the grass. Under the sky, they dance.

Mrs. Littlechap has a tall, brave husband man. He heals sick kids. Mammy Littlechap is a fantabulous cook and housekeeper. So says the story on her box. She's the best dressed mammy in town. A former model, she left her job to rear Judy Littlechap, pretty as pie.

Judy's seventeen, the secretary of her Senior Class. She "loves parties and crazy desserts." She has a handbag made of cheetah fur and her very own record player with three weeshy disks.

Mammy Littlechap looks at her fambilly, fresh out of their boxes, sitting on the convertible sofa bed in the rumpus room. The sun's gushing color through the window panes. Her heart rises in her chest, a balloon with too much air. *Bang-pop* goes the balloon. *Bang-bang pop.*

Aiiii. Mammy Littlechap shrieks and falls to the ground.

Doctor Littlechap roots in his bag for the heart-hearer thing. He strips off Posh Mam's flashy blue gown, puts the snaky thing on her bazongers and listens to her heart.

Cough, please, Doctor says. *Breathe,* he orders. *Again.*

Cold, the doctor's horn on Little Mam's heart.

O, inside her heart, she is bursting.

Then Dr. Littlechap whisks his wife into his arms, away to their bedroom up the stairs.

Down in the fambilly rumpus room Judy Littlechap spins her disks. Dancing in her mini to the spin of songs.

Cha-cha. Cha-cha.

She doesn't know that just up the stairs, just over her head, Dr. Littlechap and her glamorous mam will schmoodle and nuzzle all night long.

You fainted from love, Dr. Littlechap explains. *You fainted dead away from love.*

Mammy taps my shoulder. *Thanks for letting us sleep. Come help me fix a bottle for Giselle.*

Giselle, the new lickle squabbelly ba, is three weeks old. She has fluffy ginger hair and gray eyes watching the world. She's only chicken-big. Born early, like me. Mam says she is my best-of-all birthday present. But I like toys and friends and parties more.

Mam and me tiptoe down the stairs. I spread newspaper

and twigs in the fire. I do love the shape of a fireplace. It's like a teeny theatre with the turf waiting in the wings, ready to go on. I strike a match, patient for the paper to catch. Then the turf leaps from the wings and onto the crickety crackelly fire.

I stand up, smack the turf dust off my frock. There's the picture of Synge over the mantelpiece, the ticking clock and Nelson's sword carving into tomorrow.

The kettle is smiling and whistling like a smolloch. *Mammy, will you cook brown bread for the party?*

Yes.

Now?

I know you're excited, but it's only six o'clock. Mam sets a saucepan of water on the cooker. *I'll boil you an egg and we'll have a quiet breakfast before the gang descends.*

After my egg, I dash outside, rake the sandbox. Race up the granite steps into the side garden. Shimmy up the elderbelly tree, then onto the roof. I tiptoe along the gutter. Down below, far down below is another lane filled with parked cars and stinking ould stables. I pick moss off the roof slates and bomb the cars.

I tightrope walk along the gutter with my arms straight out, swaying forwards and sideways. I am the best tightrope-walker ever. 'Cept for my grandda. He worked in the circus in London. He was an acrobat and clown. Died ages ago. Mam never even met him.

Mam would throbble me if she saw me up here. I scootch down the elderbelly tree and pull a few white blossoms off the lilac tree. I carry the branches in to my mam, flowers heavy with the scent of spring.

The lilac is gorgeous, Mam says. *Put them in a jug before they wilt.* She's resting her poor legs on the couch, babby Giselle dozing in her arms. Mam's terrible tired lately. I heard her tell Aunty Mara something's wrong with her milk so's she's all the time warming bockles and feeding Giselle and lying on the couch. Having a babby is exhausting.

Go play in the lane before Lily arrives to start the house.

I Iug the slidey board out to the lane, climb the metal steps, sit at the top. Watch morning turn blue, flush with the music of birds. Alone, I'm in me lone, lost for long ages in thought. I'm running through the plans for my party. There'll be balloons, rides in the wagon and slides on the slidey board. We'll play hide-'n-go-seek and there'll be a play, *Hansel and Gretel.* I'm playing Gretel, star of the show. Been rehearsing all week. There's Cucumber Cottage. Daddy built it for my last year's present. It's a miniature version of our home, big enough for me to stand inside. I'm using it today for the set of the witch's sugary-pugary cottage.

Heya, Nolee. Someone kicks the soles of my Bradley's sandals, new for my birthday.

I look down the slanting trough of the slidey board to a pair of sunny red plastic shoes, the kind worn in summer. No socks. Up scrubby bare legs to just over her knee, a bruise in the shape of a hand—four fingers. You can count 'em. Cheap frock and woolly cardigan. Angry green eyes set far apart like a half-wit. A baldy head. Cut to the skull, she's a baldy.

Happy birthday, the baldy girl sneers.

Yeh, happy birthday. I hear from under the slidey board.

A second girl, same frock, same far-apart eyes, same baldy head is suddenly there beside her. The dead-spit of her sister.

Twins. Identical. One very ugly pair. The way they look, they must come from slums. How do they know it's my birthday?

Who are you? I ask them.

Who are you? the second one mocks. She has a shocking birthmark over her left ear, a deep-deep purple stain, like God flung a goblet of wine at her 'cause he detests her so much. *Huh.* That's how to tell 'em apart.

We came for your party, the first says, stepping up the board towards me. *Give us a go.*

What're you saying? Never seen 'em before. How do they know about my party?

Give us a go on yer slide, says the one with the birthmark, follying her sister. Who are they?

What're yeh, selfish? Shove over.

I'm so surprised, I let them shuttle me down the metal stairs to the lane. Then the pair a them go shrieking down my slidey board.

Party doesn't start 'til one, I say. *You aren't invited.*

Yes we are, Green Eyes says.

Our new daddy asked us. Purply Stainhead wipes her hands down her sweater, fastening and unfastening the bottom two buttons.

What daddy? Something in the way she says "new" has me heart going like clappers.

Daddy O'Feeney.

That's my da, I say.

He's our daddy now.

Just then a pram big as a tank comes wheeling down the lane. Their ma, a tarty swoggler, presses the brake to the front wheel with a high-spiked, high-heel shoe. It's Stacia from Da's Black & White dancers. Thought she got the sack.

Ma, Green Eyes calls. *Nolee gave us a turn on her slidey board.*

Lookit me, Ma, Purply Stainhead screeches. *Watch me go.* Hurtling face down onto the cobbles. She pops up pure-immediate and doesn't cry.

There's rattles strung across the hood of the pram, pale blue elephants. In the pram, Little Lord Fart-leroy decked out in a navy blue sailor suit and a white sailing cap. O, fat fucks of hell. I despise him right off, more-even than his sisters.

What a dirty crowd.

I'm here for my money, Stacia says.

What money?

For the babby.

For why? But I know before she says so. Lookit that babby fat in his pram. He's got the giant, most-biggest brown eyes. Just like Ely. My daddy's eyes middle of his chubby-fat elephant face.

We don't have your money, I say, weak in the tummy.

You tell Olly O'Feeney from me, I want my money and if he doesn't pay up, I'll tell yer ma.

Tell her what? I ask.

That Our Nelson is yer daddy's.

I steal another look at the boy in the pram. He's tucked under five pale blue satin blankets, sucking the life out of a matching pale blue soother. The blue is to let everyone know he's a boy. He's gotta baldy head like his skinny-skin, baldy sisters.

Where's yer hairs? is all I can say.

We had nits, says Green Eyes.

All the school had nits.

So we had nits.

Sister Murdo shaved us bald. Now we match Nelsey, don't we? Purply Stainhead leans into the pram, pinches Nelson so he wails, soother bouncing to the cobblestones.

In the scream, his horrible howl, I see his teefs sharp as a jackal. He's a vicious, teefy aminal.

Git. Or I'll skape yer arse down a street. Stacia knocks the purply one away from her brother. *You tell yer da.* Snot driveling off the beak of her nose. *Or we'll come back middle a yer party.*

My da, I talk loud, like my kidgang in the Green. *Goes with a girl name a Chrissy now.* Just last Saturday I seen him with a coaxing girl in the side lane by O'Donoghue's. Ciggy tips flirting in the dim afternoon, he grabbed the curves of her into him, put his tongue on her tongue. Eww—that's germy.

You are a liar, Stacia blubbers.

Chrissy is a hairdresser. I know 'cause I follied her. *She works at Jule's on the Green.* Mam took me there once for a posh haircut.

I'll tell yer Ma. I'll tell her-I'll—Stacia whimpers, the punch gone from her sails.

Tell yeh what, I say, dead cheeky. ***I'll*** *tell me ma, then where'll yew be?*

Stacia stares her fill of me, but I hold fast. Don't break, don't break.

Come on, girls, she says, swinging the carriage into gear. Squaddelling up the lane with her pair of scurry rats and a boy in a pram who is from my daddy.

How did he go into their house and have a babby with them?

Top the slidey board, I turn it over in my mind and turn it over. 'Til the birdsong burns bright and the real world goes thin.

Her sister, Fiona O'Feeney, scholarship kid at Alexandra College for Girls, is out on the lane mid the chaos of Noleen's birthday. Party guests swarm the place like cattle. Leeny's got all the boys from her class up on the roof of the scene shed. They're tramping about the corrugated tin, playing pirates, or *Gulliver's Travels,* something adventuresome.

Yip-yip yahoo. Noleen launches from roof to the side lawn, landing solid. All the boys soon follow her. Fiona's just about to put a stop to this for fear of their lives when Paddy's cab bustles down the lane. Who's inside but her Uncle Nick, home from London. Strange, for he only comes Christmas-time. Once Christmas is gone, the family has to wait the whole year round to see him again. But here it is Spring and he's home.

In the house, Noleen's fire has been ablaze straight through since morning. The three-legged pot oven sits in the glowing peat. Their Mam makes bread in the fire, slashes a cross in the dough with a knife. That's God there, baking into the loaf.

There with his suitcase by the door, stands Uncle Nick fresh off the boat from Holyhead.

Jayzus, Dominick. Shoulda sent a telegram. Olly carries pillow and covers down the stairs. *Wet the tea, will you Mara?*

Auntie Mara's in the kitchen. She's over from Dean's Grange on party duty.

Yeh divil. What a surprise. Mara wipes her fingers with a clean nappy, heading towards Nick in welcome.

Fiona hurries to the couch, clearing the way for her uncle. She moves Noleen's birthday toys to the dining table beside what's left of the two-layer cake she baked this morning. Pink icing, laden with marshmallows. It turned out spectacular. Fiona has excellent marks in cookery class. Fact, she has excellent marks all together.

I don't want fuss. Uncle Nick slinks into the pillow, bunching the covers under his arms. He's falling through himself, he's so skinny. What's the matter with him? Fiona wants to ask.

Careful. Slow. Olly rests Uncle Nick's legs on the arm of the couch.

Don't bother, Nick says. *Don't you bother.* Nick is tall, his legs stick out miles.

There's plenty of food left from Noleen's party, Olly says. *Like some peanuts? Stish-pashy-ohs?*

It's pistachios, Fee says.

American muck. Mara frowns. *From their other granny.*

Granny Volk sent two crates packed with birthday

goodies. There's M&Ms and a barrel covered with Pennsylvania Dutch hex signs. It's a tin of pretzels individually wrapped in sellophane. Printed on each package are tractors, farmers, and pigtailed girls in Heidi skirts. The pigtailed girls kick up their heels, "*Ist Gut!*" stamped next to their mouths.

Would you want a pretzel? Fiona asks her uncle. *Look at the package,* "Ist gut!" *it says.*

Don't like Germans, Nick says.

"Nicht gut." Olly jokes him. *Where's that tea, Mara?*

Bluebottle flies buzz at the kitchen window. Auntie Mara's up to her neck in bubbles, rinsing the pots and pans. *Wish you'd told us you were coming.*

Olly elbows past her to the tap. *You're good for nothing in the kitchen.* He fills the kettle himself.

You over there, so far from us, Mara says. *Had to go, didn't you. Off to magic London land, Mister James Bachelor Bond.*

It's a desperate place, London, Nick says. *I'm twenty-five year there, am I happy?*

Leave it. Olly puts the kettle on for the boil. *We might not all be here next year.*

Then Nick says, *We have more time.*

No we don't. Mara bangs a pot of water on the kitchen range. *People step out, people slip away.*

Nick glances at each corner of the ceiling in the one big downstairs room. *Must yeh start in?*

Mara won't look at him.

It's not like I'm off to Glasnevin tomorrow, he says.

Mara splits a small chicken in her hands, slides it into the pot. Tears brim her eyes.

What can I say? Nick looks to Olly for an answer. *To her.*

Say nothing, says Olly.

Say "yum-yum pig's bum." But don't let the children hear you, Mara says in a rare burst of vulgarity.

Chiselers. What's the damage, now? Nick asks, changing the subject.

Six.

Six, you hoore's bull.

Six-six-six children. Mara raps a soup spoon on the pot. *All beautiful, all loved, all wanted.*

The kettle blows. Olly does the tea.

It's a terror when people get married and have children. It ruins them, Nick says.

Ruins them, it does. Olly balances two cups of tea on two saucers. He sets each down on the milking stool in front of the couch. *Tea's up.*

Have youse anything to drink-to-drink? Nick asks.

Don't want my tea?

Not that I don't like it. It doesn't stay down, Nick says.

So, you're back on the drink? Mara asks from the kitchen. Uncle Nick's always trying to stop.

Drink? I do. Eat? I cannot. Forget? Nick says. *Never.*

Olly flicks match to fag, breathes in, it burns orange. He shakes and over-shakes the wooden match, flips it to the fire. *Say nothing.*

Noleen slams through the bottom half-door. *Mam.* She barks at the rafters, certain her mother can hear through the floor. *Quick, bring the sweeties.* Already in costume—the pigtail wig and her torn playdress for poor Gretel. *I need a chicken bone to use for Hansel's finger.* She yells at Aunt Mara like a Dublin tough. *He tricks the witch when he's in the cage.*

I know the story. Mara fetches a chicken leg from the pot, slicing off meat and skin. *I'm not a dunce.*

Don't be rude, Fee says. *Or I'll give you a smack.*

Pig. Noleen scowls in her gravelly voice.

Girls, Mara warns, giving the leg bone to Noleen. *What do you say?*

Thank you, Aunty Mara, Noleen says, so polite. *Please come see my play, Uncle Nick. It would make me happy as a birthday present.* She curtsies to her uncle, turns to the door. *Fifteen minutes,* Noleen bellows. *We're doing my play.* She clabbers out into the courtyard.

Hot Jesus, Nick says. *What an impresario.*

Let me at that cooker, Olly says. *I have drinks to brew.*

Poppy backs down the stairs, carefully holding each step.

Ready for Leeny's play, are you ready? Fee calls to Poppy. *Love your party dress. Did it come from America?*

Yes. Poppy laughs a merry, jingly laugh 'cause her new dress is sprinkled with dainty flowers. There's nothing like it in Ireland. When she reaches the landing, Poppy slaps to the couch in Noleen's old red ballet slippers. Though they're far too big, she's been wearing them since she first could waddle. Poppy sets her top teeth on the milking stool and bites.

Hello Pop-Pop, Nick says. *Are yeh hungry?*

Un-ka Nick. Poppy arches her curly head to look up at him, tips over and knocks him in the leg. Nick winces. Uhh-God. Fiona thinks. That really hurt, but he didn't make a peep.

Here, Pop-Pop. She quickly bundles Poppy to the dinner table. *Like some more cake?*

Mar-smella, Poppy says, reaching for the cake.

Just the one. Fee allows her a sticky pink marshmallow.

There's nothing like scaltheen to put you right. Olly gives Nick a mug of whiskey and scalded butter. *There's a sure cure in the scaltheen.*

They clunk their mugs and Nick downs it. ***Yew.*** *What's this now?*

Powers Three Swallow Whiskey. Daddy gives a wink. *"It's the flavor that's in favor." Scaltheen, Mara?*

I'll not go down that slippery slope, Mara says proudly, spooning powder into her mouth.

Still got you on the medicine, do they? Nick asks.

I'm still on the meddy, yes, Mara says. *Will be for life.*

Dominick. Gina comes down with Giselle who is freshly napped, nappied and fed. *Meet Giselle, our nice new baby, in her third rig-out today.*

Did someone else have that babby? For you look lethal, Nick says. *I'd get up, but—*

*Don't—Stay where you are—*Gina's alarmed at the drastic change in him. He's deathly thin. *Nick, what happened? You look—*

Don't say it. Mara, vicious for the first time in Fiona's life. *Hand me that babby bottle.*

Yeh Big Yank. Olly gives Gina a playful whap on the backside. *Too honest.* Daddy takes Giselle's empty bottle and tucks it in the sink.

I'm sorry. Mam collects herself. *We've Noleen's play at four—*

Leeny's play, Poppy shouts and everyone laughs.

It's not long, but it'll be cold on the lane, Mam says. *Noleen won't mind. Stay in, toast yourself by the turf fire—Jimminy. Get the bread, Fee, before it burns. I'll come talk when it's over.*

Poppy climbs backwards down the granite step into the front yard. Behind her, Mam carries Babby Giselle and a Williams' bag of real sweets for the witch's tempting cottage.

Bending to the flames, Fiona removes the fireguard, takes up the tongs and peers in at the state of the bread.

It's a masterpiece, she announces, dropping the lid and knocking red-hot turf onto the hearth.

Out, Uncle Nick shouts. *Get out of the fire.* Nick jumps to his feet, but winces into a tuck of pain. *Your frock,* he cries out. *Coulda caught fire.*

I'm grand, Fiona says, scraping the loose embers back in the fire.

Mara sits Nick on the couch and smoothes the arm of his suit jacket. *He was worried for you,* she says. *'Cause your Uncle Nick caught fire as a boy.*

Fee runs a knife through the loaf, piling up thick slices of steaming brown bread.

I take mine lathered in butter, Mara says, sipping milky tea from Nick's unwanted cup. *Tell her about when you burned. It's a lovely story.* She pushes Olly's forgotten tea toward Fiona. *Shall I milk your tea for you?*

Before Fee can say a word, Mara stirs milk into her tea.

Back in the war years. Nick's clutching his left leg. Squeezing the thigh at the top, sliding along his leg. Something's wrong in that leg. *Our family had, of course, you know—*

A dairy shop. Mara bites into her bread.

Hup, it's me telling this story. Nick tamps his empty mug on the milking stool. *Have I a mouth in my head?*

Olly scoots to the kitchen with their mugs.

Back, far back. Nick sings it like he's appearing in a Christmas Panto. *When we were young.*

And Nick a boy of sixteen. Nick was the eldest, our fair haired boy, Mara says. *I was fifteen and Olly not much older than yourself.*

Thirteen, Olly says. *Lucky number.*

Fiona smiles to herself, imagining them young. How dramatic, living through the war. But not really, 'cause they were safe from the Germans here in Ireland.

Just months before your grampa died. Back when—

Back when we still had our da with us, Mara cuts over.

Back when we still had a dairy for Da to run, I was saying.

Da had to come home from his worldly rambles 'cause his brother had fallen for the ponies. Mara chucks her tongue. *Your grand uncle Frankie was out at the races every day, gambling. Running our dairy into the ground.*

Before the dairy, Grampa was a clown. Olly's stooped at the range, scalding hot butter for the drink. *He was on the Moss Empire Circuit with Stan Laurel of Laurel and Hardy.*

And Chaplin, Nick says.

Charlie Chaplin? Fiona asks. *Grampa knew him?*

Before he got famous, Olly says.

It's Granny made him give up the clowns. Mara bends forward in the rocking chair, elbows on her racky knees. *"That's a mug's life," Gran said. So your grampa quit the stage game, married your granny, and along came us three kids.*

In Da's mind, he's still out on the road. Nick gladly takes another mug of Olly's scaltheen.

Still King of the Laugh, bedad, Olly says, gently seating himself on the couch so's not to disturb his brother.

Nick sups from his mug. *He was unhappy in the dairy.*

He hated it. Olly bursts into laughing.

He liked it. Mara smacks Olly for laughing.

For the dairy ran like a railway station. Cattle all over the place and the cow ploppy, horse ploppy. Thousands of flies. Blue bottles the size of doorknobs. Uncle Nick swirls his scaltheen to make it last. *I mean, talk about disease.*

Those were the days. Before the hoof and mouth, cows dead, our dairy gone. Mara's eyes flash angry. *Before he took to bed, before you left our house.*

Before the lot of that is this lovely story. Nick meets Mara's eyes over the teacups, sugar, cream on the milking stool between. *Fiona wants to hear it, don't you, Fiona?*

It's a smashing story. Fee's listening, eyes boring into the fire.

Before all that, was Grampa at the till, sorting the change, watching our customers heading home, jugs tucked under their arms.

The only time Da took off was First Sundays.

First Sundays was gas, Olly says. *We did them years.*

First Sunday of every month, after Mass, Nick says. *The uncles and aunts, neighbors and friends dropped by.*

For an At Home.

Everyone could have a turn, Mara says. *Sometimes Da sang. I loved when he sang. Surrounded by the drawing room furniture, the windy-up gramophone, the button-back velvet poof. We had a painted Chinese screen and on it, a Chinaman crossed a bridge to monkeys and birds. Gaslight streamed down on Ma's goldy hair, tucked and folded, finger-curled. Ma, young, head resting against the best armchair in our house.*

Nick shifts his hips to loosen his trouser wrinkles. *Ma's chair.*

And Ma in it, Olly says. *Sipping brandy 'til it's empty, tips the decanter, fills some more. Sipping, filling, 'til she's fluthered. Filling, sipping, 'til she's gone. Ahhh, the ma-zy, staring blank at the white marble fire.*

There was angels on that fireplace.

Angels with puckered lips, whistling and looking at each other, Olly says. *'Member, do yeh?*

Yeh. Nick scuffs his beardy underlip with the mug, thinking.

Outside, there's an upcast of cheers as Noleen's party files out to the lane for the play, her play: *Hansel and Gretel.*

That last time, Mara recalls. *The coal was heaped high on the fire 'cause it was damp.*

It was raining.

And Uncle Frankie, the pony man, ran out of stout so he sent Olly off to the pub to fetch up another half dozen.

When I got back with the stout, Nick wasn't there. Where were you?

Out in the sheds, dressing for our act.

There's Da in a loose white working shirt, the silver hair slicked back immaculate. Olly takes a slug of his scaltheen. *He had this beast of a blue bottle trapped in a drinking glass, saucer on top. The fly was zizzing at the saucer, like it was trying to push the plate off. "The Dairyman and the Fly," Da announced. "For this trick, all it takes is a fly and a hair."*

He made a big show of pulling a single hair out from Auntie Loolee's bun, Mara says. *She had the longest hair in the fambilly. It was blue black, straight down to her BTM.*

Just say it, Mara. Bottom, bum, arse, behind—

Down her back, Mara says. *Lucilia had the hair, all right.*

Da made a lasso on the one end of the hair and tied it round the fly's neck.

Do flies have necks? Fiona asks.

Dunno, Olly says. *But he done it. He fixed the other end round the button on his hatband. The fly buzzed about Da's face and he kept his eyes dead on, follying that fly. In circles, loop-dee-loops. When the fly landed on Da's nose, he stopped.*

And the fly stopped too, Mara says. *Froze on the end of Da's nose.*

Da held and held a longing time, letting the laughs flow 'cause that's where he belonged. In laughing, he belonged somewhere. He gathered up our laughter like gold.

When he flicked the fly up and into his mouth, we shrieked in disgust, Mara says. *The fly bopping against his inside cheeks. Da's crosseyed, choking. He spit that fly out of his mouth. The fly, swinging dead, dangling at the end of Loolee's hair.*

Outside, the lane rings with the shouts of children: "Hansel, look out!" But the audience is too late in their warning. Hansel's been trapped in the witch's cage.

I saw none of Da's act. Nick picks up his train of the story. *'Cause I'm in the toolshed, gearing up, fixing my hairdo.*

The hair, Olly says. *Part of the act me and Nick was gonna do.*

Ree-gardless, Nick says to Olly, shutting him up. *The toolshed's the only place in the entire dairy you can snatch some privacy. Beautiful in the toolshed, tidied to perfection. Rain pittering on the tin roof. Floorboards scrubbed clean as milk. Red raddle painted three quarters up the wall to a rail at shoulder level.*

What's red raddle? Fiona interrupts, but Nick doesn't mind her intrusion. She's the rare kid who really-really wants to know.

A whitewash paint made of lime, only we mixed a red dye through it. The red was to cover a fungus on the wall that never went away. If we left the whitewash white, the mildew bled out a purpledy gray. Nick considers the poisonous mold and shudders.

Your grandda got TB out of it, I do believe, Olly says, tapping his lips with an unlit ciggy.

Every spring, we painted the toolshed to hide it. But it was so damp it never fully dried, even in summer. If you weren't careful, it'd come off on you. The red walked herself onto your clothes, marking you.

So, I'm in there, you know. Being sneaky, 'cause I'd borrowed the lend of Ma's thrupenny box of face powder without her knowing. I was patting it on, when doesn't the door open. Christ-in-torment, I'm caught. But it's only Joe the Butterboy.

Forgot about him. Mara smiles as she thinks of it. *He was the one salted and packed the butter into shape, pressing "O'Feeney's" onto each pound block. Didn't he die?*

TB, Olly says. *He was a Pigeon House boy, I heard. Gone before my time there.*

Joe the Butterboy. Nick's lost in rememberies. *In the doorsill. Fattery pattery goes the rain. Mold rising in the wet afternoon. Joe takes his thumb to the red-raddled wall, reaches up and spreads red from my cheek to my hair. On one side, the other.*

Uncle Nick thumbs each cheekline.

"For rouge," says Joe.

Yeh, rouge, Olly mutters darkly.

Then, the daringist thing, Joe brushes raddle here, here, and here. Nick dabs the center of his lips. Top-top, bottom.

"Over the bow in your lips," Olly says. *I 'member that, I do 'member.*

Joe stands in the full of the door, feet bare and stone bruised. Sure, he's just a boy from the Rebel Liberties, but I invite him in. Out my mouth before I can stop. "I'm doing an act up at the house. Want to see?"

"Ah no."

"Come on up, everyone's there."

"The boss—Your father, I'm meaning, wouldn't like it."

And Joe dashes up the rain-mucked lane, past the cow houses, away.

Back in the drawing room. Mara's lining is bunching up her thighs. She lifts each leg, neatening the slick cloth to align with her skirt. *Uncle Frankie tossed a fresh feed of coal to the fire and it sputtered light. It was funny. It was lovely. It was the best of all First Sunday.*

Behind the Chinese screen, I pulled Da's suit jacket over my clothes like Nick rehearsed me.

Aunty Loolee had the loud pedal going terriff—"Nick and Oliver's Show Act." Olly stumbled out wearing a scrunchy milking cap and Da's dress suit for Mass. Jacket to his knees, hat down his nose, eyes squinting under, looking up. I needn't tell you, the audience was in deliriums.

Olly took a small step, skidding into a backwards somersault, feet whipping the air with a whistle. He was always a fine acrobat, your da, Mara tells Fee. *He switched his BTM, raised the baton pointing to Aunty Loolee, but—No sign of Dominick.*

Murder, I'm thinking. I'll kill him, Olly says.

When Loolee banged out the cue again in a flourish of keys, didn't Nick come on dripping. He was wearing a dress, Mara says. *He looked like a girl, a beautiful girl.*

I dance into the lampglow along the wall.

He'd on powder and rouge. Mara sucks her breath back in. *He was prancing about in Mam's blue shimmergown. She wore it the night she got engaged. Only sixteen, and Daddy thirty-two. Twice the year of her, twice her very life. Was beaded blue, she was, a nighttime blue, a shimmer flitter.*

Them beads caught the gaslight in watery mauve, Mara says. *Nick looked the spit of Ma. 'Cause she was slim and fair and he was slim and fair. He was her very twin. He'd taken up his boyish hair to goo it. His hair, like Ma's, was finger curled. And on his forehead, a brilliant star from the Christmas box.*

I picked up my baton and—Olly points his unlit cigarette at an imaginary orchestra. *Pergolesi's "Stabat Mater."*

"Stabat Mater in her arum-chair," Uncle Nick sings out. *"Stabat Mater, or she'll get you."*

The drawing room was caught in an avalanche of laughing.

I twist into the music, Nick says. *Spinning in to face the room, but when I see Da, he's not smiling.*

Da was the only one not laughing.

"You jinny-rip," Da calls and the party comes to a stop, Olly says. *Total frigid bloody silence.*

Da roaring out, "You jinny. Rip." I 'member that. Mara wraps her fingers over her chin, holding the story inside for a minute.

"*Wipe that red from your mouth, that mouth from your head or I'll give you such a clapper,*" Olly rages, spit flying. *"Parading about in your Ma's delicate garments."*

"Christ's-Dear-Mother, give me that child," Granny said.

Ma never said word one, Olly sneers.

She did, Mara says.

No. Olly strikes his empty mug to the coffee table milking stool. *After a certain point, she never stopped him from going at us.*

It was the drink, he didn't mean it, he—

When he was on the drink, he was the greatest brute in the sty. Olly shouts Mara down.

But why did he, why? Mara whispers, cringing in fear of her brother. *Why did he do it?*

Because—Nick says.

You looked too much like Ma? Olly makes a suggestion.

Because—Nick tries again.

'Cause everyone was laughing? Olly says.

Nick tilts his head. *Because I was funny.*

We were funny. Olly realizes. *Our act was funny.*

Funnier than his.

We were funnier than him is why he done it. Olly's certain now.

"I'll tear that star from your head," Nick says in a daze. *Taking off his belt, coming at me savage-hard.*

When he'd come after us, we'd run under the table to get away, Olly tells Fiona. *And Ma often said—*

"Wouldn't it be grand if he died?" Mara says to her two brothers sitting on the couch across from her. *"Wouldn't it be grand?" Indeed.*

She got the worst, Nick says. *Before we were old enough for walloping, Ma got the worst of him. Baby Michael kicked to God.*

Nick—Mara screeches. *What're you talking?*

He beat her to her knees.

Da's version of fambilly planning, Olly says with a snort of wild laughter.

That's crude and vulgar. And I . . . hate it.

Fambilly Planning.

I'll go home right now if you continue this disgraceful course of discussion—

Go *home. To your bitch-mother, then,* Olly screams in a sudden flare of rage. Takes a savage drag on his ciggy. *It's a much better story without your annoying chatter—*

I'm downfront in the parlor, Nick says to Fiona. *"Becripes, I'll nail you. Divil take your shitten life."*

Uncle Frankie pulled another bottle from behind the coal scuttle. "There'll be a murder on."

"Da, will youse stop," Nick says. *There's this bit where it all comes full stop. The party, the piano, the play goes away and it's just me and him. It's in his eyes, the ramping hatred.*

Then you charged at the fire, Mara says.

Nick ran to escape.

No, Da chases me in. Drives me into the grating. Run away, fly away, I'd run up the wall if I could. Run up the rage of a dream, Da's dream ever raging. Da's life screaming up the walls and up the walls of that room. 'Cause that's all the stage he had left to him, two foot square, the front parlor. His audience shrunk to fourteen. Sure, I'd nowhere to go but the fire.

There's a lickle tickle-tickle at the back of my ear. Violet steam, flames spool over my shoulder.

Everyone screamed all at once, "Nick's on fire."

The rank stench, them beads ablaze.

In that fat second, the very instant Nick caught fire, in the long-long time from here to there, Da comes iron sober. He leaps up, beating the flames with his hands.

Daddy tore the drapery down, rolled Nick in the curtains cross the floor, Mara says. *Our last First Sunday ended in fire.*

And me going for the doctor. Olly stubs out his cigarette in Fiona's empty teacup.

How I keep coming back to Dublin in my mind. Nick rocks, eyes closed. *It's no matter where I go in the world, I'm stuck in the parlor. Spending my days in that room with Da. Back there, damp August, 1942.*

You went into the Navy, went to war, Mara says. *Fighting for Queen and Crown, 'cause of him?*

He put me out.

You never got put out of our house.

Let me just say he put me off Dublin.

You leave us and you leave us, you do, Mara says. *You'll leave us again.*

Missus Jayzus Mercy, you're such a minger, Mara, Olly says. *It's no wonder Nick left.*

But yeah-no-no, that's not what I mean. Loosening his tie, Nick drops it to the floor. He's slurry. *I'm saying?* And confused. *No, I'm meaning.*

Let me get your drink in order. Olly collects the mugs for more scaltheen.

Stop, you're an awful man, you'll have me drunk.

For the Lord's sake, lads. Go easy, Mara warns.

Nick blunders to his feet, hitches his rumply trousers. Removes his jacket, unbuttoning each cuff. Stretching to the splintered rafters, his shirtsleeves fall up his arms. He rolls and cuffs them above his elbows. On his left forearm, a fish-leaping, blue tattoo. Under that, a burnie scar.

What happened, Uncle Nick, that you came home? Fiona asks the quiet room.

Surgery, Nick answers.

To your leg?

Nick's eyes go red and swimmy. He nods.

Will it get better?

I've bloody cancer. I'm going to die.

Cancer hangs in the air.

Cancer, then fear.

Fear bubbles up and over the foamy butter in the pan. It stands in Olly at the range. Fear in the firelight, over the coffee table, fear in the quieting room.

The fuck.

God's sake, boys.

Exactly.

Uncle Nick takes two teaspoons, cocks them, goes clatterdy-clatter-me-click, turns them into clicking spoons.

Give us the bar of a song, Mara says.

"O Missus McGrath," the Sergeant said. "We'd like to make a sailor out of your son Ted."

And Nick's away in the clacking. Ba da-da, ba da-da, bahh da-da. Spun out on his good leg.

Nick can play the spoons. Take any old tablespoon out from a drawer and clatter-the-clat, clacker-the-click, clather along his fingerbones. Rap to the elbowback, the rippling fish tattoo. Tatterdy, tattle-dee, tit-tit, dancing silver in the fire.

Nick's ever the clattering spoons.

Spoons, them-spoons wailing, battering free. Smacking on shoes, the floor, our lino. Nick's singing out loud and louder. His square yellow teeth thrump through his foxy beard. Blatterdy-blit in the ba da-da, ba da-da, bahh da-da. Ba-da ba-da, *bap* the da-da, *bap* the da-da. *Bap-bap-bap, bomb.*

Nick and Olly're stupid drunk. The scaltheen guides them into the weirds. Into songs and out again. And when they come to the end, when they do, Olly says: *Let's pop over to O'Donoghue's for a couple of small ones.*

That was a fine sing-song, don't you think? Mara asks.

It was very good, Fiona says.

We had a laugh. I need a laugh, yeh? Nick's fastening his shirtsleeves, fisting into his jacket.

Mara fumbles in her bag. *Here's a few shillings for tonight.* Dropping silver into Nick's palm.

Wait-no—Hold onto that thruppence, Nick says, returning a coin to her. *The waggling daisies, '54. That's worth three pounds. Any dealer'd give you that, maybe four.*

Fee holds his suitcase at the door. *Here's your case, Uncle Nick.* Moving it to beside the couch, picking up his tie where he'd flung it down. *I'll put it where you need it when you come in.*

If they come home, Mara corrects her.

Get a gargle, will we? Olly asks.

We'll kill the night in-anyway.

And off they go. They rip out into the yard.

At No. 11 Tolka Row, in the rear, my play—*Hansel and Gretel*—is just about done. I sneak a peek at my audience—thirty-six of 'em. A good house. Mam is there looking proud of me. She's got burpy Giselle over her shoulder, spitting on a nappy. There's Poppy, like a hoppy kangaroo, bouncing with delight, holding onto the handles of the wheelbarrow fulla birthday primroses. That was Daddy's present to me, wild primroses brought in from the Wicklow Mountains, filling the boot of Paddy's cab. Wish Daddy could see me in my play, but he's in the house with Uncle Nick.

There's no sign of them rotters with their banged up knees, their baldy heads, their stinking fuck of a brother. So glad they didn't come back, they'd have ruined everything.

It was super-brill to do my play at the party's end so the sisters and mams picking up my pals could come early and see me acting.

Be Hansel fat or lean, Des rasps in a high-pitched voice. He's the cruel and evil witch. In drag, Daddy calls it. *I will kill and cook him.* Des wriggles his fingers front of his nose. *Climb into the oven, Gretel. Is it hot enough?*

How shall I do it? I put my hand to my chin, bat my eyes like an eeje.

You stupid goose, Des the Witch shouts. *I'll show you myself.*

Des the Witch sticks his nose in the oven I made of a painted fridgebox. In a twinkling, I shove him in, bolting the door forevers.

Ohhhhhh, Des wails in agonies.

Burn to gingerbread, you ungodly witch, I cry. *Hansel, we are saved.*

Ely's playing Hansel. He's jammed in a wrought iron birdcage lent from Daddy's scene shed. He says nothing, 'cause he never learned his lines. He's like a little trapped bear, with his old teddy bear coat shrinking up his body.

The witch is dead, I tell him. *All our sorrows are ended.*

When I open the teensy door, Ely springs forth like a bird out of his cage.

Happy birf-day, Nolee, Ely yelps and my audience claps with glee.

Sunshine floods down on a fence of life-sized gingerbread girls and boys, holding hands. My school chums, frozen in place for the whole of the show.

Just then Uncle Nick and Daddy slash through the row of gingerbread children, breaking them open and free.

The kids on the lane turn real again. *Wheeee-hah.* The lane is alive with their screams of delight. They attack the witch's house and gorge themselves on a glorious feast, Smarties. Packets and packets of Smarties that Mam pasted to the outside of Cucumber Cottage.

Every day it is a party for the girl who eats her Smarties.

Buy some for Noleen.

red ring

Even though it's the last day of school and starting right now, I am free to go gluttony-books, free to tear through Stephen's Green for a summer-long of fun, I am in the downy-doops, can't get out.

I cleared my desk, my cloakroom hook. Everyone's gone from school but me.

Don't want to leave Miss Winters, our teacher in first class. She is young. She is brilliant. She went to America to learn how to teach and came back with a tan and an autoharp.

Don't want to leave our flower garden, our paints, her autoharp. I don't want to take Second Class with the Holy Terror of Kildare Place School. Old Bonks is killing-mean. She scolds and slaps. Made a girl take her knickers off and stand bare under her dress just 'cause she wet herself. Fee had her and Des had her. When summer ends, I'll have her, too.

All these things is running through my mind. Don't want to go nowhere, do anything. I kick and draggle my empty schoolbag down the front stairs of the building. Make a face at the lizarding ghouls crawling on every corner of every windowsill on the Kildare Street Club. Devils and monkeys carved in stone. Stewpid.

There's no sign of Des, no sign of Mam. I'll swing through the gates of the National Library, check for Mam's special signal. When she's writing in the Library up the stairs, she leaves a secret rock under a bench outside. If I want, I sit on the bench and wait for her. But today, there's no rock there.

No Mam, no Des. I'm browned off. I'll go up the Green and play parachutes.

Summer sunlight slashes through the black fence that runs the wholeway round the Green. That fence looks like sword after sword, standing proud, holding in fat shiny bushes with green-green leaves. So that's why they call it the Green. I search for my bam-runk-tious kidgang. Not a sign of 'em. They're all Catholicks anyway, stuck in school 'til July.

I climb to the roof of the bandstand, schoolbag on my back. Feet at the edge, just above the rain gutter, I yank the imaginary ripcord of my parachuting schoolbag and leap into the bright June day. I do a somersault, landing with a thud on the grass.

Then I tightrope-walk along the low iron railings that edge the duckpond. Eyes intent on the rail below, when I hear a voice in song.

Gó raibh míle maith agat. That's a thousand thanks to you in Irish. In Irish, they can't just thank you once.

Gó raibh míle maith agat for all you tried to do—I folly the singing. Lazing on the grass under the conkers tree in the shade is my Uncle Nick.

Alone-alone, he's in his lone. At the end of himself.

Tears run over his cheeks. He's sitting in the middle

of the day throbbing all round him. He's breathing air in through his harmonica and heaving out lonesome notes.

Sometimes Uncle Nick gives me the lend of his harmonica. It's big and stupid in my hands. When I try to make tunes come out the way he does, the square holes get clogged with spit.

Ah, Noleen, he'd say, but he wasn't angry. He'd slap his harmonica against his palm to clear it. The tap of his toes and he's well away, into a song and out again.

My Uncle Nick. O, Uncle Nick. I turn from him, run my hardest away.

On the arc of greenbridge, Dominick is moving slow, picking his way. He's bent over a cane, swallowed up in duffle coat, a scally cap pulled over his ears. Last week his hair fell out in clumps, his whisker-beard is gone. Limping over the arching stone, he stops and presses into his left leg, the really paining one. He's dripping thin and only barely stands.

A cocky bit of kid marches into Nick's day, striding the footpath towards him. With the black mane parted far left, tangled fringe flopping into his smile. He catches Nick by the elbowcrook. *Dominick O'Feeney, is it yourself?*

Nick squints, thinks, amazed. *Joeboy Tierney. Declare to God, can it be you?*

Tis me, Joe the Butterboy.

In short trousers last I saw you.

You look like a beggar's handbag, are youse well?

Nick tongues the crack in his cornerlip. *Just a sickspell at the moment.* He cups his tumorous liver in his right hand, holding himself alive. *I'm after having a treatment when I get the brillo idea to go for a stroll. I'm not up for it.*

Then take your rest here on the plush swards of Stephen's Green.

When Joe takes his arm, a blaze of strength rockets through Nick, heels to scalp. *Don't touch,* Nick says. *They'll think we're together.*

They'll think nothing. You're so took to pieces, yeh look like my grandda's grandda.

Is it really you? Nick says. *Am I seeing things, or what.*

You sausage. Joe's grin, in fullbeam.

You sausage roll.

The hard sun strikes Nick from behind. His shadow dances before him on the path, but Joeboy hasn't a shadow of his own. Slow-walking arm-in-arm they pass flowerbeds of tulips-red, white and orange daffodils, a pair of wild swans on the pond.

Look at them swans, Joeboy says. *Swimming around, eating hard bread—fools. How old yeh think they are?*

Dunno.

Never seem to go gray, or baldy, or anything. I know them years. Hello, wild swans, Joeboy calls, giving Nick a flirty wink. *Hello, wild song in yerself.*

Won't you have a smoke with me? Nick asks, looking out over the grounds.

Can't, on account of the ould con. Joeboy taps his heart. *The TB left me a bit chesty.*

They sit under a chestnut tree, upon grass dotted with daisies. From his jacket pocket, Joeboy pulls a bottle wrapped in two brown socks. *A trick my granny learned me, socks keep the heat.*

Nick and Joe take turns sipping lukish tea straight from the bottle. They're munching on a packet of Marietta biscuits—bit damp.

Have youse come from over?

Yuh. Nick digs at a sore on his ear.

Mister Rambling Sailor, Mister Royal Navy Man. Fell off the town map.

It's just I... never wanted you to see me like this, always imagined you'd—

You imagined me?

Yes.

Spent your days imagining me?

Guarantee it.

You're a rake and a divil.

No. Nick rolls a golden dandelion 'tween finger and thumb, squashing the stem to a green goo. *I fell in love quite madly once.*

Aren't you the scorcher, Joeboy says. *It's you sailed way.*

Jayzus' good sake, I waited all that summer for you to return. You never came back to the dairy.

He run me off the place, Joe says.

Who?

Your da.

When?

Went to work that August Monday and he ran me off the yard for good. I mean, here's a man who failed greatly. Even after hoof and mouth hit the stables and his fancy dairy died, when I saw him in the street he wouldn't have a word for me.

Wanted to say, I wanted—To say to him, "I'm not just some back-there boy from ago, behind, beneath you." Him shoving me 'gainst the wall and starting in.

What're you saying?

Cop on. I was your da's red-raddle boy. Where do you think I learned the red? Was him taught me. "Use the red to girl-up, now. Use the red." And me a young one only. Your da was demon of the toolshed.

So, that's why Da went for me that First Sunday. Nick sees right into the clear of it. Da knew by the rouge on my cheeks, on my lips. Da thought I'd messed with Joe. So Da banned Joeboy from the yard. His father was the reason Joe never returned to him.

Nick glances briefly at Joeboy's sandy gray eyes, looks away, looks back. Joe the Butterboy, his supple hair, a glossy satin. He's not aged, looks about fifteen. Looks thin as want.

Your da was a geeze, Joeboy says. *That was my lovely job he took from me. Why punish me? When it was him doing the dirt to me every chance he could. I allus thought it was him give me tubercu-locusts with his mucking me about. How many of your customers carried consumption home in their jug a cream? Answer me that one, can yeh? No.*

Nick nods, examining Joe's high stepping, well-arched feet on the sly. His feet, bare as a hare.

I was delighted to hear he'd landed out in Pigeon House, stained, hemorrhaged, died, Joe says. *Got what he deserved, the bovine lungyl.*

He was a gang of vicious bastards, Nick says. *What he did to you—I can't imagine.*

They don't know what to say.

They can't look at each other.

They lie together on the cropped green staring at the sky.

Nick slides a harmonica over his teeth, huffing and sucking in sorrowful notes. Nick knows every ballad that's going. He sings and plays, plays and sings a song by his old pubfriend, dead four years now. The Behan, Brendan Behan.

Twas on an August morning, all in the dawning hours,
I went to take the warming air, all in the Mouth of Flowers,
And there I saw a young man, and mournful was his cry,
'Ah, what will mend my broken heart, I've lost my
Laughing Boy.'

And Joeboy loudly joins Nick from the rough margins of the land:

My princely love. Can ageless love do more than tell to you,
Gó raibh míle maith agat for all you tried to do,
For all you did, and would have done, my enemies to
destroy,
I'll mourn your name and praise your fame, forever, my
Laughing Boy.

They don't know what to do.

They can't look at each other.

Nick plucks a jinny joe from the lawn. Round, perfect, a dandelion clock.

When most-peoples see a jinny joe, they see a silver summer dandelion. But each seed in a jinny joe is a wish. Nick shuts his eyelids tight, no lashes now, no hair.

Kiss me. He wishes. Save me from my life. Nick blows the seeds, makes a summertime wish. Silver seeds boost and scoot over the pond, wishes dervishy on the winds.

Can I see you? Nick asks. *Can't we slip into some back place?*

I can't afford foolish wishing. Joeboy treads over the green-hymned grass, feet bare. Feeding into the June-warm day.

But hang on, hang on. Nick's thinking. Where's his shoes?

In high summer it is light, light all round like heaven. Days run long and wide, nights start late and mornings early. Mam has scripts to write, so she put us in a swimming course at the Blackrock Baths. Late, we're late, we're all of us always late these days now, 'cause Fee's in the *Gaeltacht* for July, learning Irish. Since Lily the housekeep only works afternoons now, there's no one to wake us, get us outta the house on time.

Des and me and Ely rush to the Pearse Street Station. I've my flowerdy swim cap on my head, so's I won't lose it. Towel rolled in the crook of my arm.

All aboard. We fight for the seat nearest the driver, fling our towels on the overhead rack. *All aboard.*

Zoomaloom, zoomaloooom. We're speeding into the day ahead. South to the seaside towns on the Irish Sea.

Say-hello, say-hello, say-hello, I shout at telegraph poles flicking by.

Here's leaving the dirty city—her slummy houses with curtains made from old *Irish Times.*

Here's leaving. Here's leaving. Whipcracking the rails edging Dublin Bay.

And the train wraps the land.

It's Irishtown and the Pigeon House Fort. The Sea Wall at Sandymount.

Now Ringsend where the ould TB wards used to be. Where Daddy went and Aunty Mara went for years on years.

Here's Booterstown. Now Williamstown. Is it Blackrock already? *An Charraig Dhubh.*

There's the diving tower set against the sky and the smell of the sea.

We shoot off the train, through the dressing rooms and into the pool for our lesson at nine.

I'm in the pool for tall people, the pool fed by icy sea water. I'm following the pole the teacher pulls just outta my reach. If I stop kicking, I'll sink to the bottom and drown. On I splutter, I dip and bob and toss and spurt, gulping mouthfuls of salt water. I slap toward the pole and the hag barking. Lift my arms, swim on, swim on to the rusty bleed of the metal stairs.

Lesson done, I fly to my towel, teefs chattering like a woodpecker, legs purple with cold. I scourge myself with a skinty towel for a bit of warmth. There's Ely in the babby pool with the under-fives. Beyond him, the deep-deep pool with two high-dive boards. There's a bunch of big sturdy men chatting on the top one. They are in a club, the Blackrock Dare Divers. Every morning at ten o'clock they give a little exhibition for the people in the pools. The Blackrock Baths has three pools. The babby pool, the regular pool where me and Des has our swimming lessons, then the pool for high diving daredevils such as them.

They're at the far end of the platform, in discussion, studying the highboard. 'Til the one fella marches forward deliberately. He stands in stillness for a thousand years, chin dipped to his chest like a squat little soldier. *Tenn-shun.* Yanks his swimming trunks outta his arse, hands to his sides again. *Tenn-shun.* He considers the water far-far below, he crosses himself, hands back at his sides. *Tenn-hut.*

Yer man bounces on the board. Once, twice, higher, higher.

Every eye in the place is on him.

Then he turns round and walks back to the huddle of men near the stair. And before we can blink, he bolts to the end of the board, springs, pikes, then jack-knifes, turning flip-flops all the way. He lands in the water with the smallest *spuh-lash.*

The place goes mental with wild applause. Then bang-bang-bang-bang, one after the other, the strong running lads take enormous headers into the pool.

They lurch from the water, roaring, laughing, ready for more.

It is the best show I've seen in my life. Better than *Hansel and Gretel*, the Nuala Ballet, better-even than Da's Black & White Dancers, that packa hoores.

I'm good as them fellas. I could do the acrobatics my daddy learned me, or circus tricks from off the board. I'm gonna join the Dare Divers one day soon.

Every day Olly O'Feeney tells the wife he's going to hospital, when really he's dipping and darting into and out of pubs.

His gaiety is uproarious. He could do six hoores and it still wouldn't do him.

He has no time for empty moments when thought can leak in.

Yet . . . in his head and in his head, there's the should and the should and the should. Should-should, he should write to Dominick at the least. Should-he-should climb in Paddy's taxi, board a bus, walk for Godsake out to St. Luke's and visit the brother.

The world will go forward. I will pull sello off the next pack of fags, crumple the silvery paper, tap out another. Smoke it down and smoke. Suck-up, suck-in and hold. Feeling as little as possible.

The world goes on. I will step out this door. He will be gone in a minute. He will be gone. And the whole of the world ticking and roaring on. Death and the days keep coming, Nick's death and the days. Get to hell out to that hospital, visit your brother, today.

These are his thoughts as Olly scutters over the streets of their childhood, burying his nose in the pub.

That afternoon, Daddy saunters through the Georgian door, home for a change. He drags the hip bath to the side garden near where Des and me is digging a moat. We hook up the hose, fill the tub and play in our teeny version of a swimming pool. This is a puddle compared to the Blackrock Park and Seaside Baths. Daddy sprays us with the hose. We eat plums, sink into the soft, drip sugar.

What you need is a bikini, Daddy says, pulling me to him.

What's a bikini?

It's all the rage in Paris. He rolls my swimming togs below my tummy, tucks it in so there's a bulge all round my hips.

What goes on top? I'm scarlet with embarrassment from my bony ribs and naked selfs.

Nothing.

Well. That's nothing short of shocking.

On the beaches in France, the girls don't wear bras, he says, fag bopping about in his mouth. *Some beaches in France, they go all the way bare.*

Can I've sixpence for a swimming ring, Da?

I see the ring in my mind, a blow-up life preserver. I've been through all the shops and found just what I want. Miss Hoggs on Wicklow Street has great summer things: bamboo fishing poles, bright colored buckets, tin spades. If only I had the money, I'd march to her shop, slam sixpence on the counter and the ring would be mine.

I could do wonders with that ring.

She sure needs a water ring 'cause she's the worst in class. Des pinches his nose and goes under.

I'm broke, Daddy says, pulling out the pockets of his rehearsal trousers to prove that we are always broke.

Only sixpence. I scrunch my lips in disgust. He has sixpence for his friends, sixpence for the gargle, sixpence for boys off the street who've seen him on the telly, but he doesn't have sixpence for me.

I hoist the bikini back into a bathing suit, head to the house. Climb into my bunk and read *The Bookshop on the Quay*. O, it's an excitement. So real I can't stop reading. I nustle in the thin flannel sheets and read and read, loosing myself into the story, when there's a ghastly rumble from my tummy. I am bloody starving.

I go downstairs for a bowl of Rice Crispies but as I pass the open door to the MamDad room, no one's in there. There's the jumble of bedclothes, their fisheye quilt. It's an old German thing sent over from America. It has red and blue fisheyes embroidered top the patchwork.

I steal a look out the window, there's Mam on her knees weeding her flower garden. Poppy's in the sandbox, shaping sand pancakes with my red seaside spade. She takes everything-mine, before I'm done with 'ems. Giselle's napping in the Moses basket on the cobbles of the yard. Daddy and the boys are busy with the hipbath in the side garden.

At the foot of their bed, Daddy's good trousers hang on the post. Let's see if we're broke. There's change and crumpled bills. Pound notes, ten bob notes.

Daddy lied. He has his wages.

Five pounds. What if I stole that? Breaking two commandments in one go. But Daddy doesn't care for commandments, 'cause he doesn't believe in God. He doesn't go to church, 'cause he doesn't believe in God. Though stealing is a sin to the rest of us, maybe it's not a sin to him.

Sides, he lied to me.

Clink, the change clinks. Someone'll hear. Ah-Christ, no. He's climbing the stairs, three steps at a time. He is coming.

I jump into the clothes press, kick into a large square tin the size of a cigar box. It makes one unholy clatter. Did he hear? Squashed tween Daddy's two spare suits, I press my eye to the gap tween the doors.

Daddy's already got his trousers unzipped. Once in the room, he drops 'em to the floor. He rushes to the toilet in his shirt, undervest, garters and drawers.

If I strike now, I could make my getaway. But I like spending time in clothes presses, spying on people when they think they're alone.

He's back in a flash of tardy-gotta-go, gotta-move, gotta-go. He's rushing straight to the clothes press. He'll murder me if he finds me here. But no, he sees his good trousers slung on the bedpost. *Thwack*, the snap as he shakes 'em out, his money jangles.

Just one sixpence coulda been mine, shoulda grabbed it.

Da ties his shoes, checks his image in the vanity.

Aren't you the messer? Da says to the mirror, raking a brush through his hair, greasing it back with black shoe polish. He grabs his suit jacket off a hook at the back of their door. The knob clicks snug. He is gone.

Soon as it's safe to come outta the clothes press, I take the heavy box and sit on the MamDad bed. The flash of fisheyes, watching me.

It's a tobacco tin. Players, Please! stamped on the lid, white on navy.

I lift the lid to a mountain of money, every kind of

money. *Bow-wow-wowzahhh.* Sixpences, florins, crown pieces from the olden days. There's Queen Victoria, Elizabeth Regina. Bitch queens of London-town, Uncle Nick would say.

What'll I take? What'll I get? What do I want?

I shut my eyes, pluck one from the box.

Eh. Just a thrupenny bit with waggelling daisies. Not enough spondoolix for me.

I toss it back like a fish to the sea.

Shut me eyes, try again, and . . . it's a gleaming half crown from 1942.

I race to Miss Hoggs, slap it down. Just as she drops it into her till, I notice doubled horses on the coin. In the money factory, they musta made a mistake, stamped the knacker twice. So it really is just a broken ould coin no one would want.

Please. Take your time. Miss Hoggs folds her stout arms around her bazongers.

I look through her glass counter at the Lucky Bags crowded on the tray below. Behind her, shelves to the ceiling crammed with jar after jar of fantabulous sweets. I figure the prices in my head. Four two's is eight, plus threepence, no—Not that. Do I want the Edinburgh rock? No.

I'll have four Lucky Bags—two pink, one blue, one yellow. Twelve Jelly Babies, a lolly, five snakes, a pack of sugar cigarettes, four black licorice pipes, and a box of Smarties. Spending gaily like my da.

Miss Hoggs plunks the sweets in a brown paper bag. *Have you got everything now?*

Gimme a red swimming ring. I point to a ring pegged on

a string of seaside buckets and fishing poles rigged jauntily above the counter.

She rummages in a hidden drawer 'neath the cash register, hands me a square plastic envelope, white snap on top.

That little packet is my ring?

You must inflate it yourself, Miss Hoggs says, real prim. *It's non-returnable.*

What's that?

Once you've put your mouth to it, don't expect me to refund your money. You could get someone sick with your germs.

On my way home I eat a licorice snake, three purple Jelly Babies and smoke a few cigarettes, proudly blowing the powdery smoke out the end. I look like a gang-is-terr, bet people think I'm smoking for real.

My heart runs gladly down the lane. I've the red ring and all my sweeties. I duck into Cucumber Cottage, tear open a pink Lucky Bag. Inside is the fizz bag and a ring for my surprise. It has a green jewel. The second pink Lucky Bag has a ring with a blue stone. I put the rings on, my sparkelling gems. In the yellow Lucky Bag is a gold bracelet with a pearl. Love pearls. I slip the bracelet up and down me arm. I saved the blue Lucky Bag for last, 'cause blue is my favorite color. Turquoise, actually, 'cause I love the sound *and* the color. I dig out the surprise, it's a top. Diss-appointing. I'll give it to Des. 'Course then he'll wonder where I got the money.

I've got to hide my sweeties from my greedy-gut brothers. So I wrap up the rest in the bag and shove it in the oven part of the wooden cooker Daddy made for me.

I unsnap the packet, take out a flat wedge of plastic. The

skick as I unfold it. I blow air in and in. It grows fatter and fatter 'til it's the most magically red swimming ring. I will swim forever in this ring.

Check there's no nails on the wall, squidge it hind my neck and use it for a pillah.

Propped 'gainst the wall in Cucumber Cottage, book on my knees, just like the fambilly in *The Bookshop on the Quay*. All of 'em is mad for books. They read and read even during their tea. I wanna live in a house like that. I lick my lolly, dip it in a fizz bag, dipping and licking and reading my fill.

I've fallen into heaven I do believe.

The next morning I come down for breakkie wearing my flowerdy swim cap over my hairs, red ring round my middle.

Where'd you get that? Mam asks. *Eat up, Ely.*

Miss Hoggs. Mam thinks Miss Hoggs is a huckster so she'll never go there and she'll never find out I bought two shillings' worth of sweets with my red ring. I'll get diabetes if I want.

How much? Des asks me.

Sixpence.

Yeh-but where'd you get it?

Outside O'Donoghue's. The lie flows from my mouth butter-easy. *Sitting up in the pavement crack, saying: "Hello, Noleen." So I said, "Hello, Sixpence." Went and bought my swimming ring.*

You can't take it to the baths. Mam plops my Peter

Rabbit bowl in front of me. Cornflakes is hardly breakkie. *Eat that, you need your strength.*

I'll swim a thousand miles in my ring. I wag it back and forth like a tutu.

Excuse me, Madame, Mam snaps. *If you're going to wear that ring, you can eat at someone else's house.*

I kick the rungs of the *súgán* chair, but she ignores me.

You're not taking that to Blackrock, it'll get pinched.

It's never fair in this house, I never ever get my way. I push the ring to the floor, set it on the couch. Gobble down my Cornflakes and solve it. I'll squash the air out, pack it safe in its pocket, stuff it down my shirt.

Mam never suspects as we file out the door.

At the finish of our swim lesson Des and me join Ely on the flaking gray benches near the baby pool. That's so we can watch the Dare Divers do their show. I fold the gray chips of paint, snap 'em in half, to half again. The Blackrock Baths reek of toilet. There's seagulls perched on the blue railings of the top board, waiting same as the bunch of us on the benches, wondering where are them Dare Divers?

Suddenly, from out of the nowhere, they spring from the boys' dressing room, hurry along the cement decks toward the diving pool. They plunge with a mighty *whoop* to the cold seawater, swim to the farthest wall and heave themselves out, swopping back their wet heads like seals. These are country men with powerful frames, dockers just coming off a night of work on the quays.

I pull my red ring from its plastic pocket, inflate it full, and before I know what I'm after myself, I'm at the foot of the blue metal ladder leading to the sky. Each stair is half my body. I've the red ring hooked through my left arm so it won't get punctured. I start to climb. One look to the ground would petrify me. So don't look down, only look up. To the next step, the next, the next, 'til I arrive on the bottom board.

I am standing in the sky, pillowy clouds all round me. There's gangs of birds battling a fierce wind that's punching 'em seaward.

I aim my hands through the shining red ring, fit it to my tum.

In the middle of the ring I am triumphant. In the power of the red ring I can do all. I hold my head high like a Paris dancer and survey the scene. There on the bleachers far-far below are the kids from swimming class. There's Ely, there's Des.

On the top board, the leader of the Dare Divers is bollicking through the same stunts as yesterday. Only today no one is watching.

They are looking at *meee*. Ready for Noleen O'Feeney's Diving Show. I fling up my arms in a regal gesture. *Live life to the power of Red Ring.*

I can see the crowd outta the tail of my eye. *Lookit.* They point at me. *There's a girl up there.*

I streak to the end of the board, execute a wonderful standing backflip and the crowd goes wild monkeys.

The lad on the board above checks to see just who is one-upping him.

Hey-you, he shouts. *Clear off, or I'll put you home.*

I do a *plié*, two *jetés*, I spin like a top and blast like a canon off the platform. Turning three front flips on the way down. So splendidly bold.

I slam into the pool with a tremendous boom.

All my insides is shorn to pieces, I'm torn in two.

The world's a rocking bed of light. Someone's breathing in my mouth. It's the Barking Hag, my swim instructor. Think of the germs.

When I'm finally able to breathe on my own, I pull myself to a sitting position. I'm in a puddle on the cold cement.

What would you be doing on the diving boards and you not able to swim? The Barking Hag wants to know.

I can swim. I can dive. I want to say. But can't form the words.

A circle of faces towers over me—the Dare Diver Boys.

Och, yeh're a dreadful nuisance. It's the swaggery bollocks from the upper board, my rival. He's a stocky fellah, gut bulging over his swim trunks, a forest of gingery hairs on his chest. *Wasn't fer me, yeh'd a drowned.*

Guess it was him saved my life, not the ring? My-ring, where's-my-ring? I scan the crowd like a lighthouse beam.

There's Ely, his dawny face a shock of O.

Are youse hurt, Nolee? he says.

Where is my ring? Did someone pinch it like Mam said?

Sun glints behind Des, lighting the blood in his sticky-out ears. He has my ring. It's a drooping squashed red thing in his hand.

Smashing dive. Too bad yeh can't swim. He slaps the ring flat in my lap. *It burst when you hit the water.*

My poor little dead ring. I cry and cry and cry my fill. Then chuck it in the bin at the finish of our bathe.

Noleen's aunty, Mara Aine O'Feeney, is at St. Luke's. On the cancer ward where the stench is killing. Jeyes fluid, oil-cloth and wee. Bunks and windows line the walls. Outside, August hot on the smeared glass.

Nick's herded in with a crowd on the public ward, asleep on an iron-framed cot, his feet hanging over the rails. Cold, they're cold, in want of socks.

Mara's chunked in next to him, sitting tough. Sure, she's used to this. Wretched invalid for most of her life. She went to hospital straight from convent school at the age of seventeen. No college for her. No training, just sickness. She's muttering to herself like it's mass or multiplications she's telling teacher at school.

Sum es est. I am, you are, he is. I am, you are, he is.

Sumus estis sunt. We are, you are, they are.

Eram eras erat. Eramus eratis erant. I was, you were, he was. We were, you were, they were.

Ero eris erit.

Erit. She can't get beyond erit.

I will be, you will be, he will be, she chants.

Erit—Erit—He will—He will be alive tomorrow. He will be.

Nick jolts awake, face all eyes, nothing more. *Look at you and your fancy tomorrows,* he says through broke lips, dry rot in his mouth. *Day's too bright, could you turn down the sky?* His voice is paper. Older than Granny now, he's older than old. His breath and eyes and thoughts astray. *Have youse got my wooden suit sorted?*

Don't speak of it.

No lying. Breath tears through Nick's words. *No crying.*

Mara leans in close to his ear, saying soft, *No whispering.*

They smile.

Them's the rules. Nick takes a mouth of water from the drinking glass she offers him. *You are the best medicine.* He sinks to his pillow and blunks out.

One real Jesusy nun wheels a trolley of linens to the bedend. Clapping Nick on the footsoles, she shouts, *O'Feeney, where are your stockings?*

Crouched in the window well is Nick's shoes and a brown paper bundle of clothes, his toiletings. Mara rustles in his parcel, finds pale blue socks.

Now, we have to do your poolie. The charge sister shakes him by the feet, rattling the cot.

No, I—Want to use the lavatory. Myself. Nick tries to lift the covers, put a foot to the floor. Pain rucks his face. His hand drops on the bedding. He's blue from his fingertips to knuckles. He is dying up his hands.

Mara leaps to help.

You wouldn't want to lift that sheet, the Sister says. *And he hates to be helped.*

Hates it. Mara rolls a sock over Nick's hairy toes, then rolls the other.

Don't talk to me, Sister says.

What's today? Nick gasps between words, within questions.

Today is teeth-brushing and a bath.

Would you like a hand? Mara asks the nurse.

They go to work on the bedclothes, tidying and settling. Lifting sheet, Mara steals a brief glance. Crucified with the botch. A tangled journey of purple scars.

Shifting Nick, they fit him with a fresh singlet and white cottons. As they bang him about, his blue stockinged feet tip this way and that way off the end of the bed.

Sister stands back, looks at Nick. *Life. He's perished with it.*

Is he very near the last?

At the backend of it, I'd say. With the prostate, the lungs, the liver. He's already half-ghost.

Can't we have another tomorrow?

This night will see him out.

God-God-God and God-God-God, please save him. Hands a trembling knot of twined-together. Mara prays in the wooden chair, thinking, God-God-God and God-God-God, make it stop.

At the hour of twelve that night, Olly murks into the room. *I'm a lousy, I know.* Showing up in last week's shirt and teeth three-days old. Christ, he's a reek.

Never meant to turn my back on him. Olly's trying hard not to look at the room. Men slunk in their cots along the walls. Hospitals give him the terrors.

All those years in the san. Twenty-five beds, eighteen inches separating them. There wasn't room to fall out. Five small windows on each side, two fireplaces, one never lit. Twenty-five patients from all walks of life, mainly dockers. Most had dug coal boats in their day, the black lung. On the ward they were destitute, diseased old men at thirty-five. The average stay was four to six years, when they died.

When death arrived, they'd send for Burke and Hare.

Burke was tall in a workhouse suit and enormous boots. Hare was a red-haired, squat little shitter. Between them swung a large box seven feet long and three feet wide. Each end had a handle, a loop of greasy rope.

Someone would call for the Rosary.

And no matter how fast or loud they went into it, the lads on the ward never drowned out the slam of the box on the floor, or the sickening thud as they lifted the body of a pal and let him drop. If Burke and Hare were collecting from the women's quarters up the stairs, they just slid the coffin down the steps. A terrible rattle in the dead of night, and the clump-clump-clump as a granny, a girl, rolled round like a pea in a box.

All there is to do in the face of death is get drunken. Fuck deeper.

*I was meaning to come. It's just I—*Want a month of dirty fucking, want a different life. *I fecking hate hospitals.*

He's very at the last, Mara warns.

It was never him would die. He escaped the da, escaped the TB. It was us s'posed to die, never him.

There's malignancies everywhere. Mara gives Olly her seat beside Nick.

So afraid of losing him, I couldn't come.

They stay quiet and mind their brother.

The matter? Nick asks. He's there, he's gone, he's back again. He opens his eyes, sees Olly, says, *Waited for you.*

Nick—

Seeing you is my enough. Nick sleeps.

He rides a rocking bed of light, skimming the tricking halls of time.

In Nick's dreaming head, his mind stammers. Cattle-blood on cobbles in the yard. Blood in the sink come the morning, Da's bright-bright blood. The curse of all dairymen, TB.

A boy, feet stone-bruised, racing up the lane.

To never be found, never. It's that is the fear.

Death rises over the bed, Nick in her dark clutches.

He struggles to breathe.

The little buttons on his pajamas bouncing. Skatterdy skatterdy, skit-skit.

And Olly thinking:, Nick is jamas in the bed. He's the body in the jams, not my brother anymore. Sure, isn't that Burke and Hare waiting at the door, swinging the empty box between them? Olly's tears drop to the sheets.

No crying. No lying. No whispers, Mara orders. *Is the rules.*

Olly takes his brother in his arms to gather him, and gather. He holds and strokes him. *That's your enough now,* he says. *Off you go, safe home.*

Olly sets Nick back on the pillow and kisses him full on the lips with love.

The ward fills with Nick's leaving. His breath torn to rags. Breath folds into breath, climbing up the night and down, clambering and slowing, pushing out.

When Nick's breath skips a beat, his heart keeps pumping.

Is he dead? Olly panics. *That the last?*

Just when they think he's gone past living, Nick takes one more, and death breathes him home.

When Nick's breath leaves the ward, his heart slurs to a stop. Life goes *pap.* He is up and gone. Nick's let into air.

Head aslant on the pillowcase, eyes blown wide. Nick's gazing cross the room. Seems to be.

Nick hears a rapping and a calling. *This way out. Here on the glass.*

At the window, Joe the Butterboy. Pictures flash on the grubby pane—a cinema reel unwinds.

Shimmer-the-glimpse, it's boys.

Two boys back there in time.

They kneel together in the toolshed.

The glimpsing shimmers and comes real.

There on the windowglass. Two boys in love.

Joe pulls Nick in. Into the silks of him. Into the silks of his mouth. Into a never-ending kiss.

Fly with me, let's leave the land. Joe the Magic Butterboy takes Nick gently up. Kicking up-up, and up. Spoonlegs silvering. Out of the red-walled toolshed, through the blanching room of death. Hospice windows come away. Flowers fall all round. All the flowers of Stephen's Green. Smell it. Can you smell it? Jinny joes, tulips, daffodils.

They lift out of this world and shoot to the blued backwall beyond.

Not two hours before, Olly pressed his brother's lids closed. He shut them to the pale rim of blues coming over the rooftops, shut them to the day rising up like Jayzoo Easter and the bells sounding the hour. He shut them.

He felt the heat leaving Nick's poor ould eyes. That's him gassed out. That's his big brother ex-scaped on the morning.

Hardly two hours and Olly's left St. Luke's and gone maundering. Bounding gray pavements, ciggy clamped in his jaw. His clicky leather heels winding through the backlanes of Eerie-town. 'Til he turns into Blather Alley, stopping where him and Gina lived when first they wed.

None of youse are dead, he shouts at the blank windows of their teeny Georgian home. A coachman's quarters, condemned now. No one inside to hear. *No, none of youse're dead.* The Corporation moved the Liffeysiders to modern flats in Ballymun. *Sure's, youse don't even know you're not dead.*

It's Market Day on the cobblestone lanes. There's trailers stocked with fruit and veg beeping and screeching through the market gates.

Olly passes the milkman doing his rounds on Mary's Abby, Swift Row.

Passing the shag-dogs off the quays, wild-living and loathsome. Their barking joins the throng of worries in his head, the jangle. The "why-am-I-here, why?" howling up vomity.

A wobble of sad plugs him. He stops, grabs his knees. *Wuh—Wuh-uhh.* And boaks blood. *Why am I here?*

Olly scrapes a bloody tongue 'gainst his top teefs. It is blood. He can taste the metal. He spits in his palm. It is blood gone thick, dark red like a piece of liver. What? Sick again? Is it back to the ward? He spits once more to the gutters-all-muddy.

Mister Lugubrious, remains of his fag glued to the corner of his mouth somehow. He takes a long, slow pull on the butt, burns his lips.

Olly steadies himself on the riverwall. O, the wicked

smell off the Liffey, mud and salt. Keeps walking, aiming for O'Connell Street. At the crest of the bridge he stops, gazes into the shimmering river, flowing seaward.

Olly stares and stares, clearly mesmerized. There's a thrust of wind, his hair floops and sways.

The gay lights of the neon signs flicker on the water's surface as though a second city lies below.

A pair of lads wander up from the docks, and happen upon O'Feeney. Mid-the-bridge, such a head-down sense of despair to him.

Something's not right in his manner, Liam, the red-haired one, surmises. Then yer man hurls himself onto the parapet. *By the hokey farmer, that man's gonna jump.*

And like he doesn't want to know what's next, Olly does an abrupt about-face and sits back into the river.

He jumped. Peadar suddenly twigs something's wrong.

But his pal Liam has already removed boots, cap-n-jacket. He rushes down the moss-slippy steps, diving from the bottom stair.

Olly tumbles 'neath the beneaths. The Liffey's currents buck and chaw, sucking him beneath beyond benunders. Into the cold, the cold, where he'll join his brother in the land of the dead.

When he comes to himself, for that's what it is, a coming back into himself after, O'Feeney squints at the dockmen looming above. Burke and Hare, is it? This pair of rough-looking country rubes.

Olly curls on his side. Alive, I'm alive.

Isn't it a shame? The state he's in, Peadar says, handing Liam a lit ciggy.

A lie, I'm a lie.

Hey Dublin. Liam prods Olly with an unlaced boot.

Life-lie, life-lie. Down by the Liffeyside.

Tis a dreadful sin. River-bilge streams from Liam's ginger colored eyebrows, the scant hairs on his chin. *To be acting the jackeen, flinging yerself in the Liffey—hoore of rivers.*

Olly sits, suddenly asking, *What is the difference 'tween life and lie?*

Life, what? Peadar's baffled.

Liam takes a deep drag, studying the smoke as he blows it out. *F.*

Only one letter 'tween life and lie, O'Feeney says.

True for you. Liam decides to joke him out of it. *Ja hear that, Peadar? What's the differ 'tween life and lie?*

F?

Yeh, F. Liam explodes in hilarity.

F? Peadar's most confused. *Don't encourage him, he's a nerve case.*

You should go on the stage, Liam says to Olly. *'Cause you are capital F for Funny.* Liam screeches with roar upon roar of laughter.

Yeh, I'm funny all right. Sooooo-so funny.

Life-lie, that's laugh.

So F off, yeh spud-eating, culchie wankers, Olly shouts, launching off the bridge.

He's not.

Och, he has, Liam says, kicking off his boots again.

Where you going?

Back in.

Back in?

First I'll save him, then I'll kill him. Giving Peadar his ciggy. *Keep this dry 'til I return.*

And Liam dives into the Liffey's filtheroo.

Peadar shivers on the bottom step, scanning the water, most concerned. Liam's fag has long gone out. Consternation. Should he go for the guards? But if he leaves, Liam could drown. But surely not Liam, star of the Blackrock Dare Divers. Och, blasted consternation. He will wait.

There's a quick-thrash, Liam jolts to the surface. With burly ferocity, he lugs O'Feeney that last length to the stairs. Peadar grabs a fistful of Olly's suit jacket, hauls him aground.

Liam and Peadar shudder and gasp, catching their breath, gathering their strength. Intent on vengeance, och-aye.

But as Peadar goes in for the first kick, he sees that is no man there, but a black-coated cur.

Begod, Peadar cries. *Tis the blackdog.*

Slicked in Liffey-stink, collapsed on its side. Ribs heaving in-and-out, in-and-out.

Life-lie. Life-lie.

Hsst, Peadar. The blackdog. Liam backs away, clutching boots and cap, bare feet padding. *It means death to wake him.*

Then let's skedaddle.

And they scram.

Olly wakes with a pain in his eye, opens to a blinding flash. He's jumbled in bed covers, the fisheye quilt, in the MamDad room. Tucked on his side. Ribs heaving in-and-out, in-and-out. Day gushes through the window squares. Sun so alive, it's a-ripple. The glass itself is a river flowing left to right with dark bodies. There's phantoms murmuring on the glass. Hallucinating, is he?

No, it's birds flying by on the other side of his pains.

Ah, fuckery. He's gone blue, gone blasted. He's climbed Mount Misery again.

Can't get down.

He shuts his eyes and he's off to sleep. He's off to Catatonia.

Deep in his melancholy he misses it all, misses the awfuls.

Misses Aunty Mara's snooveling, her prayers and self-admonishments. "Treasured memories of a brother."

His brother's Mass at Saint Theresa's. The swinging of the censers, the ringing of the bells, the Latin-groaning, the slow parade out to Glasnevin.

Misses the dig-out of their plot—the six-by-three of clay. The sickening thud of his brother's body. The terrible rattle. A pea in a box.

Misses the laying of the coffin sangitch—Father, Son. The flogger, the flogged. One top the other *in perpetuam*.

Misses the lightning strike and the slashing rains, the lean-dog slinking near the tombs. The mud and Dominick under.

Misses Granny who stayed home. Refusing to put her sailor boy to earth is her fist of dirt flung in the face of tomorry.

What a fambilly, a shambilly, I tell youse.

Ghost in the House

1968

man at the far end

There's an inkwell in my desk at Kildare Place School and blue ink in the inkwell. Kildare Place School is a Church of Ireland Primary School. It's a private school which means we go here for free.

Tired, I'm gassed-exhausted.

On the side wall is a map of Ireland in blue, green, pale orange. There's a pointer for following routes of war and agro-cultural growth over time, through all of our histories.

My feets is killing me 'cause they're far too big for my Bradley's sandals. I begged and begged Mam for a new pair, but nooooo, we've to wait 'til our ship comes in.

Pull up the wooden desk top. Inside is jotters, pink blotting paper and pen nibs. I'm hungry. Ate a boiled egg this morning, all we had in the larder. Nine eggs in the small fridge, nine eggs to feed the fambilly. Fiona cooked us horrid porridge, Odlum's Little Oatlems. She added milk to thin out the lumps and it turned to gruel. Gruel's all right if you like it. And I don't. But I ate it anyway.

Under my desk top I tear off a hunk of blotting paper. Sneak it to my mouth, soften it up, chew it slow. Hoard it in my cheek so Old Bonks doesn't think I have a mouthful of chewing gum.

Old Bonks's proper name is Mrs. Bankson but the O'Feeneys call her the Bonks on accounta she's a beef-to-the heels, stodgy ould pounder. Slappy, she's blutz and whack-happy. But you wouldn't know it now 'cause she is smiling. You know how some people smile. Like my mam, say. When she smiles she has forty-three smiles in her face. Then some other people smile and there's no smile there. Well, that's the Bonks to a tee.

There's a young man just learning to be a man standing beside her desk, front of the room.

Today we have a visitor. Old Bonks is using her talking-to-parents voice. She has a blue-gray perm curly as a poodle. *Say hello to Mr. Hagan, class.*

The class dutifully stands. *Hello, Mr. Hagan.*

I mouth the words, pretend to fit in, hiding behind Birdy Sally's chirping. Birdy Sally sits smack in front of me. Every time I look at Ould Bonks, I have to duck around Birdy Sally, a pretty. The perfectest girl in Ireland. Socks well pulled up, ribbons tied smartly in her piggy-pig tails. The part in her head is straight-so-straight, rubber bands pulled so the brains of her stretch like a tightrope ear-to-ear though her measly mind.

Birdy Sally slapped me on the first day of school. Weeks later, when I tripped her back she went mewling to Bonks, who stood me among the wet macs and wellies in the cloakroom for a full-day of school.

Mr. Hagan holds a super-colossal box of expensive chockies tied with a purple satin bow. Bonks pushes her reading specs up her bulbous nose, smiles her smirking empty smile.

Thank Mr. Hagan for the lovely sweets, class.

Thanks for the sweets, Mr. Hagan. Everyone joins in, shouting hard.

Hoo-hooo, it's thank you, class. Old Bonko glares at us.

Thank you, Mr. Hagan.

And Birdy Sally? Would you come up here and open the box, then pass it along to all your pals in second class? Not my pal. Hardly. *We mustn't be greedy, let's save some for another day.*

Today Old Bonks is wearing her burnt brown suit, silk. Little coat jacket, a V in the front where the cleave of her huge bonking boobers swells with pride.

I'd like to tell the class why I'm here today and why I come here every year. Each time with a super-colossal box of chocolates for Mrs. Bankson.

Would you like to hear the story, class?

Yes, very much, drones the class.

"Yes-very-much, yes-very-much." These eeje-bombs would of course say "yes-very-much." But I don't say "yes-very-much" 'cause I neeeeed them chockies more than everybody's needings in this room put together. If I told them how much I'd like to wallop down the boxload, the walls of the school would fall away with my roaring. 'Cause I'm starving like a Biafra baby.

When Birdy Sally takes the chockie box from Mr. Hagan, he flicks her hair ribbons. *Hello, Birdy Sally of the bonny cheek and bonny eye. Woncha keep that chockie box ribbon for your fair rosy pigtails?*

Mr. Hagan's rusty-colored hair spikes up like weed grass. He's got freckles like Birdy Sally. That's prolly why he thinks she's the pip of the class.

Thank you, Mr. Hagan. Birdy needs no prompting from Mrs. Bonko. She knows all by herself how to brown her nose. Birdy Sally undoes the bow, quickly winds it round her hand. Slips it in the big square pocket of her plaid pinafore, with the waist dropped low, kicking into a spray of pleats above her knees.

I am here today to tell you a very important story, Hagan says. *One that could lead you to your future endeavors. One that could save your life.*

Birdy Sally, neat and slim, queens through the lanes tween the desks, allowing each kid to pick what chockie he wants. Like they're her box of chocks, like she owns 'em. Miss Birdy Strut, Miss Birdy Slamper works it so that she comes to my desk at the very last.

When she reaches me, she won't let me lift my sweet from the paper cup, nooooo. Birdy Sally plops the smallest chockie right near my inkwell, almost dropping it into the blue.

What a stinking snob. I take aim, shoot my wad of blotting paper straight to the heart of her pinafore. Her eyes go wide, she wants to scream, but she doesn't 'cause she's such a goody-gumdrop. She quietly picks it off and pockets it.

She'll tell on me when Hagan's gone, yeh, she'll tell all, later. She's keeping my crime secret for now, so Old Bonks won't be shown as the torturer she is.

Do any of you know what you'll be when you grow up? Young Hagan asks.

Petrol pumper. Mammy. Yeh, a mammy, a mammy. Car mechanic. Zoo keeper. Nurse. Solicitor.

Confederate soldier, Ignatius Isaacs says.

Mr. Hagan laughs. *But that war's long over.*

Hmm-hmm-hmm, goes the Bonks, pretending to laugh. She loathes Ignatius 'cause he's left-handed and Bonks says that makes him evil. Well, Old Bonks is evil incarnage. Lookit her clenching her meaty hands, wiping 'em briskly on her skirt. She grabs the throb of her thighs and shakes 'em 'cause under her jollity and vacant smiles, she's worried something could go wrong with the kids in front of Hagan.

If I can't be a confederate, then I want to be in the IRA.

With that shocker, Mr. Hagan and Old Bonks stop their snickers and move on. But Old Bonks will get Iggy later. Like she'll get me once telltale Birdy snitches. Nothing gets past the Bonks, ever.

What about you? Mr. Hagan scratches a shaving cut on his jaw, making it bleed. He's waiting on my answer. *What do you want to be?*

Actor. There's spits running over my teeths, I'm that hungry for my chocolate.

*Don't you mean ac*tress*?*

Actresses are ninnies, I say. Meaning hoores. All the ones my daddy loves.

Ninnies. Mr. Hagan licks a finger, presses it to his jaw to staunch the blood. *Think so?*

I know so. And—I already am what I want to be. I've been on the telly. That said, I toss my chockie into my mouth. Ew-pee-yucks. Coffee. That's ghastly.

And what about you, Miss Sally? Hagan winks at her in encouragements. *Will you be a model? Or an air hostess?*

Veterinarian. Vetter-rin-airy-an. Miss Superior with her six-syllable word. *I'm going to Trinity College where I'll study animal species. I'll learn to save their lives and heal them.*

Excellent. Young Hagan claps his hands, marches the length of the teacher's desk. He spins to face us. *All right, squad. To look at me, I might seem like nothing. But everything I am—bank manager, happily married, scholarship to Trinity College—*

Who cares? My mam went to Trinity College for her Pee Haitch Dee.

This. All this... He puts his eyes to the side looking at Old Bonks. They're in cahoots, it's clear, 'cause she already knows what Young Hagan's going to say. *Is due to Mrs. Bankson.*

The Bonks glances to the floor, bashful. She tucks her hands into her armpits pressing up her titters in a tub of lust.

When I was a lad. His tongue laps his lips like he's thirsty. *I fell in with a malicious lot of laze-abouts. I scorned my school lessons. I failed maths and failed Irish. If it wasn't for Mrs. Bankson, I'd have sunk to the gutter and wallowed there. I'm proud to say I'm nobody much but what she made me.*

Young Hagan smashes Bonks in a hug of joy. She thumbs a tear from under her specs. *I hope you believe me and take my example.* He finishes with a flourish. *Be good, do your schoolwork diligently, and you'll prosper. Squad dismissed.*

Say goodbye to Mr. Hagan, class.

We stand in unison. *Goodbye.*

Mr. Hagan, she corrects us.

Goodbye, Mr. Hagan.

Must dash, bye-eee. Hagan flies out the door. His chockie box sits on the Bonks's desk like a prize.

When I grow up, I'll visit Old Bonks with a chocolate box bigger than Mr. Scholarship Spunger Trinity's. I'll give her a box bigger than Trinity College itself. But she'll lift the lid to... not one chockie inside. Just stones, pebbles and dried up hunks of ould dog poo.

While we diligently, so diligently, work our sums, the Bonks tickles about in her desk searching out chockie after chockie. Such a greedy heap of flab. She munches slowly, false teefs slipping and clicking as she chews.

When it's time for religion Bonks makes Carmel Dignam stand out in the drears of the hall. Carmel's a Catholick, the only one in school. Religion Class's not much to miss, staunch Proddy hymns and the grueling lessons.

So glad I'm not Catholick 'cause Christian Brothers hit more than the Bonks, if you can believe it. Daddy went to school with them Brothers who took the cane and the strap to him every day... all for making his friends laugh.

Old Bonks wanders the aisles keeping her eye out for cheaters and sneaks. She has the thick ruler in her hand. As she walks the room, she strokes her thigh with it. *Just warming it up*, she says. *Keeping it warrrrrm.*

Let us rehearse the articles of thy belief. The Bonks pokes the ruler down her front, itching the sweat-tickles on her bazoomers-galore.

I believe in the Holy Ghost. The kids in the class mouth meaningless words. *The Holy Catholick Church*, even though they're Prods. Wish I could join Carmel in the hall.

And the life everlasting.

Amen, I say, glad it's over.

All to the line, it's missionary time, The Bonks says. We

snake along the map wall for the weekly collection of missionary money. I end up next to Ignatius under the border dividing the six besieged counties and Ireland, free.

Bonks takes the missionary box out of her massive desk and *plink*, her thrupenny piece hits bottom. She stands in front of Birdy, who slips a silver sixpence in the slot. Gloating 'cause every week she gives the most, she gives her pocket money.

Ignatius is next and has no money, not even a hayporth in his kick. Iggy Isaacs, socks aslouch and poor as stink. I've a mad urge to kiss him. He's so sweet 'cause he's poor. He's a sad little boy all in his lone. Like to fix him up, clean his clothes, hug and love him. O, my darling kid, my gorgeous.

Isaacs, Bonks scowls, expecting him to crumble with that one word, but Ignatius holds strong, holds mightily. *Where's your missionary money?*

He out-turns his pockets, full of nothing but holes.

Evvvv-ery Thursday you forget your missionary money. I don't mind how much you give. You can give tuppence, even a penny, but you give nothing. Those poor starving children in faraway lands living like beasts of the pigpen. What does Jesus say about charity, class?

The-panics fly through the missions line 'cause Bonks could turn on anyone.

If you've two coats, give away one, Birdy says, triumphant that she has the answer.

For weeks you've given nothing to the missions. But we're aware of your troubles, aren't we class? What's the trouble with Isaacs?

He's poor, mumbles the class.

The Bonks cocks a hand behind her ear. *Can't hear you.*

Igga-natius is poor, they shout.

No, he's a thieving, lying, tin-whistling beggar. She seethes with loathing. *Didn't I catch him yesterday busking Grafton Street after school.* The ruler rushing down and up her leg. *His cap was packed with a fortune in change, but could he spare one farthing for the Lord?*

No, yells the class, though they're quaking. It's only a few weeks into the year, and she's been at everyone in Second Class. 'Cept for Birdy.

As if God can't see into his busking cap. God sees all, knows all. God cannot be mocked. Stand out of line.

She grabs his right hand and throttles him. Six quick sharp smacks. Ignatius tucks his tender palm under his arm, but doesn't cry.

Then she gets to me. *O'Feeney. Where's your money for the missions?*

I pretend to search my dress, but I know I don't have it. How did I forget my missionary moolah? Coulda helped myself to the Players, Please! tobacco tin. Not much left but a handful of florins and a ha'pence or two. I've been doling 'em out to my kidgang in the Green. When shopkeepers won't take the blackened, bent pennies, I put 'em in Miss Hoggs' gumball machine.

Sides, I can't get to the money box 'cause Daddy's been slonked in bed for weeks. Since Uncle Nick died he hasn't left the house. He's in there with the gray tweed blanket nailed over the window like when I had chicken pox. In the darkened MamDad room it smells like ashtray and rotty dog.

Daddy's fighting his troubles, staying off the drink, lighting a fresh ciggy off the burnt-down one, flicking ashes from the quilt. He sends me to Dolly's of Baggot Street for his fags. Wish I could see into his mind, understand what he's thinking. There's heaps I want to tell him. When I try to talk with him, he looks at me like he doesn't know me, or turns his face to the pillow slip.

Miss Smarty, with your American frock. Old Bonks prods the hem of my turquoise dress with the rule-tip, batting the skirt in a taunting way. *Your parents have money.*

Not anymore. Daddy got the sack from *Our City* for not going to work. Aunty Mara said he must stop his sulking and pull himself together 'cause we're dropping to ruin.

It's a desperate thing to have the Bonks down my neck this early in the day. The top of it is, Birdy Sally picks this time for revenge. She shoots up her arm, wagging it for the Bonks's attention.

Yes, Birdy?

She smoothes her skirt pleats with her nails, savoring the attention. *Noleen spit blotting paper on my pinny. She did it deliberate. While Mr. Hagan was here, but I kept the evidence.* She points a gun hand at me. On her fingertip is a teeny bullet, my blotting paper wad.

O'Feeney. Put out your hand.

I do.

Twelve smacks for incivility to your betters and for forgetting the missions.

I hold out my hand and hold out my hand.

But does Bonksee-Bunghead start the smacks fast to get them over with?

No.

She circles the ruler against her palm, flipping it like you'd butter the bread. Bonks wraps her hand round the bottom of the ruler. Then she dunks it up and down like a pecker in the woods. *Let's get this ruler good and hot.*

My hand is trembly, fingers twitch in anticipation of the pain.

And whoosh. She strikes, but I flinch back so-quick she misses.

Don't pull your hand away.

I hide my hands behind my back.

Put out your hand, or you'll get four more for insubordination.

When I stick out my hand, she clamps my fingertips. I'm caught.

Whack cross the palm of my left hand so's I can still do my schoolwork.

One. Two, she calls in rhythm. *Count along, class.*

The class chanting. *Three. Four.*

Don't break, don't break. Give nothing out, give nothing away. Ignatius didn't cry. I'm brave as him.

Seven. Eight. If I cry, I'll die down dead of shames.

Let that learn you. Slashing my hand again and again.

Eleven. Twelve. I hold my breath, gird my lions. Pain is shooting and stinging from my palm, along my arm to all over the place.

Fifteen. Sixteen. The class comes to the end of their counting.

Made it. I didn't break. I'm strong as Ignatius.

Then Birdy sticks out her tongue at me. The world tilts up-over and I'm crying.

Cry baby, Bonks says. *Only babies cry.*

The class looks on in silence.

The kids in this class are a shower of shite.

Swallow your tears.

But I can't stop the crying, once started. I choke on my snots, shake my left hand. There'll be bruises soon.

Birdy. Go get the baby chair.

Birdy careers to the front of the room, dragging a pink chair from Babies Class.

And the bib. Bonks squeezes her claws into my shoulder blade, guiding me to the chair where Birdy ties a bib round my neck.

Aren't you forgetting the pacifier, Mrs. Bankson? Birdy says, aiming to take me down three pegs, or seven.

What a clever clogs you are. Bonks smiles her empty smile.

When Birdy Sally pops the soother in my mouth, the class laughs. With Mistress Sally laughing loudest of all.

I'm disgraced for life.

Old Bonks pushes me into the baby chair where I'll sit for the day. Thinking over my miseries. Small in my sin. In my sin. In my sin-sin-sins.

Olly climbed in the MamDad bed one morning, late August. Here it is October and he's still there, awake. Inside one more of them nervy, brain-rioting nights:

There's a hole in the bed where I am.

There is hate in the bed where I am.

There is rage in the bed where I am.

Round it goes, round and round, these thoughts. An avalanche of sads and anger has been whirring his mind these black weeks now. No sign of a let up.

The matter with him? Not like he's in hospital, restrained in the head box, lashed to the spine board. Things were done to him, medical things. Waiting for months while his ribs healed after them operations. Years spun out in a gas dream on the wards.

In the theatre of his mind there is so much sad. He soothes himself with pictures. What he's done and what he'll do when he's out in the wide world again. The laughs he'll get, the money he'll earn, the stories he'll tell. Sure, it's just stories in the end, mere stories.

Isn't true at all.

Here in his house? The door, the door, the door is open.

Just walk through, g'wan out . . . to free.

There's a hole in the bed where I am.

There is hate in the bed where I am.

There's a dog in the bed where I am.

He has nothing, he is nothing.

Can't bring himself to leave the bed.

There is rage in the bed where I am, where I am.

There's no me in the bed where I am.

How plundered he feels, like rubble. He'll have another cigarette to hold himself together, he's fallen apart.

O fuck. Fuck everyone. Fuck everything. Fuck.

Hate going home to our house 'cause with him up the stairs, it's a prison. We're crammed so tight, we've hardly room to turn. We've to be quiet all the time, good as gold.

There's a ghost in our house, it is him.

Once in the door, I drop my schoolbag. The hand is falling off me from Bonko's walloping. I set my fingers over my swollen palm, feel the heat and the throbbing. It hurts. Wish I could kill her, bash her face.

I hump off my pinchy sandals. Want a new pair of shoes so I don't get crumpy-toed like my mam with her bunions and lumps and her bent-in toes.

Mam has my shoes marked on her shopping list. There's a slate board on the kitchen wall where she writes all the things we're needing:

Milk £6

Pay for turf

Music lessons £24

Pay Mr. O'Reilly – Chemist

Pram wheel

Piano tuning

Buy Noleen new sandals

Typing paper – carbon

Owe turf £8.15

Not one of them things has a tick beside it.

We're heading into winter with no turf in the shed. There's a collection of bits in the turf basket to keep us warm, wet sticks from the corners of our backlane and garden. Des and Ely dug up armloads of wood from Da's scene shed. There's crates from the market, old scripts from plays done and gone, yellow pages full of their notes. Da paces the room telling jokes, Mam writes 'em down. She's the Ideas Girl shouting out things as they come along. Daddy laughs, Mam scribbles away. Later, she types it up at her writing desk. I hear the clack of the keys in the early morn.

But that hasn't happened in a really long time.

Then bossy boots Fiona gets the idea. *Let's play cleaning.*

I wanna go for sweets.

We've no money for sweets. Fiona's at the dinner table, organizing dry clothes from off the line. She's folding our underthings, the short pants, bugsers and frocks, tucking back the arms of blouses and shirts so they're weeshy packets of cloth.

We've money for bunk-nuffins these days, I say. *Not a damn ha'penny.*

It costs nothing to clean the house. Fiona stacks five neat packs of clothes on the seats of the *súgán* chairs 'cause Peter Rabbit dishes cover every inch of the dinner table. Been there since breakkie with dried egg-skroook and gruel, hardened crumbs 'neath the plates.

I want sweets. If Lily were here she'd give me some. Her son works at Urney's Chocolate factory so she keeps a secret supply of broke chockie bars in her apron pocket for me.

I know you want sweets but there are none. I was going to make razzer jelly for tea tonight but when I went to the cupboard for the jelly blocks, know what I found?

What? I say, almost cheeking her.

The boxes were empty.

What about the lime?

Four empty boxes.

Do you think it's Poppy ate them? I ask, all innocent.

No, Poppy says. *I is a so-good girl.*

You selfish-selfish greedy gut, accusing your little sister when it's you were at the jelly blocks again.

How does Fiona know? Is she a witch can read into minds? I was so starving last night, I went down and had a root through the kitchen. Took the catsup from the fridge, licked the crunchy globs off the ridge where you twist the cap. Tipped back and drank, pouring it down my gullet. Then I gobbled up the Birds Eye Jelly—two raspberry, one orange, even the grocky lime. I left it 'til last thinking I'd be full, but when I got to the lime I ate it.

When Mam comes home I'll tell her you ate the jelly blocks and she'll punish you.

You know she won't. I am dead lucky 'cause Mam doesn't believe in hitting. 'Cause Mam's own mother, Granny Volk, used to blutz her with the hairbrush when she was bold.

You know she won't. Poppy copies me. *You know Mam won't.* She's practicing talking, practicing having ideas.

Fiona crashes her fists into the table, making the Peter Rabbit dishes jump. *This place is a pigsty. Anyone would think we live in a stable.*

We do, I say.

Don't get snippy.

It's true.

Well, it's a shattered ruins. Poppy, bring these upstairs, but shh-quiet. Stay out of Daddy's way.

Poppy wobbles up the stairs, her chin holding a tiny pile of clothes in place.

Fiona's carrying on like a tornado. She scoops a fistful of toy soldiers off the couch, flings 'em at me. *Throw these in the bin.* She punts Mrs. Littlechap under the piano. *Throw her in the bin. Clear the decks.* Fiona stomps round the room, attacking our toys. *If you lazy-pie kids can't put things away, in the bin. Everything will be chucked out, 'cause I can't stand it anymore.*

Aw, Mammy Littlechap, her posh hair-do's come down. There's teeth marks on her baldy head from where Poppy bit her. Look at the state of this place, disgusting. Worn shoes and schoolbags at the landing stair where we toss 'em at the end of the day. *Let's make this house fit for a magazine,* I say. *As a present for Mam.*

I get to work like a fiddler's elbow 'cause I don't want Fiona to go into one of her big-huge conniption fits.

Fiona goes back to doing the clothes. It's Fee washes them now 'cause Mam had to let Lily go. Due-to-you-know-why, not enough moolahs.

Mam's taken Giselle in the pram to pick up Ely at Montessori and Des is over at his friend Packey's. He even sleeps there some nights rather than put up with Daddy's moods.

Why don't you do the fireplace? Fee says.

It is the perfects to get the fireplace. Since there's no turf, there's nothing to clean, 'cept dirt. Fiona drags over a bucket of sudsy water. I soak a ratty nappy, wring it out and dunk again.

I'm on my knees scrubbing the gray slates. I'll soon have it shining like gold.

O, Mistress Mother. Mary, meek and Mary, mild. Forgive me, please. Forgive my child. I slap out the raiments of Jaysoo Easter on the rocks of the Jordan River. I have sinned and I have sinned. I weep for all sinners sinning on earth.

I'll wring out Christ's clothes for him. *Ochón agus ocón, forever. Life is sad. Ochón agus ocón, an ice cream cone, O.*

I do love being an actor. I have real tears stroobelling over my cheeks. That's 'cause I feel terrible-awful for the Jesus dying. I must wash His hair with my feets like Mistress Mary Mandolin, that lubberly wrench. I'll clean the Holy Body's bloody wounds, dress Jayze in His burial clothes, swaddle Him in the raggy nappy. Lay Him cold on the bench of stone, roll the heavy rock, closing the door to the cave of the dead.

What are you going on about? Fee asks.

Leave me alone, agus ocón, ocón.

I duck into the fireplace, stand inside, tip my head back, and look up. Through the charred passage, out our chimbelly pot, the day's still bright, and birds fly by.

Helloooo, I cry, but them birds ignore me. Wish I was a bird. Wish I could fly.

I scour and scrub 'til the nappy catches on a sharp corner. There's a weensy wooden door set into the chimbelly. I search for a latch or a knob, pick at it with my fingernails but the door won't budge. Passing my hand over the face of the door, I feel writing, or something, carved—No, *pecked* on the wood.

It's the imprint of three birdy feet in a V.

Like this:

Wind screams through the chimbelly. At least, I think it's the wind. Every rib of hair stands on my neck and on my arms. I swallow my spits and knock at the door, four knocks. The door opens.

Halloa, my dear. A tinkling voice, inviting me in.

Is there a witch lives in the wall of our chimbelly?

A thousand welcomes, wee Noleen.

Why, this is no witch but a weeshy-dear graylag goose, small as a thrupenny bit.

Come in, come on in, she is saying.

I step inside a box of sparkelling Wicklow granite stone.

Shall I wet the teapot?

I'd love some tea, got any bikkies? I say. The graylag flits about making tea.

She tells me the stoney built this teeny cupboard into the chimbelly piece to ward against evil. That this is her house within our home. And it's her job to look out for the O'Feeneys.

Then she fills a silver thimble with a sweet-smelling China tea. Wait, that's Growler's thimble, the silver tarnished with the years.

Where'd yeh find that?

In the fireplace. You wouldn't believe what I find there, she twitters. *Won't you sit down?*

I sink into a splendid settle-couch made of leaves.

Thank you for the tea. I stick my little finger out. Sup it and it's gone. After all, it's only a thimble-full.

In my fairy cupboard, I am never in my lone. For I've the glorious company of the heavens, says the graylag. *Look at this.*

She shuts the door. The room goes bang-black. 'Til one by one, pinpricks of light come aglimmer. There's galaxies of glittering gems, constellations of all the worlds, the land of the living and the land of the dead-and-gone.

They are pure gorgia, I say.

On the many nights I've wasted, locked in this house, I study them hard so I can find my way when I'm out in the world again. The graylag's grin goes cruel. *I've never forgotten how you trapped me. You didn't think—No, you wouldn't.* She spits with anger. *Across the evening sky, this night, my flock will leave without me. But you came for me, didn't you, Nolee. You opened the door.* She strokes my face with her feather wings. *For loosing me this night, I will be the making of you forever.*

With that, the graylag goosie flies up the smoot and is gone.

Growler's thimble, emptied of tea, is burnie-burnie in my hand. It's all things good and wishes answered.

The voices of the Cornerboys echo in the hearth.

Antrim, Armagh, Fermanagh, Tyrone
Derry, Down, County Down

Get back to work, Fee shouts from the room beyond. Her voice is muffled 'cause she's running the tap, rinsing clothes. *Stop your playing.*

Thought we were playing clean the house. How does she know I'm playing?

She is a witch can read into minds. I step out of the fire-place.

Hate you, Fiona. I think in my head. I hate you so hard. If she's over there reading my mind she can bleeding well feel all the hates I have for her.

I pull a *súgán* chair to the fire, step up to start tidying. I hate that sword, Lord Nelson's sword, hate to even touch it.

I wipe the clock case, lift Mam's picture of Synge off the nail. Swipe it with the cleaning nappy, kiss him on his sweet nose tip. Oop, left a schmooch-mark on the glass. I swab it again and replace it. Tipping the portrait this way and that 'til Mister Synge sits firm in his glass.

Fiona's balancing two enamel basins of wet clothes, one top the other, hurrying to get the washing pegged while there's no rain. She leaves the door thrown wide.

Then of-a-sudden, Synge's picture drops, bounces off Nelson's sword, clatters to the floor but fails to shatter.

And there. Standing in his bare feets, middle of the room, is my daddy.

Daddy—

He's half-shaven, vague. Wearing his yellah tartan dressing gown and rumpled jams, he's cradling the Players, Please! money-box. Tears drip from his chin.

Alls I have. Olly tries to speak. *Alls I have left.* Coughs, tries again. *Of my beautiful brother.* His voice is crushed, dry. *His coin collection. In a box in the clothes press. But no moolah remains. Someone stole my brother from me.*

Olly sinks to the floor in a heap.

Somebody stole my brother from me.

He curls up and cries, cries the bitters.

Olly is crying, he is the saddest little boy in all the land.

She goes to him, takes her father in her arms to gather him, and gather.

Holds him, she rocks him, strokes him, soothes his blacky hair.

She can't bear to see this, she—

Must pull the sads out of him, she—

Puts her hands to each cheek with such care, such loving, 'cause Noleen is certain-sure that she can love him saved.

Fiona O'Feeney stops in the open doorway, wash basins shielding the swell of her breasts. She wears a bra now, is no longer a girl. While she was down the *Gaeltacht* this past summer, her first period arrived and she thought she was dying. No one had warned her. Certainly not her mother, who wants her to stay a girl but loads these responsibilities on her. Like minding the childer, for one. And for two, stopping the kids from tormenting each other.

O Jay, there's her father, the sullen lump, in a puddle of sad, middle of the living room. First time downstairs in two months. Noleen's hugging him, saying,

Don't be crying, Daddy. I'll get the money back somehow. Please don't cry. Like Olly's the child.

Please stop, Noleen says. *Da, stop.*

The brat. What's she done now?

Here's a thrupenny bit, a half crown. She scrambles in the metal tin, holding out coins to him. *I didn't spend it all.*

Yeh bloody rip. Helped yourself to your uncle's coins. Rage, red in his face, Olly goes to kill her. *I'll kick yer arse up the lane.*

Noleen ducks and dives under the table to escape. Olly heaves it up-over. Peter Rabbit dishes slide clashing to the floor, Fiona's clean clothes are knocked from the chairs.

And there's Noleen, exposed, turned in on herself, shivering with the terrors.

Daddy, don't do it. Fiona pulls at his sleeve. *Da, stop.*

Olly turns to shrug Fee off and in that moment, Noleen bolts for the door. Never makes it, 'cause Olly bashes her one with the Player's tin. Catches her under the cheekbone, lifts her from the lino for a moment.

In her face a shock of O.

She sails cross the room into the empty fireplace.

Olly watches a small coin turning on the lino, a spinning blurrrr. That stops, tips, drops flat. It's harps.

Olly crosses to the open door, steps out into free.

He wanders from the house in his pee-jays and tartan robe, feet bare on the cobblestones.

Daddy, come back, Fiona calls after him. Can't go out in that condition. *Where're you going?*

To my other fambilly. They love me, he says. *They love me.*

Fiona's stomach lurches when she sees her sister lying unconscious, like one dead. Heart beating in jerky thuds, she swiftly lifts Noleen, carries her up the stairs, leaning against the wall for support. When she reaches the kids-room, Fiona settles Noleen in her bottom bunk.

Wake up, Leeny. Fiona gently touches her cheek. *Please, wake up.*

But Noleen sleeps deep, far beyond her sister's reach.

Fiona turns her attention to her next worry. *Just where is Poppy?* During Olly's drink tantrums, Poppy often hides beneath her cot. *Is she under the bed?* Fiona tilts her head to the wooden floor, making it a game. No sign of Poppy.

Is she in the clothes press? Pop-pop, Fiona calls. *Come on out. Daddy's left the house.* Fiona opens the lavender cupboard and her little sister peeps from between the frocks. *He's gone.*

Gone for really? Poppy claps her chubby hands with glee.

Downstairs, the dining table rests against the unused fireplace. There's a clatter of shattered crockery in the hearth, broken carrots and bunnies from Mister McGregor's garden. She must clear this up before Mam gets home. Collecting the metal Player's box from off the floor, there's the few spare coins Noleen was offering to Daddy. Sellotaped to the lid is a piece of yellow paper folded in half. Fee opens it to find a drawing of Nelson's Pillar done by her Uncle Nick.

"A necklace of—" She recognizes his writing from the postcards and inscriptions in the books he sends her. Used to. He'd pass a bookshop in London, think of her, buy five, send 'em over. Brown paper parcels wrapped in string, sealed with droplets of blood red wax. There will be no more books, no more presents from Uncle Dominick.

"A necklace of bombs," reads his note. An arrow indicates the lookout platform where these bombs should lie. Up Nelson's Pillar, below the statue. What a fine picture, she thinks. A draughtman's drawing. It's the only thing left of her beautiful uncle.

No. Her heart loud in her chest. He blew up the pillar? Uncle Nick? He was in England when—

On the mantelpiece, Nelson's sword.

Evil scamps up her spine bones as she comes to realize. *Daddy.*

What came over him? What was in his mind? Why bomb the Pillar? He'll end up in Mountjoy.

If there was a fire, she'd burn the drawing. It is evidence.

Hide it, hide everything. Say nothing. Don't tell a soul.

A calm comes on her once she's decided. She refolds the yellow paper, slips it in the Bible on Mam's writing desk. It won't be found 'cause no one reads the bible here.

When I come in to myself again, for that's what it is, a coming back into myself after, I'm nestled in the graylag's settle-couch made of leaves, and the door to her magic cupboard is gaping.

Blue moonlight floods the shaft of our chimbelly.

It's blacknight, halfway to morning.

And I'm holding Growler's thimble he lost ages ago.

I'm squeezing Growler's thimble.

Draw down power from the heavens.

Draw up from the earth, the sea.

Power from all three kingdoms.

I am inside the chimbelly, the walls of our house.

I can see through passage stone, through shale.

There's baby Giselle, a weeshy treasure, asleep in the Moses basket on the dinner table. Five months old and still the skinny scrawns. She's stretchy and reachy in her dreams.

Giselle frets and whines. It's Mam she's wanting but Mam's dead-out in the storytelling rocking chair waiting on Daddy.

Giselle's wailing, in full cry but Mam doesn't wake up.

I step out of the fireplace. One step—onto the lino. Two steps—back into the world.

I check Giselle's piss-stained nappy. It's dry and clean, too. She's purple-faced from hunger. I throw off my turquoise frock, my undervest and pick her up. Careful, most careful. Left palm under her head, I press her mouth to my winky nippies. Giselle stops whingeing immediately. She has that baby powder smell. It's easy to see why she's the pet of Tolka Row. Giselly goes to sup, to suck. She teethes and gnaws but finds nothing. She scratches my chin with sharp new nails so I smack her.

Giselle shrieks. Mam leaps up. *Don't hit my kids.*

Sorry, I say. Mam's very cross, the crossest.

She rips Giselle from my arms. *What are you doing up?*

Trying to feed her. I'm bad, blamed for everything. The empty Moses basket goes slurry, tears splat to the lino. *Giselly was crying but I couldn't wake you.*

Mam doesn't want to be looked at. Daddy's sads has got their way into her. Her hair is rankled. She hasn't been to Jule's on the Green in an age.

She plods to the sink, pulls a bottle from the small fridge, holds it under the hot tap. Her hands shake with nerves as she tests the milk.

Get back to sleep, she says. *There's school tomorrow.*

Don't wanna go, I feel sicky.

Mam looks at me. Sits on the couch, studies the swell of my cheekbone, left eye almost closed. *How did that happen?*

What? I dodge her, glancing away. She mustn't know Da knocked me flying. Mustn't see the lump at the back of my head, it's a whopper.

That bruise. Her voice is shrill with alarm. *On your cheek.*

A swing, I say. *After school. I got hit by a swing in the Green.*

The lie flows from my mouth like cream from a bun.

Lookit my hand. I hold it out so Mam can see.

O, dearie. My good kid lollipop, Mam says, coming out of herself with concern for me. *Mrs. Bankson?*

Yep.

She is vile and despicable. Mam strokes my palm. *You had a terrible day, didn't you?*

Yes I did. Had no money for the missions. Grab my frock and vest from off the floor. *I need new shoes, Mam. They're too small, I'm in agonies.*

I climb the stairs to my bunk in our room. To sleep again in the mortal worlds, to dream. Can't wait for my dreams.

o dark hunger

I'm sitting on the bench outside the National Library, wagging my feets. Holding Mam's secret stone in both hands, wishing for my mammy. Why won't she come out the door like she used to do? With a grin and a fresh script for the BBC. Mam's always trying for the BBC.

"A cat may look at a king," Granny Volk said every time I tried for a part or a scholarship. Mam crosses her fingers, shakes 'em with hope. So much hope. *Why don't you post it for me? And wish it luck.*

Good luck, I say, dropping her script into the blank mouth of the green letter box.

But Mam's not coming. She's teaching a hellecution class, helping people from the guts of Dublin talk posh and get better jobs. After that she'll stop at the shops, pick up bibs and bobs of food, whatever she can get on the strap from shopkeepers who still like us and feel for our troubles. They think Mam has nine kids like Daddy's fambilly on *Our City*. Even though Jimmy Downs is playing the Jackser now, that yunk.

It's raining, pounding down like a sewer. I'll hop into the National Museum, take shelter 'til the rain slacks. I rush up the street, ducking the drops, schoolbag on my head for an umbrella.

It's Halloween week. They're giving a special program to a mob of kids wearing sheets, their mams' gowns down to their heels and fearsome masks. Girls dressed as boys, boys as girls. I've no costume, will they let me stay? I edge in among them.

In Old Ireland there were three great festivals celebrated each year. May Eve, Midsummer, and All Hallows. A man wearing a museum uniform stands next to a table loaded with bowls of apples, almonds and hazelnuts. *Halloween marks the end of the farming year. According to folklore, the supernatural realm has great power at this time. The veil between our life and the Kingdom of Souls is slim as the skin of an onion.* He bites his lip, real solemn. *So creatures often slip between, creeping into the world of the living and down to the world of the dead.*

At that point in the Museum Man's story, there's a thunder burst above, a crack of lightning. The kids scream and rain pounds down, comes hard in a sheet of sound.

Also called November Eve. Yer man goes on. *This is a time when the old gods allow the dead to return to pay off debts, or fulfill the terms of an enchantment.*

Rain-the-rain ratters the roof of the museum like the souls of the dead trying to get in. When will yer man shut up and give out the food? Once or twice, I tried to go out of a Halloween to sing and dance for fruit and nuts. Well. Tolka Row is only offices. No one had a smile for me, let alone nuts.

The Museum Fellah's yammering on and on. There's no sign of the treats, so I sneak down the hall to pay a call on the Gallagh Man. I peer in at the bog body coffined in glass, polished so I can see myself there like a mirror. The bruise on my cheek that Daddy gave me is fading to yellow. That's my face there on the glass. I am twinned in the case with the bogman. He is shrunky short, same height as me, same skinny.

In eighteen hundred and twenty-one, he was found in the bogs of Galway by peat-cutters snegging the turfs.

How did he die?

This is not known for sure. But there's a card stuck to the case with the history.

His belly was axed by a hatchet. Then they slid him to the slud-waters. Murdered him, buried him in the bog.

There's his tools laid out in his glass box. A whetstone, or hone, a metal stave. One carved stone snake—a serpent curled in on itself—a spiral in stone.

What does it mean? What did he use it for? Could I make one meself? Scratch into Mam's secret waiting stone for under the bench at the Library. I take it from my frock pocket.

Here. I set it on his little glass box. *Happy Hallow Eve.* Leave it for Bogs the Gallagh. Happy—*chuh.* I'm anything but happy.

I wipe my breath from the glass and examine him. Skin like a battered suitcase. Can you believe, after two thousand years Mister Gallagh's got a goldgrain beard, roughly cut for war. I can see him astride his noble mare, clapping along the Bridge of Leaps. Off to war—*hup-haw.* The wife by his side, a warrior, too. Wait-stop—

Might his wife be Nuala the Dagger?

At that thought, the Gallagh Man twists to life.

Meela murders. He's alive.

With great amounts of effort he moves his lips. His voice is throaty-low, unearthly.

Howya, he manages finally. *Nuala the Girsha.*

Not Nuala, I'm Noleen.

Nuala Ní Fearna is your name for true.

A shiver blows through me.

How do yeh know that? I ask him.

I know you ages, I know you years. I seen yeh each time yeh come take a peep at me, he says. *G'wan home, your big sister needs you. If you go now, I'll stop the rain for you.*

And, of a wonder, the heavens dry as I leave the museum. I spunch my toes in my shoes best I can, picking my way over the puddles, feet howling with each step.

By the time we push in around the table and sit down to tea, Mam's still out scrounging. Where is she? If she doesn't come home, we'll have to live here by ourselves. And how will we ever pay our way? But Fiona cooked liver'n'onions and boiled spuds, magicing dinner out of the air. The way, O-the-way onions fry and frizzle, smelling up the house something gorgeous. My mouth is a flood of waters, I've a hunger headache. Ely's stomach growls dark and low.

Poppy wipes her mouth with her sleeve and roars like a lion. *I hungry now, I hungry.* Kicking her legs.

Stop kicking, Ely cries. *Or I'll blutz you.*

Simmer down, Fiona says. She's already dished out each

kid's din-dins for 'em, chopped the rubbery meat and spread it about each plate so it looks like more.

That it? I ask Fiona.

She answers with a tart nod. I want more, but there is none. Just three gray slivers tangled in onions and smashy spuds. There is not enough onions and never enough liver for me.

There's a tumble of chatter around the table. Since Daddy's gone, we can run up the stairs, make noise. Will he ever come home? I miss him terrible all the time.

Don't slurp your food, Fiona says to the boys. *And stop stabbing Des with your fork.*

He thumped me while I was practicing my scales.

Liar, Des screams.

I'm getting him back.

Swine, Des says. *You lying pig.*

You yie-ing pig, Poppy echoes, waving her spoon, flicking a splotch of taytoes at me.

Be quiet, Fiona orders. *Any more of this boldness, it's up to bed with no tea.*

So we simmer down really quick.

Giselle's propped in her pram and Fiona's spooning mashed bits from the one last unbroken Peter Rabbit bowl. There's bunnies and carrots flying round the edges of Giselly's tea. She feeds Giselle, then feeds herself. Bite for Giselle, a bite for herself. *Eat up, you Babe of the Dribble.* Spooning the groopy mess back into Giselly's mouth. Glancing at us kids seated round the table. She's all the time watching over us, checking to see we're a civilized fambilly, milk in glasses by our plates.

I have a tricky-smart way of eating food so it lasts. Drink

the milk first, that fills the tummy. I gulp my milk and—*Pew-wahhhh, the milk's gone.*

Fiona sniffs it. *Smells fine to me.*

I drink again and... *Wuhh. Sour, tastes like boak.*

Fee drinks a mouthful and has no trouble swallowing.

Could be your milk's turned because it's Halloweeeeen, Fiona tells us, going into her storytelling voice. *On Hallow's Eve down the country, they stay in the house. 'Cause if you wander away on that special day, you can get drawn down to another world, lost to your life and family.*

Fadó-Fadó, that's Irish for Long Ago. Fiona's doing it again, keeping our minds off the meager tea, keeping us fed on story.

Fadó-Fadó. On Hunger Hill there lived a mother and no one knows her name. For it was many and many the years ago, when famine tore the land. People still tell of this woman 'cause her husband had died, leaving her alone to raise twelve handsome sons.

Long before the rise of day, their Mother set out from Hunger Hill to forage for food and sup. Each time her search took her further from the Hill 'cause there was less and less to find. 'Til the one time their mother was gone for a week.

Her lads waited and waited. There are those in the town shake their heads at it still—the boys, her precious sons, were so hungry they ate the grass. They ate the field to cure the gnaw.

Back she came, their mother. She was running for once, you see—For in her apron she carried home food for her family, twelve delicious laughing red apples. One for each of her lads. But when she reached their courtyard, she found her boys black-dead from hunger and want.

The wail then, her wail. Her grief-cry loud as thunder.

Their mother sinks to the ground, her apron bulging with laughing red apples. What could she do? But bury the apples one by one in a circle in the field. Upon planting the last apple, there sprung an orchard, twelve full grown trees, branches heavy with hundreds of apples more.

It is said that her orchard fed Hunger Hill for years on years. She lost her boys, but saved her town.

And there on my plate when I look down, liver piled high on a heap of spuds. I drink my milk in one huge gulp. *Mmmm.* Tastes like cows in a glass.

Was it the magic of Hallow's Eve that made it so? Or my sister Fiona telling me, we will be well, we will be fine. Our life is good.

Gina flicks the switch to the hot water heater, goes to her bath. She's fleshy in her middle with the new one coming on. Sinking 'neath the waterline in the tub, washcloth laid over her face to take the tears.

Nick died on August twentieth. Not three months ago, Nick died and along with him went her husband. It is a sad thing 'cause Olly and Nick were always close. They had a million dreams and schemes between them.

Olly's mind was badly disturbed by Nick's death. Something's changed in him, he's nothing but ugly-natured now, drinking his talent away.

July, it was. The final weeks of Dominick's life. She'll call the new baby Dominick for their beautiful, laughing brother.

If she tells Olly? It could save him. Give him something to work for again? But the thought of telling him only brings a drowning terror.

Seven children. My God, how will we pay for them?

Wind shrieks through the chimney stones.

Why another? People will want to know. Her sister, her mother. The shame.

Facecloth sucks to her tongue, then out to bulging. She's taking two-three sucks in for every exhalation. She's gulping down her sads, doesn't want to wake the kids.

Olly, pushing in without asking. She woke to him on top of her.

"Let me catch up," she said. He never waited.

Pushing into her, with no permission.

This conception is so different from the early kids. How they'd loved for each one, brought Desmond down, brought Noleen up from the Kingdom of Souls to join their growing family. This is what he believes, what Olly told her:

All Souls rush through the worlds. On the sands, swim the seas, fly the skies. They're waiting and waiting for their lives to start, wanting to be ours.

We bring them down, bring them up with our love.

How she remembers the first time, her first ever. Running her hands over, all over his pale skin. Such softness. Petting him, stroking him, soothing him. Gentle, O gentle. Her weeshy boy, her treasure.

The heat goes from the facecloth, goes from her bath water. She spins the hot tap, heats and reheats. Covers her face again. Under the warmed cloth, Gina hums.

Lie down now, lie down now. Ye small birds, ye small birds.

Go to sleep now, O sleep now. Bird-een-ee, Bird-een-eee.

We'll be fine. She assures herself. We'll be okay.

Gina lurches from the water, pulls a nightdress over wet skin 'cause she hears it before her kids do. Someone's thrumping the cobbles of the lane, stabbing a key into and into the lock. F-ing and blinding. There's kicks and roars at the Georgian door 'til the key hits home, clicks and turns.

Hoore, hoore. The hooring boy is home.

It's her troubadour, ransacking in from a week abroad. He is in a temper, a filthy temper. Olly thugs into the house with the washline and soaked clothes wound round him.

You. Get down here.

Gina pads down the steps, snicks on the music lamp top the piano, then the kitchen light over the sink. Why does he come? It's happiness here without him.

After being on the dry these past months in bed, the drink's got into his head, got in and done its business. Olly's stocious. Where'd he get that slicky suit? Cheap.

Don't come here, disrupting our sleep with that rotten talk.

To hell, he says, distangling himself from the washline, leaving it on the floor.

Don't come here. Gina's at the far end of the sink. *Expecting dinner when there's nothing to have here.*

Not talking food. Olly's not eating. He's not eating. *What about money then?* He's brought the stales of O'Donoghue's into the house with him. *Money, now that would totally... Tranquilize me.*

How we'll eat this week is the real question.

Olly draws on his half-burned ciggy, flops on the couch, unbuttons his suit jacket and presses up under what's left of his right ribs, stroking his liver with thin fingers. *Me liver's scalding me. Couldja? Getcha me? Some hot water and... Salt in a glass.*

Gina runs the hot water, searches for the salt, fighting back the panic. The salt, the salt, where'd the kids put the salt?

I'm on the hot salt water these days. Taking salt in with the—with the—the water? That'll make you feel better when you're on the—By the dogs, me scaldy liver. Yeh scalder. Olly knuckles his liver. He has the four-finger-liver, see. His liver's swollen to the size of four fingers.

Gina swirls the mixture together, setting his glass on the milking stool.

Olly, we have to get money.

Who's paying the bills here? Olly downs the salty brew in one long swallow.

The only work you've done lately is blot your copybook at the RTÉ, she says, exasperated. *Got yourself sacked from your own show.*

They can fuck off and get fucked. I was sick. I was in agonies.

Not anymore. Now you're out on the party circuit, throwing our money away.

There is nothing wrong with me, but you.

In any civilization it is just to feed your children before you pollute yourself in O'Donoghue's.

If I want a lecture I'll go to Mass.

Do it for the baby coming.

Olly sits, suddenly sobered. *Be the divine Jayze, another?*

Yes.

That's it, Mother, off to Engalund. Olly dances to the door like a music hall comic. Pants well pulled up, elbows pumping. *Get your suitcase, let's go.*

Don't joke, this isn't a telly show.

You stupid girl, Olly says.

You're the one—Never asked me, you pushed right in—

Get rid of it.

It, Gina repeats, stunned. Off balance, she can't figure this—Just run, fly out the door. But the kids would be trapped with him. *This it is your child.*

Children, the enemy of promise.

Children are the promise.

I'm the bluggy promise, Olly whinges. His spent cigarette falls to the floor. *Perishing with you, thief of my life.* He doubles over, hugging his legs, bashing his head on the milking stool. *Such a glorious failure.*

Just stop with your mad behaviors.

I'm befambillied, beshambillied, Olly roars into a ferocity. *Get me owt, get me owwwwt. Or I'll kill youse all.*

Up in the kidsroom, we are asleep or pretending. I fling an arm over my eyes, pressing tight to the sockets. It's black-so-black inside me.

In the dark, I pray and I pray. Make it stop, God. Do something, save her, help us. Prove you are God and do this for me.

A really-God could come into my head, read my mind and answer.

I listen for God in my brain.

Help us save her.

It is black-so-black in the cave of my mind. It is black, it is black, no . . . it's blue. A blue flash rips through me.

Ruirteach springs from the doorknob hole in the wall across the room.

Ruirteach rolls long the bottom of the world.

Ruirteach-ruirteach, Da's howl.

Please, God, won't you kill him for us? Won't you smash him? Won't you put him away?

And no answer from the Holy Man above. God turns his face.

If I can't have God to my own, and He won't watch over me, then I wish I was a magic person. Wish I could stay in the magics for the rest of life.

Downstairs, Gina's feet are thrangled in clothesline. Olly's heart loud in his shirt, his open-mouthed bully breathing. The hot water flows in the sink. Water down the drain. Gina's face goes blank in disbelief. She can't believe this is happening again. And splittery lick, in the splitters, his hand whips the air. But the blow goes wide on purpose. Olly is only messing.

Fear shoots long the length of her. She numbs her mind so she feels nothing. Backs up, steadying herself on the piano. A gash of notes and thrashing scales.

I am sick to the dones with your cringing flinch like I'm about to crash you.

She goes to her knees, she goes to crouching. She scrams

under the piano, knocking her head on the soft pedal. She pulls the piano bench front her body but there's nowhere to go.

Git out from under there. Olly snatches a *súgán* chair by one leg, slashing it fast to the piano. He'll drive the bench into her, crush her under the piano. But no, he pulls the chair back at the last second.

She grunts in terror.

I'll give you such a doing, he taunts. Stamping at the bench, lurking away with the *súgán* chair. Then charging again. Wild, unpredictable charges. So nearly on her, but not so nearly on her. His tactic is designed to terrify more than if he really hit her.

So he surges. Bashing things close to her face, but not her face. Her arms, but not her arms. Her flanks, but not her flanks. He dances the fight, making no actual strikes to her person.

Gina gives over. Pushes the bench out. Stands giddy before him.

She flattens herself, goes to nothing. She has no will at all.

Olly puts the chair aside and sits upon it. In order to rest and—Gather strength.

He crosses his legs.

Good girl, he says to confuse her. *Goood girl.*

She stands, makes a fist of her own at the small of her back. Meaningless.

Inside that awful moment, from here to there and there to here, Olly's slipping through to chaos raging. A rush, a snarl, his hand comes round and—He smacks her across the face. There's the snap of solid contact and it all goes to smash.

She buckles in a ray of pain.

She was not raised into this. A minister's daughter can't hit back, can't hit at all. She was not raised for this. Fourteen years with him. The last ten, the slowly mounting violence. After a few rough-ups, one night he tossed whiskey in her eye then moved on to kicks, back-kicks, kicking her up on the floor. All these years of him hunting her late at night in the dark down the stairs, in his snare.

Olly circles Gina and before she has time to protect herself, he bulls forward, clouts her to floor. She's on her knees crawling into the empty fireplace.

Bloody sow. He snatches her by the backsides, flips her, gets her down.

She cannot stir.

His wolfish panting.

A forearm cross her throat, her cheek against the flags.

There's a pushing stink, the waste of chimneys, ashes burn in the room. Hooves beat on the drumlins, the troop of horse and four thousand feet.

She blacking out. Stay awake, don't break. She reels, sucks a breath. *Get off me.*

Stay down or I'll kill you. Olly hits her twice with the fist—to the mouth, to her head. Then he fires tween her legs.

That punch, that one punch.

Olly staggers away.

In the fireplace, a bright bubble of blood drains from Regina.

Olly stares at the blood branching in every direction.

Nothing, he says aloud. *I done nothing.*

And he's out the door.

Blood puddles in the hearth.

He was their boy, was love. He was hope-itself. And hope is lost this night.

Their son, their love, dear Dominick, spills clean out of space and time. Slips into air and is flown, is flown along and away to the land of the *Sheee.*

Mam-Mam-Mam and Mam-Mam-Mam opens her mouth, calling out with the bare grief. Her grief-cry echoes like legends.

Mam made bloods. Poppy's sleepy face filling the square at the top step.

Fiona is silent at the foot of the stairs.

Des and Ely stand stiff before the unused fireplace. Noleen, her face blanked by terror. Upstairs in her cot, Giselle's bald cries split the rafters.

I'll run for the Guards, says Des.

Fiona goes to the sink, twists the hot tap, stops the running water. The *Gardaí*? Not worth the bother. There was one fight when she learned her lesson. So incensed by one of Olly's beatings, Gina put on her coat and went for the police. When they came back, Olly'd changed. He smiled at the guards like a fil-um star, cracked a joke or two just to prove he was indeed Olly O'Feeney from off the telly. The Guards were falling about the place laughing.

Then Olly suggested Gina was the one drinking.

After the laughing stopped, Fiona told the truth, tried to

tell her mother's story. The sergeant whirled on her, told her not to interfere in her parents' affairs.

"Sure, they'll make it up in the morning," the sergeant said.

Should I get the police? Des asks again.

No, Des. It's better not to pursue the matter, Fiona says. *Go out to Dean's Grange and bring back Gran.*

nuala rising

On the first of November, a ghosty blue Mourn, Nuala's brought from the Kingdom of Souls to breathe, once again, the warm air of this world.

In Noleen's bottom bunk, Nuala rises from the soils of nightland. Nuala, a filthy poor boggart girl, heels off the bedclothes, stands straight-naked mid the kids' bed quarters. She rifles through dresser drawers, the clothes press. Looking for a rig-out, the right rig-out, so's to sort things for wee Nolee and protect this fambilly.

The frock. O, the turquoise frock with the sparky-starred brooch from Noleen's American granny. That'll do it, all right. Noleen's grotty sandals suit her fine. Her feet fit merrily-snugs in Noleen's shoes. It's been thousands of years since she's had the shoes. The last pair fell off her feet, what with running the six and twenty counties, over bog and moor, paying off the sins of her bloody ancestors. Doing messages for the *Sheee.*

Socks-socks, a pair of socks, she needs 'em. And pantalets, *hoo.* Lookit the ruffles. Bit gray, but they'll do.

Nuala gathers the clothes in her arms and pads, bare but for the loose jangle of undone sandals, into the lavo. She nudges the door closed with her beam end. Does she need a tidy-up? She does. She'll use Noleen's toof brush with the mashed bristles. Unscrews the toothpaste cap. *Buhhh.* Tube is empty. Nuala spits into the mouth of the tube, spitting and sucking, spooshing the foam over her back-teefs, brushing 'til her smiling gleams.

"Did she MacClean her teefs today?" You betcha. She'd sing a song, she's that pleased with herself, but—Sure, it'd wake the kids. Let 'em sleep. They had a night of it last night, din't they. Triple a tragedy.

She scours herself with a skinty towel, assesses her face in the looking glass. But as she moves, a second person blurs behind, a shadow, a fetch, her mortal twin. Noleen, with white-blonde electricky hairs. She glimmers, floats, then swiffs away as Nuala overtakes her reflection in the glass.

Nuala, Noleen's cunning other self.

She steps into the turquoise dress, zipping the zippy up the back in the rear. Zippers is easier than armor.

The bloomers—Toasty warms.

Step outta the shoe, left sock.

Step outta the shoe, right sock.

Then the sandals. Strap and buckle, strap and buckle.

Nuala the Girsha, she says to the girl in the sink mirror. *Nuala the Bold.*

Stop acting in there. Des pounds the toilet door. *Gotta go po.*

And Nuala slinks out the windah, shimmies down the elderbelly tree to land *spack* in Mam O'Feeney's rockery.

Nuala crouches to look and to look at all the world around her.

Be-dammy. Here in the tumble of the granite rockery lies

one of her old cursing stones. No, she's telling a lie, here's a curing stone, too.

Take two chanting stones gathered 'fore sunrise...

Cure in her right hand, curse left

Nuala claps right over left

Three times

Each strike rings clean like a bell

Throughout the land

Draw down power from the sky

Draw up, draw up from the earth, the seas

And Nuala's brought to her full strength. For the first while in a hundert ages she's up on the land and living. Not smanging round, a mind figment, in someone's imaginations, or dancing in some cruddy ballet.

She heads through the side garden door, past the cartwheel hung on the white-washed wall. She peers in the living room windah. There's a dark stain on the flags of the hearth. Olly O'Effer, that mauler, pawned his soul when he loosed Foul Nelson.

It's then she remembers the sad errand Des ran this morning's early, collecting Gran from Dean's Grange and bringing her to home here. When Gran saw the state of the place, saw the state of the mother, she took Ma O'Feeney to the Rotunda in a taxi.

They back yet? She wonders.

Nope.

House, shut like a mouth.

Nuala nips in, shoulders Noleen's leather schoolbag, ducks back through the lower half-door. She is out and on up the lane.

It's fuck-cold in Dublintown and she hasn't coat nor cardigan. Tis killing cold. At the end of Tolka Row she visits the secret hole in the street. Nuala fits her mouth to the gap in the tarmacadam and calls to the river neath the road.

Hellooooo.

Nuala the Girsha, the river cries back.

Hellooooo.

Nuala the Bold.

And so, padoo-padum, fists chopping the air, she pappels long the footpath. Makes a great leap, catches a low-flying thermal. She's in the wind, riding the air itself, the very molecules.

O, ride, ride, ride ride. Nuala glides up-up-uppp, bounding goat-like to the roof of a Georgian on Merrion Square.

She roves, flashing silver, lifting clear over the slanting roof peaks. She rears and vaults housetop to housetop, street to street.

'Til she reaches Kildare.

At the rounded entrance to the National Museum, Nuala sets a magic injunction. And *zip-zap*, she's in the hall with the Gallagh Man.

She raps on his lickle glass box. *Git up, Bogsee.*

Nuala, yeh sleeky bitch, yeh. The Gallagh Man speaks in an elder-Irish, forgotten now. *What's cracking?*

Give us the lend of me whistle, I've a message to run. As Nuala reaches for the carved snake, her hand melts the glass.

Take me with yeh, Bogs says, propping himself on a leathery elbow. *I've been stuck in this enchantment far too long.*

Don't go whingeing 'bout the burthen of your duties, Nuala chides him. *You're in this museum to mind the young wans 'bout our gah-lorious pasts.*

Nuala pulls the ripcord to Noleen's parachuting schoolbag, strings shoot out the back. Nuala rockets the sky, flying on Dublin breezes high over *Átha Cliath* sleeping below.

The soles of her sandals slap on the tiles of the Rotunda Lying-In Hospital. The walls, the walls teeming with coming souls, all those new lives starting. Nuala can see 'em.

Three more weeks, only three more weeks. Noleen's glad song of earlier days. *And Mammy's gonta have the new baby.* Echoes before her, leading up the stairs to the labor ward.

No private room for Mam O'Feeney. She's on the ward, curled in a blue wash of light. Swingy baskets at the bottom of each cot, each with a babby, safely sleeping. Save hers.

Beyond the windows, the stars, stelli-ferocious.

Ye kind stars, Nuala calls.

Draw down, draw up from the earth, the seas.

Nuala raises the stone snake to her lips, blows.

And the wide air shakes with gold dust at the kiss of day.

Nuala lays her whistle on the locker next to Gina's bed and disappears.

Dawn tickles the windows on the ward. Gina stirs, opens her eyes and stares. She's fixed on the panes, mesmerized by the faint beams of... light.

She must flee, escape time, country, life itself. She could walk right into the cold sea, she could die. But she's gotta rescue her kids from this nutcase. Really, what sort of masochist stays? Fourteen years of faith and goodness and squelching self.

Endure-endure ‘til the self is emptied.

She poured belief and love and service into a man preoccupied with self-hate. He will never have enough, get enough. There is not enough love in the world to save him.

No one will ever love him as much as Gina, but Gina loves her children more.

Her mind runs through the days of her own childhood. After Gina's father died of pneumonia in `36, Granny Volk went to bed with a sick headache. Mourned and mourned her whole life long, choosing husband over her children. Gina will not make her mother's mistake.

She must get out of this bed. She moves to fling off the covers, put a foot to the floor. But pain bores through her. Can't, she simply can't.

Gina thinks of Baby Dominick never brought to life.

She grieves for values forgotten, love forgotten.

How could he let this happen to them? Upon a time, they were the happiest family in Dublin.

Tears roll down her, drop to the sheet.

Bronagh Malone—nurse, midwife, handywoman—is heating a teapot with a splash of boiling water. Making a cuppa for the poor woman on the public labor ward. Gina O'Feeney, would you believe, can't afford a private room.

Gina was on the radio last week. *Day to Day* and *Women's Own*.

Wife to the famous actor played Jackser Molloy on *Our City*. So funny, so Dublin.

Wish to Christ she could get her hands on that bowsie. What he did to her.

Gina arrived by taxi this early morning. Hair full of blood, body gashed and bruised. Two fractured ribs, twelve stitches, a D&C.

Bronagh scoops tea from the caddy, swirls the water in the pot, lets it steep.

Lost a baby at three months, she did. Louser. The no good, bloody louser. Beat the lard out of her, murdered their child.

Bronagh, heavy braid of chestnut hair wrapped at the nape of her, arranges a few biscuits on a saucer. Jug of cream on the tray, two spoons.

No report ever made. He'll pay no consequences.

She wheels an iron tea trolley along the corridor, turns the doorknob, steps onto the ward.

Can you sit up? Bronagh asks, pulling a chair beside Regina, avoiding the wicker cradle hanging empty at the end of the cot.

Gina, neck ringed with red abrasions. Her eyes, vessels burst in each one. Right eye? Shut with it, like she could take no more.

Cup of tea?

Love one, Gina manages.

Bikkie?

Not able for it, Gina says, meek and defeated. Can't raise her head from the pillow on account of the choking.

I'd say you must really mind yourself. Bronagh, with her

lively brown eyes, gently lifts Gina, raising her so she can drink.

I can't describe the danger I feel, this terrifying sense of danger, Gina says. *He could do something monstrous, something—Against the law.*

Trouble is, Gina, he already has.

I live in his house, my kids. If he could do this to me, he could...

You are in peril, Bronagh says. *Get the children safe away.*

I feel—Gina says. *Feel the only*—Dried blood blacks her front teeth. She sips, milky tea washing them white again. Dried blood swallied down. *The only way to keep my sanity is to get back to America.*

My women, the many I see here, Bronagh says. *Are often trapped in a life of fear. So few people can undo their lives and go on. But Gina, you're American, you can. So, get out. Leave the bastard. Go.*

Did she dream it? Gina wonders. Did that happen? Bronagh telling her, *Take courage. Don't tarry. Hold your nerve.*

Must have. Here's a teacup. Empty-empty, just like me.

Empty me, empty me. *Caveat* empty me.

She's playing with words again. Must feel a bit better. Sure, tea is a tonic, as they say. She reaches her teacup to the night table tween the beds.

Himmel, Gina says aloud. It's their secret signal, Noleen's library stone. How'd that get here? Is she here? Wouldn't put it past her. Nolee, crouching under the bed, listening in. The snoop.

Gina grabs the small stone in her fist.

Heat, in her palm, heat. It goes and it grows, the-heat, the-heat, with love.

A mighty power courses through her and she sees it now.

Swing in the Green. Her little one said about that bruise on her cheek.

A lie.

Noleen's learning to lie about life, about her father, about everything in her world.

Just like Olly.

At some point in his life. Age of twelve? The year Olly's TB started. Or at eight, say, when the Christian Brothers, his very own da, groped him, shamed him, beat him blue.

That's when Olly started in on the lies. Finding rooms inside his mind more potent than life itself, building fantasy mansions where he found escape. It's that ability makes him such a charmer, such an actor, Mister Marvelous on the stage.

And her Noleen, this little girl would cheer the world.

If—If Gina doesn't get them out, Noleen will be ruined. They will be ruined.

Don't tarry. Hold yer nerve. Get the children safe away.

small world, big airline

No. 11 Tolka Row
Dublin 2
3 November 1968
Dear Mom—

Runs Gina O'Feeney's first letter.

Dear Mom—

She tries again.
Then she tries this:

Dear Donald:

I don't know whether Violet told you or not about the trouble that we have had. I am in a very bad state and need help. Olly and I have to separate. Certainly for the sake of the children, it is impossible to keep going on together.

The only way to keep my sanity is to get home to normal good living and work hard for the children. I must get back to America and get a job as a teacher at university, or public school, or substitute like Vi does.

I am, I realize, in a very awkward position for I have practically no money and such a fool I feel. ~~Do you~~ So I will have to be advanced ~~me~~ money or quietly ask Dutch ~~or mention~~ I will pay you back ~~unwelk~~ as soon as I can.

This is not an impulsive gesture. Olly has hurt me now for nearly two years with no sign of ever improving. I can't describe by letter the cruelty of it.

I don't want mother to know the worst and certainly don't want to worry her as she is so marvelous. I know this will hurt her so, but if she saw what things are she'd say I'm right to leave him as he is crude and difficult. (Ironic to think mother predicted this.)

The doctor says Olly needs psychiatry but won't of course hear of it. When I mention going to a marriage counselor. Olly says, "I could write the script." If I don't get out from this ~~embarrassing and~~ hurtful situation I know I am heading for a breakdown.

And so I have to start all over again. Trying to build a home (as a widow) all the clichés of modern, pointless life when the magic is gone out of marriage. I feel so shocking, Donald help me. I was always ~~too~~ soft and now I need help. ~~And was always~~ I was always a fool.

~~My~~ I don't know how to ask for what I have to—would I be able to rent an apartment somewhere near you—would you—

MUST I COME HOME IN DEFEAT? HOME PENNILESS.

Gina stopped there, never finished that letter. Like she already knew she'd get no university job, but work three jobs instead for buttons.

That first November Monday, Mam took the kids and their birth certs to the American Embassy to get a mootch-along going on their passports. She spent an hour miserably crying in the Ladies' before she could face the officials. But she somehow did it. Got 'em inoculations against the polio, smallpox, the three-in-one and the BCG, so her kids don't get TB. She put make-up over her bruises, got their passport pictures took. Lookit, wouldja? Mammy O'Feeney and her kiddos.

Ely, apple cheeky, with the fat smile, striped jersey. Poppy's clutching Judy Littlechap in her arms. Mam's got Giselly on her lap, spanking a plastic rattle to keep her happy.

There, tucked into Mam's left shoulder: Our Noleen, drab and sad, the Bold O'Feenian no longer. She hides out in Cucumber Cottage, reading books and reading. She's moved some tweed blankets out there and a pillah. She'd camp there if she could, but the light goes and cold drives her in. Once in her bunk, can't sleep for the nightmares. Can't eat, she is living on air.

Some days she rambles the streets looking for her da. Not in O'Donoghue's, not in the Green. He's not anywhere anymore. Where did he go? Where is he living? When Olly wakes up today, will he not think of her? Her heart is breaking after her daddy because he likes her most of all the kids. She knows it. When is it he'll come home?

While the fambilly was out on the town getting prodded and injected and passport snaps took, Da O'Feeney stole into their house, he—

Found a fresh lock in the Georgian door, he—
Din't own the key to, he—
Locked out, he—
Scaled the whitewashed wall, he—
Broke in
Sooo sneakery
Left his wedding ring side the ticking clock, he—
Pinched *Sord Nelson*
Sold it for the price of the brass, he—
Swiped the pawnbroker's payment in coin and bills
Shoved it in his pockets-all-holes
And fell to drinking hard's he could, he's—
Set on drinking himself to death

Dearest Vi:

We got confirmed 6 seats (no seat for Giselle):

26 Nov Dub/Shannon departs 1:45 arrives 2:20 Shannon

26 Nov Shannon/NY departs 5:40 arrives NY 7:35 pm

I hope you have listed all our expenses:

Air fares in full

Transport to house

House downpayment

Other expenses (Furn? Beds?)

I have received from Olly only £7 in 4 weeks for our support. We are not getting out too soon.

I am so full of relief that you are able to come to our help. And we won't be a drag. I feel very healthy now and raring to go. I know I'll get on over there. I have confidence that I lacked before. A very fine lawyer is getting a deed of legal separation (least expensive) and wonders why I didn't get it years ago.

Olly is in the latter stages of alcoholism—blackouts, lapses of memory. He is a bit verrucht in de kopf when he harms his own. The self-righteous shit. "I love drink," he says. "And I'm not changing." He is so mental, not even worth pity. I have hideous dreams he'll commit suicide.

My children are my happiness. They can't wait for America.

"We're going to America," Des said when we were getting the shots at the clinic.

"We're in America," Ely said, bold as you please.

"No, we're in a hop-is-tall," Poppy told him.

"We have triumphed over his evil" is all I will say when I climb off the plane. I do hope you won't feel hampered by our invasion but I know you will love the kiddies and I won't be in debt to anyone for more than a month. As Poppy says, "I can put my slip-slops on all by my selfish." Well, we can manage all by our selfish, too. Love and so many thanks to you dear people.

—Your one & only schwester, Gina

P.S. Won't we have the watermelon eatin' contests?

In the space of three days, they tore everything upside down packing the house empty. 'Cause each O'Feeney was allowed to pack and carry one suitcase only. And that's it.

Imagine, going to America with just one bag and a self.

Then there was the Sellups, terrible-appalling. Ma O'Feeney invited all their fambilly friends in for the show and sale of household items. They came round the backa Tolka Row to have a poke and a root through their meager belongings slanting on the cobbles in the lane:

5 *súgán* chairs for £10
Cucumber Cottage – a Wendy House £10
Hammond Lane Bunk Beds – £10
Wellington desk – £30-35
3 Donal Davies Tweed Dresses – £2 each
Wagon wheel – £2

Mam even sold the wheelbarrow fulla crinkly-dried, dead things—Noleen's birthday primroses.

The Sellups was a great idea. It brought in an extra hundred quid and then the house was empty.

On the night before their leaving, *Clan na Feeney* slept somewhere's else. Aunty Mara took Noleen to stay at Granny's cottage in Dean's Grange. All the rest dossed down with the Lanigans who drove the bunch to Dublin Airport the next morning. Off to America on air tickets. Gina lugging a typewriter in the box, her violin. Noleen with the portrait of Synge under her arm and Fiona with babby Giselle packed in the Moses basket among bundles of clothes.

Welcome aboard this jet service to John F. Kennedy Airport. There's a life jacket in a packet under your seat and a whistle.

At a quarter 'til two on the twenty-sixth of November, off they go, the O'Feeneys.

Aunty Mara on the tarmac waving them on long after any rational person would have.

Olly didn't ring to say goodbye to the children. He never came, never saw his family away.

Divil scorch and scald him. Mara folds her lace hanky, tucks it in her handbag, snaps fast the goldy clasp.

She ran into Olly a month ago. He was strolling along the Liffey, wheeling a pram. It stopped her heart.

This is my other wife, Olly said, bold as you please, introducing her to this one by the name of Stacia. He's staying with her out at the flats, Ballymun Corpo Estates. Stacia has a pair of twins from some other lunkard. They're raggy and scabby with wild spunker hair. One of the girls has a purple stain over her ear that looks like murder.

He's dirtied his bib this time, Olly has.

And this is our Nelson. Inside the pram, a two year old monster boy. An illegitimate. With Olly's eyes, round and brown, big as Ely's. He has goldy ringalets and bitey teeth. That's not natural, the squirmy beast.

Dear knows, that's what he gets for trying for more than life has in store for him. Something went wrong with Olly when he was young. Born with a hole in his heart, certainly born with a hole in his pocket. Bloody fool, with his rough tricks.

He killed Gina's new baby. Fiona told her. And they saw it, all the kids.

Just like Mara, like Olly, like Dominick.

Watching their father beat Mam down.

We couldn't stop him for nothing.

Dear knows.

But the children got away and that's good.

She looks to the sky, a great flock of swallows flying up, like black salt tossed to a blue blanket.

Her Nolee. When will she see her again? How many year?

And it's so far, America.

Yesterday was their special day. Mara had Noleen all to herself, picked her up on Tolka Row. Noleen, carrying the wee case she took with her on the plane today. They went to Bradley's Shoe Shop on Nassau Street for a new pair of shoes with room to grow. Caught the bus to *Dún Laoghaire*, bought socks, a cardigan and a smaller one for Poppy. That's so Poppy won't borrow it off Noleen. Poppy loves her big sister so much she wants to be her, tries to be her by wearing her clothes.

After, Mara walked Noleen along the granite pier among the boats and the ships, the Holyhead Ferry docked in the harbor.

The site of so many coming-homes.

Dominick. No more, no more.

And them leaving, always leaving. They leave us again.

Noleen stood at the green rail looking out over sea and sky.

The poor girl. So vague these days, she's with the fairies. She's a ghost of herself.

They'll malefooster her in America.

Mara wanted so badly to ask Gina if Noleen could stay in Dublin out in Dean's Grange with them, but no—She'll have more of a chance over there.

They strolled the strand. Noleen went on alone. She stood on the sand as the tide went out, rapt and still. Looking her fill of the glorious bay.

Wonder what was in her little mind.

outta goosetown

On the day before everything, Aunty Mara took me to *Dún Laoghaire*. The sun was low in the sky, dipping under the sea and into tomorrow.

Tomorrow and tomorrow we'll go to America where everyone has gorgeous clothes, tans and autoharps.

Shallup-shallup. Tide's going out. *Shallup-shallevers.* Sky's going blue, going violet.

The church clock chimes three times, though it's five. Like the bells is giving me more time here in Ireland.

Up along the streets, the bells ring. Reminding me of yesterday, Sunday morning's early.

Sunday, before church, not a soul in the streets, I went out walking Dublintown, searching for my da.

When I come upon him suddenly, he's sitting on the curb outside Dolly's on Baggot Street, wearing a second hand coat and scrunchy hat. Two teef punched out of his smile. Looks like a one man slum. Daddy.

He is crying, petrified of the world.

Daddy. I finally get the word out.

He lifts his head. His eyes is gone red with blood. He is smelly.

Daddy's living a wild life now. Always getting in the paper

for his rows. He put a brick through the window of the *Irish Times* 'cause the notices were so bad his show closed.

Just then, the church bells sound the hour. One. Two. Three. Summoning our souls to God.

Won't you come home? I ask him.

Four. Five. Six.

Please.

He shambles to standing and staggers up the middle of the road. He's walking in his socks in the street. His shoes are lost, gone somewhere.

What're you doing, Da? Stay home.

She hates me, you hate me—

I could never hate you.

Everyone detests me. He's in a very stocious state, mad as a feckin' brush.

No—couldn't hate him. He taught me to tie my shoes, cross my eyes, leap, soar, flee. He taught me to laugh when I couldn't—Laugh when I laugh when I laugh. When I couldn't, he taught me to lie.

'Mere to me, Nolee.

He leans heavy on my shoulder and we lurch towards the Green.

O'Donoghue's for breakfast, t'would be—Mighty. Blashers and rack pudding. Black pudding, scrambled uggs, rasher sangitch. I'd kill for a rasher.

But we're just round the corner—

With the Cornerboys, heh-heh. Wuhhh. He coughs, boaks blood. Spits it to the street. *Them Lumps leaving me behind, living in the face of Papacy? Popery? No, poverrrrry. I'll murder them, I'll—Ahh. Annihilate them.*

A cab pulls in close to us. It's Paddy, rolling his window down.

Please take him, I say, handing Da over. *Would you take him to wherever he lives and see that he doesn't get killed.*

Where to, Olly? Paddy asks.

Ballymun, Daddy manages. *To Stacia, babby Nelson and the girls.*

Purply Stainhead, them twins? He lives with them now?

And putt-putt-putt, there's a blast of soot out Paddy's tailpipe as they hang a left towards Merrion Square, heading North to the other side of the city.

On the beach in *Dún Laoghaire* the church bells ring in the salty wind above a peacock colored sea.

Shallup-shallup. Tide's gone out. *Shallup-shallevers.* Sky's gone blue, through to violet.

I wriggle me toes in me brand new sandals Aunty Mara bought for me, left the ould pair in the shop. They gave me a pink balloon, *Bradley's Shoe Shop* stamped on it. Once out the door I let it free to go soaring out over Dublintown.

That'll be me tomorrow. Up above earth, flying far and flying. Into the peach, the tan, the blue-pink fairy floss. Jetting off into wonders.

Sandal-slap and sandal-slap. I kick at the waves as they pull away.

Wish seven times, take seven pebbles. Sheela said, so long ago. At the flat where she lives with Mahree. *Make seven trips round the worlds.*

That'll be me. Going the farlands, traveling all the worlds.

I wish seven times, bend to take seven pebbles and see:

Black straps of seaweed, white boulders, slippy stones. There in the shellicoats and bottleglass is jagged humps and burlap sacks.

There's suitcases coated with mossy scree, bundles of rags, belongings. Sea-water tricks at the cases, immigrant cases from all of time. These rocks is a trail of treasures. His bindle-stiff, his paddy spindle. The shimbits, their meagers, their *theirs*. Water slamps the satchels. Each satchel a rock, a place to stand, a perch.

I take a step

And take a step

I go

Folly the multitudes that went before me. I walk the suitcases into the sky. Onto Ontario, off to Cairns, Australia, to Brewkillin, the Boston wharfplanks.

There's meelas going the farlands, into the wide world and all its branches.

They go and they go

And the waves bang away 'gainst the land they left behind

And the waves bang away

At their land disappearing

on writing *Smarty Girl*

I grew up in a house filled with music and stories and song. A robust language rang off the walls as the family freely quoted Synge, O'Casey, Shakespeare, or Bubbles, one of the Dublin characters my father collected. Both of my parents were theatre artists dedicated to preserving a Dublin vernacular that split a two-syllable word into ten, giving it a hundred new meanings. There was lively poetry to be heard on the streets and in the markets that was rapidly fading. My mother took notes and wrote radio scripts, but my father wholly *absorbed* these eccentrics and mimicked them perfectly.

Over the thirteen years it took to write this book, I drew from stories that my older sister, Shivaun, wrote about our Dublin childhood, John Molloy's recordings and his book *Alive, Alive O.*

I am especially lucky to have Yvonne Voigt Molloy for a mother. She gave me complete access to her journals, letters and radio scripts. I picked around in my parents' past in an effort to understand what happened that led her to jot, "darling life finishes" in her 1968 pocket diary. These artifacts capture her joy, her intelligence, her optimism, her incessant scheming for a lively theatre, as well as her love and high hopes for her family. They provided a glimpse into what lay beneath my father's alcoholism, for that is what drove us out of Ireland all those years ago.

Brooklyn, New York
Point Pleasant, Pennsylvania
November 2011

acknowledgments

The Indispensables:

Joe Goodrich, Yvonne Voigt Molloy, Trish O'Hare, Susan McKeown, Chris Lynch, Jan Werner, Gordon Dahlquist, EJ McCarthy, Aedin Moloney, Brenda Copeland, Sarah Carradine, Patricia Schneider, Thalia Voigt Gubler, Eileen Connolly, Silvia Saponaro, Michael Connolly, Bronagh Murphy, Jim Flynn, Esq., Kevin Holohan, Elisa Shokoff, Erica Glyn, George Miller and Kate Scuffle.

The Comrades:

Peter Quinn, Gemma Whelan, Laura Shaine Cunningham, Stanley Crouch, Naomi Guttman, Ursula Shea, Christopher Fitz-Simon, Jon Harris, Noel Sheridan, Ronnie Drew, Deirdre Drew, Todd London, Victor Lodato, Tony Jarvis, Nick Faust.

The Organizations:

New Dramatists, Radcliffe Institute for Advanced Study at Harvard, MacDowell Colony, Yaddo Corporation,

Hedgebrook, Mary Clark and Andrew O'Brien of the Dublin City Library and Archive, the New York Foundation for the Arts, and the Brooklyn Writers Space.

The Family:

John Molloy, Marguerite Molloy, David Molloy, Nicole Molloy Ix, Sajeela Molloy, Simon Molloy, and our beloved sister, Shivaun Molloy.

about the author

Honor Molloy was born in Dublin and came to America at the age of eight. She holds an MFA from Brown University and has received fellowships from the National Endowment for the Arts, the Radcliffe Institute for Advanced Study at Harvard, as well as a Pew Fellowship in the Arts. An alumna of New Dramatists, she has held residencies at Hedgebrook, Yaddo and the MacDowell Colony. She has been a keynote speaker at the Sydney Mardi Gras Festival and has read her work at the Dublin City Library and Archive. The recipient of a 2011 New York Foundation for the Arts Fellowship in Non-Fiction, Honor Molloy lives in Brooklyn.

CPSIA information can be obtained at www.ICGtesting.com
Printed in the USA
BVOW020945280212

283948BV00001B/6/P